MICHAEL NAVA
editor

FINALE

Boston: Alyson Publications, Inc.

Library of Congress Catalog Card Number: 89-85942

ISBN 1-55583-161-3

CONTENTS

to
Richard Labonté

Introduction

Though it is the bastard child of literature, the mystery has always attracted first-class writers. I came to mysteries in college through Jorge Luis Borges, whose *ficciones* frequently employed the conventions of the mystery for metaphysical ends. Indeed, one of the first mystery writers I read was G.K. Chesterton, to whose Father Brown stories Borges acknowledged his debt. The other mystery writer to whom I was initially exposed was Rex Stout who, on the whole, I preferred to Chesterton, because his stories were free of Chesterton's religious baggage.

This brings me to a related point about mystery writers. The best of them are respectful of the form in which they work, and work within its limitations (which can be formidable). One's audience requires it. Although few readers are as willing to suspend their disbelief as mystery readers, they are as sensitive to condescension as they are to artless execution of plot. Rightly so, as anyone who has suffered through a bad mystery can attest.

I try to avoid the are-mysteries-literature fray on the grounds that such a judgment cannot be made of a class of books but only of individual books on their merits and, at any rate, it will not be made by those arguing the point, but by future readers. All I am sure of is that certain mysteries have not only given me great pleasure, but I retain them in memory and happily re-read them. In putting together this collection, I hoped to accomplish the same thing for its readers.

The writers represented in this collection are gay men and lesbians. What I think is most interesting about this fact is how little it has limited their scope. In these stories you will find a broad spectrum of human types, and while aspects of being gay figure in these stories, homosexuality *per se* is seldom the central or motivating force behind them. In other words, these are not stories about the experience of being gay, they are about gay people's experiences. They look outward rather than inward and do not make a fetish of what should be simply one of many features of our nature.

Of course, I acknowledge that it is this society's unrelenting hostility to us that compels us to view the private matter of our sexuality as a political issue. I do not fault gay and lesbian writers who choose to write about the experience of being gay. I am glad, though, that some of us write from a slightly different point of view.

Oddly enough, the mystery seems to have liberated many of us in this respect for the reasons I mentioned earlier. First, the form attracts good writers; second, the conventions of the form cut down on our potential for self-indulgence. You need all kinds of ingredients to make a mystery work and the mystery writer must cast her nets far and wide into her experience to populate her story. This kind of imagining forces us to think beyond ourselves and our immediate circumstances into the greater world we all live in.

The two stories in this collection that best illustrate my point are Katherine Forrest's "Jessie" and Richard Hall's "Death Writes a Story." In both, the issue of homosexuality is so subtle as to appear absent and yet, try to imagine them if homosexuality did not figure in them at all. I am particularly proud, by the way, to be able to include both these writers. Katherine Forrest's Kate Delafield novels, popular among women, deserve a wider following among men. Both Katherine and Kate are first-rate. Richard Hall is a venerable name in gay crime fiction; his *Butterscotch Prince* first appeared in 1975. (Even so, it was not the very first gay mystery; that title would seem to go to George Baxt's *A Queer Kind of Death*, published in 1966.) Hall's "Death Writes a Story" shows no abatement of his skill and wit in the interim.

I am also proud to present a new story by another pioneer of gay fiction, Phil Andros. In "Death and the Tattoo," he provides a graphic demonstration of how rich the narrative voice can be in this kind of fiction. "All About Steve," by my friend Vincent Lardo, is as dry and skillfully mixed as the martinis that one might expect his characters to have always in hand. As does "Jessie" by Katherine Forrest, "All About Steve" provides a good introduction to another fine writer.

Gerald Lebonati, the author of the wonderful novel *Tropic Lights*, turns his hand to suspense for the first time in "Reunion," with great success. Read the story carefully — there are little surprises throughout, for instance, a reference to a stained glass window, that contribute to the story's overall theme.

Also, I welcome two new writers, Ivy Burrowes and Alan

Irwin. This collection marks the first-time publication by each. An editor ought not to have favorite stories but, having worked so closely with the writers of these, I must admit they have a special place in my heart. Read them, you'll see why.

Finally, I contribute a story of my own. I'd hoped to take a vacation from Henry Rios, the lawyer-protagonist of my two mysteries, but he wormed his way in at the last minute. I did, however, manage to banish him to sidelines for most of "Street People."

I would like to thank Sasha Alyson for the opportunity to put this collection together, and his patience while I did it, and my dear friend, Richard Labonté, bookseller extraordinaire, snowback, scholar, and keeper of secrets. This book is lovingly dedicated to him.

Michael Nava
West Hollywood

RICHARD HALL
Death Writes A Story

The guy from *Writer* magazine keeps asking me how I got started. Maybe he thinks I'm not the literary type. So I decided to write it down for him — amazing how easy the words come now. The guy who said artists have to suffer had the right idea.

You see, I've always loved stories. A funny taste in a grown-up man who also loves ball games, fishing trips, family reunions, old cars, dogs. I guess I got it from my old man who read *The Saturday Evening Post* all his life, the stories of Clarence Buddington Kelland being his favorite. When he finished one, he would slam down the magazine and say, "Son, that's what I call genius." Naturally, this made an impression on a growing boy.

When I was going to night school (Pace College, Manhattan, Commerce and Accounting), I took some writing courses. I could almost see my father beaming down at me when I signed up, when I started my first journal (Eugene Ebbler,

Writer's Notebook). I think that's probably why I wound up in the printing business instead of something else — insurance or computers. I wanted ink on my fingers. With eight employees, I wasn't in the pressroom much, but I still liked to hear the big webs humming, to know that words were being inked onto paper.

Of course, I always tried to make up stories of my own, even if I didn't do too well in the writing courses. My main trouble was that I couldn't figure out what people would say and do in an imaginary situation. My mind tended to freeze up.

However, some years ago I came across the solution to this, in an article in *Writer* magazine. "Clip newspapers for fascinating story ideas, because truth is just as strange as fiction." Well, I went them one better. I clipped newspapers, also I took notes on TV shows, true-life adventures, even from great works of fiction. Once I had collected enough tips, leads, ideas, I would fit them into stories of my own.

This was easier said than done. Tying one event to another wasn't that easy. I would get a good start ("Gobi nomad finds cache of jewels left behind by Marco Polo") and maybe even a decent middle sequence ("British industrialist caught smuggling relics behind hubcaps of vintage Rolls–Royce") and then it fizzled out. I was left with loose ends.

Sometimes, after having sat up late in my den, trying to fit these pieces together, I would climb upstairs, really swacked out, and peek at my kids, Tommy and Annie. A sleeping child is one of the most beautiful sights on earth. Watching them, I would ask myself why I bothered with stories. Wasn't this enough? Wasn't this life itself? But a few nights later, after the headaches in the office, the union problems, I would start to think about my stories again. They would glow in the distance, like treasure. Maybe this evening I'd knock out the big one, the grand slam. And sure enough, after dinner Roz would get her patient look, the kids would slide off their chairs, and I'd find myself drifting toward the den. They had spotted my mood before I did. That's what happens when you have a family. Everybody got their antennas out, twitching. But no matter how long I stayed in the study, how hard I tried, I couldn't find the stitches, the seams, to my stories. Nothing came together. I had Writer's Block (also covered in the magazine mentioned above).

Roz would never ask about my work when I came to bed. In fact, she'd pretend not to wake up. She could probably tell just from the way I moved what had happened.

I remember clearly the first time I laid eyes on the person who would end my Writer's Block. It was at our liquor store, Eastbrook Wines & Spirits, on a Saturday in September. I was buying the usual, two bottles of Heublein's pre-mixed Manhattans, which is our standard for Saturday night. A thin, crooked man with a battered face was peering at the wine display. I would put his age at just over the half-century mark. But it was his hair that made me look twice — two-toned, like a '67 Buick. The sides russet, the top burnished gold, though the colors blended together at the edges, which you don't find on a Buick. He picked out a couple of bottles of French wine and walked to the counter.

"These are rather overpriced," he said to Angelo. His voice was high and flutey and very British.

"We'll be having a sale next month, sir, maybe you'd like to come back and stock up." Angelo was giving his number-one-customer treatment.

"Perhaps I shall." The customer didn't carry a wallet. No. On one slim hip rested a leather bag, from which he took a small change purse, the type old ladies carry to the supermarket. He pulled out some crumpled bills. This took a long time. Angelo and I waited.

While Angelo was ringing up the sale, the customer turned and gave me the once-over. His eyes took me in from top to bottom and back to top. I had a feeling he saw all of me and liked it — even the hair on my chest and the family jewels. It was the kind of look a woman would give you if she thought you wouldn't catch her at it. Then this guy smiled — not apologetic for staring. Not apologetic at all.

After he swung out the door, Angelo let out a heavy breath. "I didn't think they liked small towns."

"Times are changing, Ange," I replied. Then we talked about the league play-offs. I had the funny feeling we were fumigating the store.

You can imagine my surprise, on reaching home, to find that the person I'd seen in the liquor store was moving onto our block. That's right, a new neighbor. I saw him unloading a Merc as I swung by. Roz, who is a member of the Welcome Wagon, had the preliminary details.

"You wouldn't believe it, Gene," she said, "his name is Storrs, he was a dancer with the Royal Ballet, and he's going to open a school right here behind the Stop 'n Shop."

"What kind of school?"

A dumb question. Roz got her patient look. "A dance school!" She paused. "Do you suppose he's got a wife?"

I thought I had the answer to that but didn't offer it. Roz likes to find out things for herself. Besides, the Welcome ladies would pay their first call tomorrow, and she'd have the whole pitch. Just then Tommy came in with two mitts and the ball. Time for our Saturday catch. Afterwards, we were going to Shea to see the Padres play the Mets. We are both very big Mets fans.

It was the next afternoon, Sunday about five, when Roz got back from the Welcome call. Neil Storrs — that was the guy's name — was renting the Gabler house. The ladies had intended to roll out the hospitality but he had gone them one better. He had served tea using a special blend, Roz said, sent over from Fortnum & Mason. "They have a file on him," she said. "It's like registering your silver pattern at Tiffany's." During this tea party he had told them about his brilliant dance career, including five command performances for royalty. When I suggested to Roz that she look this up in the local library, she didn't go for it. In fact, she seemed to be more on his side than mine, for some reason. I didn't argue — it didn't seem that important. And then she dropped her bombshell.

"He's a writer, Gene. He's had several books published. Novels."

"I thought you said he was a dancer. I never heard of a dancer who writes books."

"Well this one does. He paints, too."

"What is he, some kind of one-man band?"

She didn't answer. Instead, she got up and started dipping around the room, straightening the blinds, smoothing the doilies. All signs she had something up her sleeve. I started to sweat.

"I was thinking, Gene," she wiggled the wand for the Levelors, "since he lives so close, you and Mr. Storrs . . ."

I got it in a flash. "Goddammit, no!" I jumped up, suddenly wet under the collar. This is a hormonal release I can't always control.

"But there are all kinds of famous collaborations. There's . . . Gilbert and Sullivan."

"That's words and music, for God's sake."

"What about Nordhoff and Hall? What about Beaumont and Fletcher?"

"Who the hell is Beaumont and Fletcher?"

"I'm not sure, it just popped into my head."

"Well, there's also Bonnie and Clyde and the answer is no."

I was really sore. Did Roz think I couldn't make it on my own? That I had to have assistance — and from a type like this? Had she lost faith in me?

I took out my handkerchief and started mopping. She was staring at me, feeling bad, but she didn't feel as bad as I did. If my own wife didn't believe in me, where was I? I'll tell you where —in a crowd of businessmen who ride the subways till they drop dead.

"Well, I hope you're not upset, dear, I was only trying to . . ."

She was only trying to. Half the trouble in the world comes from people who are only trying to. I decided it was time to get a little fresh air. I left her opening and closing the doors to the TV cabinet like she couldn't make up her mind how she wanted them.

I didn't intend to walk past the Gabler place, but my feet took me there. I didn't want to look in the windows, either, but my eyes swung over. And there he was, dressed in a caftan, though I didn't know men wore them. Blue, with long sleeves. He was sitting in a room full of crates and cartons, reading a book. He should have been unpacking, for God's sake, but he was turning over the pages of that book like it was the most important thing in the world.

I tried to wipe out the picture, but as I walked down to the village to buy some claros, it went with me. A dancer, a writer, a painter. Of course, he didn't make babies so he made other things. This thought should have calmed me down but it didn't. In fact, it only made me sweat more, though the afternoon was cool.

By the time I bought my cigars and had a chat with Charlie, I felt better. I had even stopped sweating. Roz meant well. There was no reason to take it personally. She had my best interests at heart.

When I got home Tommy appeared with the two mitts but I said it was time to help Annie with her homework. By suppertime everybody was feeling good. That night I didn't go into my den. It just didn't appeal to me. Roz was extremely affectionate to me later on, although Saturday and not Sunday is our regular time. It's amazing what a woman can think up if she's in the mood. I told Roz that she was the one that ought to be writing stories. She got a big kick out of that.

My big idea came to me after a rotten day at the office a few weeks later. To be honest, I didn't make any connection at the time. It all seemed like happenstance, which shows how little we know ourselves.

First the office news. When I walked in the door I found the big Miehle shut down because Bruno had lost the tip of his index finger through carelessness. Blood all over the rollers, the fingertip on a bench. Next, my bindery calls to say one of their cutters went haywire and they ruined half the sheets we had just sent over. And last, an urgent phone call from my number one customer. His boss found out he was on the take from me, and he was being transferred out of

Production.

By the time I got home that night my shirt collar was black. Roz took one look at me and announced Manhattans, a special treat. Why not, I said, that's why National Distillers makes the stuff.

I was on my second round, beginning to unwind, Tommy giving me the rundown on the Mets' chances for the Series, when there was a tap at the door. Both kids jumped up, Roz rushed to the mirror—all par for the course—but imagine my surprise when who walks in but our fruity neighbor. I put down my drink and stood up. We hadn't really been introduced, just that stare in the liquor store, so I put out my hand.

"Gene Ebbler."

He replied with his own name, which by then I knew by heart.

Tommy and Annie were introduced next. They stared, of course — you know how kids love weirdness — but he didn't seem to mind. In fact, he kind of smiled and preened, like he was onstage with the lights shining.

Roz made him come in and sit down. "We're just having a cocktail, Mr. Storrs, can we offer you one?"

"Oh, dear." He looked around like he never heard of alcohol, but I know a taste for sauce when I see it. "Well, perhaps a tiny one, since you're having one yourselves."

Roz went back to the kitchen. The kids sat side by side on a stool. I could see their giggles like frozen waves just under the surface.

He wasn't wearing the blue caftan. Maybe that was his house-dress. Tonight he was wearing a flowered sports shirt (orchids and ferns), tight Daks (puke-pink), and white shoes on which he had covered up the original color.

When Roz came back with the Manhattan, I noticed a maraschino cherry in his glass, which she had not bothered to put in mine. This was not a pleasant comparison.

"Well, how do you like Eastbrook, Mr. Storrs?" she asked after the guest had muttered, "Cheers," and put away half his drink in one long slurp.

"Charming, charming." He widened his eyes which were lined with mascara. "I've always wanted to live in a small American town, and this is perfect."

The kids were getting loose again, the elbows digging back and forth. In a minute we'd have hysteria.

"Didn't your mother ask you to set the table?"

After a few groans they got up. Did Storrs's glance linger on Tommy? Or was I imagining he took an extra interest in a twelve-year-old boy?

Roz started to pump him. He had a dozen students lined up for his school, of course he couldn't give them the real classical stuff because for that you have to start in the womb, but he'd do his best. I could see Roz enjoying this. She was using her cultural voice.

Before long we were on refills and tongues were flapping. Especially Roz's.

"I'm dying to hear about your books, Mr. Storrs, you didn't really have a chance to tell us the other day."

She gave him her googly eyes at that, the kind she turns on the butcher sometimes. I could see her tits straining against her dress. Once or twice she strained too hard and our guest looked away, like he was embarrassed.

I was getting a little embarrassed, too. Why was she bringing up the subject when she knew how I felt about it? Did she intend to spill the beans about me? Suggest we collaborate? I could feel the old brain heating up, sending juices down my neck. Pretty soon I'd be wringing wet. But don't misunderstand. I wasn't jealous — I was just trying to figure it all out.

"Well," our guest fluttered his eyelids so the mascara showed. "I write novels. Gothics and thrillers mostly."

"Have they been published?"

"They've been published in England. I have an agent here now, who's trying to find someone to bring them out in America."

There was a slight pause. I could hear Roz's mind squeaking. She glanced at me, opened her mouth, and closed it. I guess she saw the sweat.

"How're things at the Gabler house?" The words sounded hoarse, even to me, but I had to speak up. Things were moving too fast in the wrong direction.

"I'm so glad you asked." He flapped his hand in the air. "The most ghastly thing just happened. That's really why I came over. I thought . . . someone said . . . you're very good at fixing things."

"Gene can fix anything," Roz said, not in her cultural voice.

"I'm so glad. My fridge just went out. I called the G.E. people but they're closed for the night. I've got tons of food and it will probably spoil."

"Probably a condenser," I said, taking out my handkerchief.

"I didn't know a fridge had condensers." He flapped his hands again. "Does that mean it can't be replaced?"

"I could probably rig up something that would last overnight."

"Oh Mr. Ebbet, could you?"

"Ebbler. I'd be glad to." The sweating had stopped, thank God.

We got up soon after that, Roz looking a little annoyed because her Q-and-A had been interrupted. The kids came back to say goodbye, their faces bright with excitement, and Storrs shook hands with both — daintily with Annie and a bit longer with Tommy. We made a detour to the garage, where I keep my tools, then down the street to the Gabler house.

While I poked around the motor, he kept up a babble. About being at the mercy of ruthless repair people, how kind the neighbors were, on and on. I didn't pay attention. I like to concentrate on one thing at a time. But when I finished, and the motor snapped on, he was all smiles and gratitude. He even suggested a drink, but I said I had to get back.

It was while I was heading for the can back of the kitchen, so I could wash up, that we passed the spare room. The Gablers had used it for laundry, but now I could see that a card-table was set up with a portable Olivetti and a pile of typed pages. On another table I saw several shoe boxes. Something clicked in my head and I stopped.

I didn't hear him behind me. He was a creeper — the sort you can never hear coming — which had probably come in handy for his type of life.

"This is my sanctum, home of my muse!" he sang out, coming so close I stepped aside. "I dream up everything in here, come see."

I followed him in.

"This is a new Gothic with a ballet setting, *The Ghost Dancers of Rue*, rather a good title, don't you think?" He tapped a pile of manuscript pages. Looked like he was almost finished. I started to ask him how long it took to write it, but stopped myself. That kind of information doesn't help anyone with Writer's Block.

"And these are my story ideas." He went to one of the shoe boxes and lifted the lid. It was jammed with 3x5 cards. "These are books I will probably never write. Don't have time. I'm too busy with the wretched business of earning a living." He fluttered his eyelids and smiled for the fiftieth time.

I looked harder at the box. It was about the same length as the one I used in the office for ink suppliers, of whom I have a great many. "You mean all those are story ideas?"

"Every one of them would make a marvelous book." He flashed his eyes again. "I have this penchant," he gave the word a French twist, "for plots. I dream up one a day. If I could afford a secretary, I could dictate a book in an afternoon, like Barbara Cartland." He let out a little screech. "That old bitch."

I shook my head slowly. What I'd been working on for years — all my life, really — this guy could do in an afternoon. A fucking afternoon. No wonder Roz had given up on me. The kids, too. I could feel the old body heat starting to rise. And then, moving toward the back, I caught sight of something I had missed at first — don't ask me how. A painting on the wall. A young boy about Tommy's age, sitting by a window, a vase of lilies on the table next to him. Storrs followed my glance, "Beautiful, isn't he?"

I don't know what I said. Between the sourness in my gut from the Manhattans, the troubles at the office, the confusion over Roz and the kids, the sweat old and new, I was too confused to say much. I don't even recall how I made it to the can and out the front door, finding a passage through all the crates and cartons. But on my way home, the painting stayed with me. A kid about Tommy's age. *Beautiful*, he said. Some other details of the evening came back to me. How he'd stared at Tommy. Held his hand a little too long.

And then, walking up the front steps of my house, the house I had bought for my bride Rosalind DeMarco fifteen years ago, I had my bright idea. Funny how one second can change your life. I had concocted, without even trying, the greatest story in the history of the world.

❏

The family noticed the change right away.

"It comes from being a good neighbor," Roz said, a day or two later. Then she went on about virtue being its own reward, a statement I have never had occasion to agree with. The kids, who are like walking pieces of litmus paper, turned blue and pink with bright ideas. Annie was planning a big Halloween costume. Tommy had a scheme to sneak into Shea for the last game of the season. All because the old man was full of jokes and cheer.

What they didn't know, of course, was that I had already made my first move. Called up my friend Little Richie Lubanski, who had once helped me clear up some Teamster problems, and set up a meeting the next day at the town dump, a terrific spot for an opening scene. At that meeting, Richie agreed to talk to some of his people. He would get back to me on the weekend.

Next night I went in the den and took out a clean sheet of paper. The time had come to line out the big one, the home-run. A few lines for the opening scene went right down.

The gulls wheeling over the mountains of garbage in the town dump did not, for all the keenness of their vision, notice the two men talking alongside a green Lincoln Continental. One, in his mid-thirties, tall and dark blond, with the build of a natural athlete, appeared to be giving instructions to his companion — a small man with black hair and shifty eyes.

Came out just like that, no problem. Next I would have a little conversation. Dialogue opens up the page and is easy on the eye. But, believe it or not, I couldn't get a handle on it. Even though I remembered every word Richie and I spoke, down to the five-grand part-payment he wanted in advance and my instructions for delivering the shoe boxes. I wrestled with the sentences, the spacing, even the punctuation, but no go. Something was stopped up.

Then I remembered a piece of advice from the experts — Make an Outline. I'd never been a star at this, ever since Miss Osborne in the eighth grade spent an afternoon telling us about I and A and 1 and a. Looked like a lot of hard work for nothing — I mean, whose hand can fit around something like that? It's like trying to make a shortstop wear a catcher's glove. Still, I decided to give it a try.

I was still working when Tommy turned up. I hadn't even heard him open the door, I was that wrapped up. He was dropping the ball into his mitt, right hand, left hand.

"Would you like to play catch, Dad?"

His eyes, big and sweet, searched mine. It was all I could do not to rub my knuckles over his skin, smooth as coated stock.

"I'm working, son."

He looked at the page with the few lines written. Had Dad finally made the breakthrough? Was he about to pole the big one? I couldn't resist telling him. "I think I'm onto something exciting, Tommy."

In his smile, his love, I saw what I'd been waiting for, coming my way at last.

The next minute, the doubts I'd had about the whole operation disappeared. My first responsibility was to my boy, wasn't it? Maybe Roz and the Welcome ladies had been taken in by the tea from Fortnum and the command performances and the rest of it, but not me. I could add faster than any of them. Besides, they hadn't seen the painting, heard it described. I looked at Tommy, at the hope and trust and newness of him and thought, yes, he's beautiful, but not in the way that guy thinks. And so my conscience eased. Any father on the block would go along, even if he didn't have the guts to take the responsibility.

As agreed, Richie Lubanski called Saturday afternoon.

"Hey, Gino." I don't know why he called me Gino instead of Gene — maybe he saw *The Godfather* too many times. "It's all set. One night next week. We have to make that little transfer we talked about."

The phone is in the hall and the door to the kitchen was open. Roz was in there making spaghetti gravy.

"Uh, yeah, I'll meet you at the same place. Monday night about seven."

"The town dump is closed Mondays, Gino."

Why hadn't I thought of that? It's the details that matter in writing, like everything else. "What about meeting me at the railroad station?"

"Good idea. Tell ya what, I'll park at the end of the lot. Seven o'clock. Then we'll wheel over to your block and view the premises."

I hung up to find Roz standing in the doorway. She likes to monitor phone conversations. "Who was that?"

"Ed Miligan from the office."

"He's going to meet you at the station Monday night?"

"Yeah, so I can check some color proofs, then go right back to the city."

I'm not sure she believed that, but finally decided it didn't matter. I waited a minute, then went into the den. *The following Monday evening, the men who had met at the town dump made their second contact, this time at the railroad station. The bigger and huskier of the two, whose name was. . .*

What the hell was his name? Stumped again. I cast around. Ted, Lennie, Frank, Bill. For some reason I couldn't make up my mind. Why was that?

All of a sudden, Tommy was there. The Mets had gone two innings already. I'd been wracking my brain for almost an hour.

We were in the fifth, a 3-2 pitch coming up, when Roz walked in and dropped her bomb. "I've invited Mr. Storrs for dinner. I thought he might be lonely on Saturday night. What's the matter?"

"Nothing's the matter. You made me miss my pitch."

"Oh, the pitch!" She made a face and flung out. Sometimes I wonder if she resents the closeness Tommy and I have developed over sporting events. My mind started working fast. Did this visit mean an extra scene for the story? Was there a chance for dramatic irony? I read an article about that once. It is something much appreciated by editors.

I went in the kitchen for a beer. Roz was nowhere around, neither was Annie. Probably gone to the Stop 'n Shop for some fancy food. But when the game was finished (Mets lost) they weren't back. I went upstairs for a nap while Tommy went visiting. I was tired from all the excitement.

I didn't find out where the distaff side had gone until we were sitting around with our Heublein's before dinner.

Roz had painted her fingernails, all ten of them, silver. This is the sign of a big event, though why she would consider a visit from Storrs special, I don't know. Maybe she was looking forward to a conversation about the decline of the novel.

"I'm going to study dancing with Mr. Storrs, Daddy."

I guess I wasn't paying attention because Annie repeated it, her voice looping higher.

"I haven't told my husband, yet," Roz confided to our guest.

"He won't mind, I hope," Storrs replied.

I had the sudden impression I was not in the room.

"Well I'm not sure." Roz let out a little fake laugh.

It was time to speak up. "How much is it gonna cost me?"

"Oh let's not talk about that, Gene." Roz shrieked gaily at the idea of discussing money.

"Oh Daddy!" Annie was adenoidal with embarrassment.

I hitched around in the wing chair. No point in making a big deal out of it. There'd be no payment of any dance bill around here.

"While you and Tommy were glued to the TV this afternoon Annie and I went to Mr. Storrs's studio." Roz flashed her silver fingers. "He thinks Annie is just loaded with talent."

"Oh, yes, quite. Definitely." Storrs, who was wearing a leatherette outfit this evening, vest and little tie of vinyl with matching pants, gave his eye flash.

Well why not, I thought. "I think that's a great idea."

I was rewarded by a hug and a kiss from my little girl, the sweetest sugar in the world.

"I knew he'd go along," Roz was confiding to our guest again, who flashed his eyes and flapped his hands. Then they started discussing classes for adults — a project Roz had dreamed up. Seems like all the ladies on the Welcome committee were dying to cram their butts into leotards and prance around. That's a bill that won't come due, either, I thought, aware that I was beginning to drip a little. I got up and opened a window, then went to the hall to mop up. Funny, I was self-conscious about my body fluids with this guy around, even in my own home.

Dinner was okay, though we took sides at first — me and Tommy against them. I wasn't surprised to find the spaghetti and gravy had been replaced by lobster newburg. Conversation wasn't too difficult because the guest did all the talking. He told us about his season in Monte Carlo and his adaptation of Maori hunting dances and his invitation to learn kabuki in Tokyo and God knows what else. The kids, even Tommy, kept asking, "What happened then?" which upset me a little. But, of course, remembering his shoe boxes and his 3x5 cards, I wasn't surprised he could spin a story. In a week or two I'd have my own story, I thought, just hang on. That made me feel better.

It was when I came back downstairs, after seeing the kids to bed, that I got my big shock, though. They were both sneaking out of my den! That's right, Roz and Storrs, guilt plastered all over their faces, were in the act of stepping over my private threshold!

When Roz saw my face, she gave her fake laugh, now crossed with a sputter. A minute later she lost her poise, which is her favorite possession next to the kids and the house. She stammered, looked around, and took out her hankie. The guest who, to give him his due picked up signals fast, decided it was time to split. Which he did very gracefully, with a remark about the pleasure of having Annie as a pupil. At the door I thought he was going to give us a curtsy, but he did his seal flipper movement and departed.

Roz was quiet, cleaning up. I went to the TV. A "Love Boat" re-run is not my favorite show but it didn't matter. I didn't trust my mouth at that point. Every so often, Roz came in for a check-up but I didn't turn around.

She was already in bed, very innocent, when I finally went up. I gave her a hard look. "Why did you take that guy in the den?"

She wriggled under the covers. "He asked to see the house."

"It's private in there."

"What's private about a desk and a bookcase?"

You can never tell with Roz, or any woman for that matter. Lies come natural to them. "Did you show him any of my papers?"

"Oh Gene, you know I wouldn't do that."

She was either telling the truth or giving an Academy Award performance. Probably the latter. "You didn't say anything about us collaborating?"

She widened her eyes, probably having learned that from our friend. "You said not to."

"That's right, I said not to."

As I mentioned earlier, Saturday night is main-event time in our house, but tonight I wasn't in the mood. Even though Roz reached over and turned on our special light — red, inside an abalone shell, which we bought in Bermuda. When I made it clear how I felt she flipped on her eye mask and said no more.

❏

One of the advantages of having your own business is the freedom of movement, cash-wise. There was no problem making out ten checks to petty cash for five hundred each and back-dating them. This might trigger an IRS audit, but Roz would never find out I needed five grand in a hurry.

Just before seven on Monday night, I drove to the station. Little Richie turned up in his Continental, which he parked alongside me. I switched off my motor. When he released his passenger door I slid in. The money was in a number ten window envelope, no return address. He put it in his jacket pocket without counting. A nice detail, I thought, something to remember.

"Let's go, Richie," I said, thinking this was not a good line of dialogue. Just as we pulled out, the 7:02 from the city arrived and the usual wrong-way housewives, meeting their husbands, gummed up the lanes.

"There's number 134." We pulled up in front of the Gabler place. It was dark tonight — no lights at all.

"What's the set-up?" Richie asked.

I laid out the ground floor to him, including the back door. Then I warned him about noise. "This street is one big radar trap, Richie. The Elm Street Ear. Your man has to be careful."

"No problem." Richie looked easy. To tell the truth, now that we were getting close, I was sweating around the clock. Richie studied me. "This is a piece of cake, Gino. Relax. We got quite a bit of experience."

"Maybe you do. I don't."

"You'd feel better if you knew the plan but. . ." he trailed off. "Tomorrow's the night."

"Tomorrow," I said, mostly to myself, taking out my handkerchief.

After I got home — Richie had driven me back to the station to pick up my own car — I stood in the yard a long time, not ready to go inside. Roz was still in a mood, the kids were always fretful on Monday night, and I was not in top shape myself. Still, there was no place else to go. Only as I turned to move did I check out the Gabler place again. The lights were on in the back now. Probably in the study, I thought, writing up new 3x5 cards.

The next day was the worst in my life -— or should I say the next to worst? My ex-secretary, Sabrina, needed more money. I'd already paid for the goddam operation, even though she'd probably been banging half the guys in the pressroom. Also, her kid sister Norma had been blabbing, so now there were some very nasty statements coming over the phone.

"Okay, Gene," Sabrina's voice sounded just like a man's — women get this hormonal change sometimes, don't ask me why. "I want another grand by Federal Express tomorrow or Norma goes to the D.A."

Now why should that make me feel guilty? In ancient times, 14-year-old girls were practically grandmothers. Still, listening to Sabrina talk about some of the cases now getting publicity, I decided not to argue. What's another grand?

But this wasn't all. Right after lunch we had a press break-down, followed by an accident with a messenger on a bike. All this was in addition to my little problem on Elm Street.

But everybody was happy when I got home, not even noticing Daddy's discomfort. Annie had had her first dance class, Tommy had just got a signed photo from Howard Johnson, and Roz's mother was coming for a visit. I wondered if this was more dramatic irony coming down on me.

Once or twice during the evening I went to the front window, craning my neck to look at the Gabler place. I was having my doubts again. And then the worm really began to gnaw. Was I doing this because I was jealous? Because God had given this creep the talent I deserved? My forehead started raining, and then I was saved by a good thought, the way a great catch can save an inning. I was doing this for Tommy! I pictured him being invited into the house, offered some Perugina chocolates (only the best), lured upstairs. I pictured all that innocence being corrupted. And then I knew I was doing the right thing, not just for Tommy but for all the kids on the block.

I lay awake most of the night. I guess I was expecting a phone call. Or a police siren. Or maybe a scream. But it was silent like the grave. I tried to pass the time by picking a title for my story. I decided it should have death in it. Death sells books. I finally decided on *Death of an Artiste*. The little "e" at the end was dramatic irony, in case you didn't recognize it.

Then I thought about my Writer's Block. I still had it. All of a sudden the cause came to me — I didn't know the details of the ending! How could I write the story before I knew the most important thing? For example, would Richie's friends use a silencer on a Duromatic .22 target pistol, the kind the mobsters used on Sam Giancana? Would it be a garotte — the old Sicilian method? How about something more American, like an axe? Flopping over the hundredth time, listening to Roz complain in her sleep, I realized the story would pour out like syrup once the ending was set. There was nothing to worry about.

The next morning was like nothing ever happened, everybody going about their business, kids spilling milk, Roz making an appointment at the beauty parlor. I hung around, not going for the 7:42, even though I had plenty of time. I went out back and straightened my tools, putting a little oil on the blades. Roz looked out the kitchen window, but asked no questions. Antennas waving all over the place. When I missed the 8:13, she came to the back porch. But by that time it didn't matter. I had just seen the patrol car.

I got out the power mower and moved it to the front. A good way to listen and watch, hunkering down, tinkering. I didn't know the guy who got out of the car — a rookie, probably. I watched him knock, then go into the Gabler house.

Like I said, I'm slow. It took me a few minutes to realize. There was only one person who could have let that rookie into the house, and that person should have been on his back with his legs sticking straight up. Talk about sweat! In thirty seconds every article of clothing was stuck to my skin. I would have to change before I went into the city — that is, if I ever went in.

When the rookie came out, ten minutes later, he made a U-turn and drove my way. I flagged him down.

"Any trouble, officer?"

"Not serious, sir. A break-in last night, nothing taken. We'll check it out."

He nodded and pumped the gas. The car shot off — those babies have extra horses inside of them. For the first time in twenty-four hours I began to relax.

"Gene!" It was Roz on the front porch. "What's the matter?"

"A little trouble over at the neighbors, honey."

She came out fast. "You mean Mr. Storrs? Is he all right?"

I nodded. "A break-in. No damage."

In two seconds, Roz was on her way across the street. I just had time to call Richie Lubanski.

Richie's voice was low and fast. "They muffed it, Gino, what can I tell you?"

"Tell me anyway."

"He wasn't there, that's what. We didn't figure he'd be sleeping out. Maybe he got a girlfriend."

"Believe me, there's no girlfriend."

"Well, we gotta lay off for awhile. I'll be in touch."

Richie hung up and I went upstairs to change. My head was clearing. I'd been given a second chance. But to do what?

I caught the 9:08, and, believe it or not, everything was good at the office. Barney, our messenger, was off critical and doing well. Even Sabrina called to say Federal Express had come through and she wouldn't bother me any more. By the time I got back to Eastbrook, I'd more or less made up my mind. I couldn't take another night like the last one. Even a great story wasn't worth all the hassle.

Once again I was too slow. Way too slow.

The doorbell rang at seven that night, just as we were settling down for the league play-offs. It was Storrs, dressed to the eyeballs in fur. You heard me — a mink coat. I thought only Joe Namath could get away with that but I was wrong.

Roz was all girlish glee when she saw him, invited him in, doling out the "oohs" and "ahs" like a massage. I didn't say much, just nodded to keep it polite and stayed with the game. But at last I heard something that broke my concentration.

"It's my what-if technique," he was saying. "I always use it when I'm plotting a new book."

I heard Roz egging him on, like he was some kind of wizard.

"What if someone wanted to steal a writer's story file, which is really his capital?" His voice rose slightly, cutting through Howard Cosell's solid baritone. "What if, just to take it one step further, that someone planned a murder to cover up the theft?" I turned and looked at him. His eyes — lots of mascara tonight — were focused on me. I could read hate and arrogance in them, a one-two punch.

"Now what if the assassin's wife, trying to be helpful, shows the victim a plan of the crime, outlined rather stiffly as a schoolboy might do it? And the victim, now warned, attends a rendezvous at the local railroad station and follows a green Continental to his own home?"

All of a sudden my body hormones were going crazy. Tommy came over and stood next to me.

"But, and here's the interesting twist, what if the intended victim, with the help of the local constabulary, sets up his house with some discreetly-placed Camcorders — high resolution and autofocus in a low light? That would rather put a crimp in things, wouldn't it, especially when it is learned that the driver of the Continental is not only a mobster but a coward, eager to shift the blame to the person who hired him?"

He paused. Nothing could be heard but a baseball bat connecting and my pores opening and closing like slats on a venetian blind.

"Yes. If all those what-ifs were put into place I think we'd have a plot for a mystery, don't you?"

Nobody answered, but Roz's eyes moved from Storrs to me. I started to speak but Storrs raised his hand.

"Of course, one must have a title. I have decided to call it *Death Writes A Story*. It's always good to have death in the title of a detective novel. And the cover has been selected too — a painting of myself as a very young boy. A very beautiful young boy almost forty years ago. That, too, will figure in the plot, in ways I am not at liberty to divulge at present."

He stood quietly. Nobody else moved until Roz went to the TV and switched it off. Then I heard a fender scraping paint against the curb out front, followed by a slamming door. I had a good idea who it was but Storrs filled me in anyway.

"Detective Marceau is a perfectly charming man," he said, buttoning up his mink coat. "His only shortcoming is that he never reads mystery novels. He thinks they clutter up his mind. Rather a pity, don't you think?"

He held the door open for the new arrival, a big man with a tough face, then swept out with a last wave to Roz and the kids. After that the visitor took out a pad and pencil and started asking me questions. Mostly out of curiosity, of course, since he already knew the answers.

I will skip what happened next because by now you must have a pretty good idea. But let me say one good thing came out of all my troubles. I overcame Writer's Block. I'm on my third book now, which is based on the true-life experience of an inmate who was scalded to death in the kitchen. I'm calling it *Death by Degrees* and it's coming out in big chunks every day. I'm such a success, believe it or not, that *Writer* magazine is doing a profile on me. They say my life could become an inspiration to others.

Of course, I have pointed out that nobody can become an artist without suffering a lot. I thought I used to suffer, what with Roz and the kids and Sabrina and her baby sister — to say nothing of that creep down the street. But that agony was nothing compared to this. Believe me, in here it's the real thing.

KATHERINE V. FORREST
Jessie

I

"It's a bad time for you to visit, Kate," Sheriff Jessie Graham offered in quiet apology.

"I'm glad to be here, Jess," Kate replied with equal quietness. "I know how close you are to Walt. Right now you need your friends."

Kate Delafield, sipping coffee from a styrofoam cup, sat beside Jessie Graham's desk in one of the plain wooden chairs the county of Alta Vista provided for visitors to its Sheriff's station at Seacliff. She said to Jessie, "As I recall, he helped you get this job."

Jessie nodded. "I owe it to him."

"You say he disappeared Friday. Any theories about why — or where he might be?"

Jessie contemplated Kate Delafield, the strong face framed by fine graying hair, the intelligent, somber light blue eyes. Kate had last stopped here for a visit more than two years ago, and Anne had been with her. Anne's accident, her death, had happened two months after that, and Jessie had not learned of it until a week after the funeral. . .

"Woman, you're on vacation," Jessie growled, reaching to place a hand over Kate's arm, and pointedly surveying Kate's jeans and the hooded white sweatshirt adorned with a small LAPD insignia. "You're not four hours out of that smog-ridden cesspool, I'm not about to—"

"The smog's a little better in L.A. these days, Jess," Kate said with a faint smile. She slouched back into the wooden chair as if it were comfortably cushioned, and crossed an ankle over a knee. She picked up her cup of coffee. "My friend, tell me about it."

"It's a hell of a thing." For the first time in two days Jessie felt the pressure within her ease, felt a sense of comfort. She pushed herself back from her desk, rested a foot on an open desk drawer, folded her arms across her brown uniform shirt. She said in a rush of words, "There's no damn sense to it, Kate, I played cards with the man and four friends of ours Friday night, I swear he was the same as always. He left my place making jokes and waving twenty-seven dollars in winnings, he'd taken most of those dollars from me. The next morning Walt's wife calls me, claims that in the middle of that very same night he'd taken off in pouring down rain with a bag of money under his arm, without his car, and nobody's seen hide nor hair of him since. There's no *sense* to it."

Kate shook her head sympathetically; her eyes narrowed in scrutiny of her friend. "Any theories, Jess?"

"Theoretically," Jessie said with all the confidence she could muster, "he's a missing person, he may just turn up like a lot of them do." Then she felt a stinging behind her eyes and looked quickly away. "Kate — dammit, Kate, I know in my gut he's dead."

When she could control her voice she said almost angrily, "My gut feelings don't always turn out to be fact." She forced a semblance of a grin. "I had a gut feeling about Irene, too. That we'd be together forever."

"I know the feeling." Kate gestured at the case file on Jessie's desk. "Could I take a look?" Jessie handed it over. "Tell me everything, Jess. Everything you've got, right down to the fine hairs."

Jessie nodded gratefully. Then scowled, remembering the Saturday morning two days ago in Walt Kennon's house.

❏

Velma Kennon had been seated in an armchair in the immaculate living room, her red-checked apron clashing violently with the pale lavender of the upholstery. She pulled a grey cardigan loosely around her shoulders and said in soft, reluctant tones, "He had me draw out the ten thousand from our savings Friday."

Jessie's voice was sharp with skepticism. "Why'd he have you do that? Why wouldn't he do it himself?"

"Maybe it was his way of telling me." Her voice broke. "I think he was in some kind of trouble."

If she expects me to fall for this horse manure . . .

"I *know* him," Jessie said. "You're Walt's wife—but it's only been a year for you, Velma." There was hostility in her tone that she had not intended, and she added more gently. "I grew up knowing the man, we've been close friends ever since I came back to Seacliff. I *know* Walt. There's no sense to this."

Velma picked up a corner of her checked apron and dabbed at a cheek. "Well, I thought Walter loved me."

Jessie asked with renewed brusqueness, "What'd Walt say he needed the ten thousand for?"

"He said I should just trust him." The voice throbbed with injury. "Said he'd explain it all later. I think he needed that money to pay someone off, I think he was in some kind of serious trouble. Maybe trouble from back when he was Sheriff here. And whoever it was took him somewhere and . . . Maybe the ocean."

Jessie pushed herself to her feet, shifted her hands down to rest them just above the wide belt and holster. "He'll have to be missing forty-eight hours before it's official. But I'd like to have a look around now if it's all right with you, Velma."

Velma uncrossed her thin ankles and rose to her full height, not much over five feet. Her dark eyes were reproachful. "I'd never have called you if I didn't want you looking into this any way you can. Go right ahead, look everywhere."

Jessie radioed for a car to pick up Cowan, the deputy who had accompanied her; she wanted to be alone as she sifted through the possessions of Walter Kennan. She knew she might spot something odd, some little thing Cowan could miss.

After Cowan was gone, she sat in her Sheriff's car trying to collect her thoughts and fight down an almost paralyzing foreboding. Not for a moment did she believe one detail of Velma Kennon's story.

In two days of hearings before the seven Commissioners of Alta Vista County, Jessie had learned all she needed to know about the character of Walt Kennon. Ten years a retired Sheriff, he had challenged the Commissioners to ignore Jessie's superior record, her solid years of experience in police work in both Los Angeles and Alta Vista County, her administrative ability, her leadership qualities. Jessie knew that she owed the position she had held for the past year and a half entirely to Walt Kennon.

Groping for objectivity, she reviewed the facts she readily knew about him. He was sixty-four. He'd been released from Veterans' Hospital in '46, some months after the war. Had finished his education at Cal Poly in San Luis Obispo, then come back to Seacliff and taken up police work, rising to the position of Sheriff. But the shrapnel fragments still scattered throughout both his legs and the persistent severe pain had led to his early retirement twelve years later. Of his wartime experiences she remembered him saying only, "Duty. Loyalty. A man owes it."

He had settled into the town of his birth just as Jessie had — like a thirsty plant sinking deep roots. And like Jessie, had grumbled at every evidence of the oceanside town's growth. Walt's only vacations had been to Los Angeles to visit a brother afflicted with emphysema, and he returned each time even more contemptuous of big city life. He was Jessie's kind of person: quiet and leather-tough, his friendship a hard won prize, a man who kept to himself until some interior principle signaled him to speak — as he had for Jessie, as he had again just recently when a consortium of builders tried to force re-zoning of a section of mobile homes occupied by elderly residents.

Her mind dark with apprehension, Jessie climbed out of her car and went back into Walt Kennon's house. In the bedroom she inspected Walt's familiar plaid shirts and windbreakers, the baggy corduroys he usually wore around town and to her card games, his khaki gardening pants, the fleece-lined jacket for the few really chill days of winter, the well-worn cardigan sweaters, the one good blue suit with the white shirt protected by plastic. Like herself, Walt had few clothes; he preferred what was tried and true and comfortable. Jessie noted that the clothes Walt had worn last night — gray corduroys, a blue plaid Pendleton shirt, a black plastic raincoat — were not in the closet. Everything there seemed orderly, undisturbed.

As did Velma's closet. The contents were modest: house dresses and cotton robes, a few skirts and frilly blouses, three good woolen dresses. But inside several large zippered plastic bags were smartly styled suits and dinner dresses, high-heeled sandals and evening shoes stored in plastic compartments — all of these apparently relics from Velma's past, and all of them useless in quiet, informal Seacliff.

Jessie was glad to move her scrutiny from the bedroom to an area less evocative of Velma and Walt Kennon's marriage. In the living room, dozens of *Field and Stream* back issues on the inconspicuous bottom shelf of the small bookcase were the only concrete traces of Walt Kennon. In heterosexual marriage, Jessie mused as she browsed around the carefully appointed room, precious little of a house ever really belonged to the male; his part of the closets maybe, and the yard and garage. The living room *always* belonged to the woman. Yet there was no evidence of Velma in this room either, Jessie realized — or anywhere else. Odd that the house had changed so little during the entire year of Walt Kennon's second marriage.

Remembering how swiftly she'd made her own quarters austere again after the three year disaster with Irene in Los Angeles, Jessie moved into the den adjoining the living room. She looked at a framed photo of Velma and Walt on the small, leather-topped desk, and admitted that she disliked Velma Kennon intensely.

And yet she'd accepted her at first, and willingly. Walt had been five years alone with his grief, and it was good to see him happy. And Velma was a pretty woman, and vivacious. But the buoyancy had soon left Walt's step. And Velma's prettiness and high energy seemed to fade with each succeeding month of her marriage to Walt. Only once in the past year had Walt invited the Friday night poker group to his house — when Velma was away visiting her parents in Garden Grove. Walt and Velma seemed to be two people who had leeched the vitality from each other.

Jessie could easily account for Walt's faithfulness to this joyless marriage — the same reason he had never questioned his wartime obligation: *Duty. Loyalty. A man owes it.* As for Velma's reason, it appeared to be the classic one: she had no means of support other than Walt Kennon.

Jessie opened the top drawer of the desk. She found a twenty-five thousand dollar insurance policy, Velma Kennon beneficiary; a copy of a deed to property in Santa Barbara which had been signed over to Bergan Construction Company on January ninth — only two months ago; and a bank book. She opened the bank book. It showed a ten thousand dollar withdrawal made this past Friday and a current balance of two hundred and eighty-six thousand dollars; two hundred and fifty thousand of that amount had been deposited on January nineteenth.

Jessie gaped at the numbers for only an instant. She knew all the surface details of Walt's life, he'd willingly shared them; but never had she heard him speak specifically of his finances. No more than he had ever shared his grief and loneliness for Alice, or talked of how his leg had been shot from under him during the assault on Guadalcanal. He'd muttered about the cost of living — had grumbled at the card game about expensive repairs to his Toyota — but she knew he contributed to the support of his chronically ill brother, and he always seemed to have sufficient money. She had assumed that he lived in relative comfort on a combination of military and police pensions and social security.

"Velma," Jessie called, "could you please come in here a minute?"

Velma glanced blandly at the bank book. "It's Walter's money. His savings, and proceeds from selling a house in Santa Barbara that belonged to his first wife." Her voice took on bitterness. "When my first husband died I didn't have two thin dimes left after probate."

Jessie tapped the bank book with a fingernail. "Says here it's your money as well, Velma. As joint tenant." Then she added reflectively, "I remember about that Santa Barbara house — Alice wouldn't sell it. Amazing it was worth so much money."

"The land it's on was re-zoned commercial years ago. She never did one thing with that place for years," Velma said harshly. "Never even raised the rent of the people living there. Him either, after she died."

"Alice liked the tenants," Jessie said mildly, picking up the executed deed, turning it over in her hands, her mind lighted with the image of Alice Kennon. Genial, comfortable Alice, with mink brown hair that had suddenly gone gray and then whitened over the years, and hazel eyes always radiating humor and spirit, conveying that everything about Jessie — everything — was just fine with her. She had given Walt

Kennon a glow of quiet contentment for twenty-six years, until the diagnosis of pancreatic cancer. Just a scant six weeks after that, Jessie Graham had borne one of the heaviest burdens of her life — the casket of Alice Kennon to her gravesite in Rolling Hills Cemetery.

Replacing the documents, Jessie brushed a finger along the lock mechanism on the drawer. She bent down to examine it. "Walt mentioned a couple of weeks ago he'd made out a will, to make sure his brother was taken care of. One of those handwritten wills. Holographic, they call them."

Velma looked startled. "I don't know about any will." She added with belligerence, "I never saw it."

"Drawer's been forced open," Jessie stated, watching her. "You know why that'd be?"

Two thin furrows formed between the penciled brows. "The drawer's never once been locked so far as I know. I don't know what anybody'd take."

Maybe that will.

The yard was neat, well tended, the grass wet and spongy under Jessie's feet. The pain in Walt's legs had limited how much he could do but he loved gardening, and well-cultivated flower beds bordered the front of the house and the side hedge. Last night's heavy rain had separated and caked the dirt around the bushes.

Jessie walked up the driveway past the house and opened the garage. The gray Toyota was parked against one wall; garden utensils lined the opposite wall. A few woodworking tools lay on a scarred bench. She picked up a plastic hood and covered the circular saw that Walt used to cut his firewood. A movement caught her eyes; she glanced over to catch the flutter of curtain at the kitchen window.

So Velma was watching her. With heightened senses she examined the garage minutely, donning a pair of Walt's work gloves to pick up and study each tool. She found nothing unusual until she came to a well-used but very clean shovel. At the kitchen window, Velma Kennon watched openly as Jessie studied it. She replaced the shovel and went into the house.

Velma stood at the kitchen counter slicing a tomato; its rich earthy odor reached Jessie. It occurred to her that she had always seen Velma Kennon in a colorless dress covered by a red-checked apron with big pockets.

Jessie said evenly, "That's a mighty clean shovel out there in the garage."

"Walter left it out in the rain last week," Velma said, her eyes on the knife slicing through the ripe red tomato.

"Didn't rain last week," Jessie informed her.

"Well, whenever it last did," Velma said in exasperation.

Jessie said, not bothering to soften her skepticism, "Being careless with one of his tools isn't something Walt would do."

Velma's knife stilled. She stared at Jessie, then said with asperity, "It doesn't sound like Walter to just go off and disappear without a trace, either."

"Don't think that's what he did."

She locked eyes with Velma Kennon. Velma's unreadable dark stare did not waver. Finally Jessie said, "Could I trouble you for the keys to the Toyota?"

She followed Velma into the living room. Velma picked up her purse from the desk.

"Could I trouble you to look at the purse," Jessie said. "Just routine."

"Of course," Velma said with distinct sarcasm, and thrust

the leather bag at Jessie, her fingers rigid. "As I recall, I think I've got thirty-two dollars in bills, and a little change."

Jessie did not reply. Of course Velma wouldn't be stupid enough to carry any of that ten thousand dollars in her purse. Removing one object at a time, she carefully placed on the desk a comb, wallet, lipstick, compact, metal nail file, package of tissues, ballpoint pen, checkbook. The checkbook register showed ordinary transactions.

"The ten thousand," Jessie said. "What denominations did the bank give you?" She examined the zippered pocket and lining of the black leather purse.

"Five hundred in twenties," Velma muttered, her lips in a thin tight line, "the rest in fifties and hundreds."

Jessie nodded. "That's quite a wad of cash." She handed the purse back to Velma. "I'll let you put everything back the way you want. We have to look at everything, Velma. Just routine," she added absently, thinking that Walt had bought chips at the poker game with two tens.

Jessie unlocked the car. The Toyota Celica showed the usual signs of five-year wear, and smelled of Walt's pipe tobacco. She added the powerful beam of her flashlight to the morning sunlight, and examined the interior. She'd impound the car; Elbert and Ron over at Martinsville would go over it thoroughly. But there were no visible stains. Of any kind.

Deep in thought, she walked slowly to her own car and replaced the flashlight in its sprocket. Money and property were the reasons for many marriages — and the motives for the vast majority of crimes. Most people would say Velma was not the type to kill, but she knew anybody was the type. Knew it from those years of police work down in Los Angeles and fifty-two years of plain hard living. Only their Maker knew why people did the things they did.

Something had happened to Walt — and Velma had done it. Of that Jessie was certain. She shifted her gunbelt, adjusting the heavy holster, wishing she could do the same for her leaden heart. Velma had done something to him, and taken him somewhere to dispose of him.

But where? And how? It just wasn't physically possible for a hundred and ten pound woman of nearly fifty to do much with a man Walt's size, certainly not against his will, and not if he was dead weight, either. Walt had become heavier recently; he was a good hundred and seventy pounds, maybe more. He'd joked ruefully about it just last night as he helped himself to potato chips and dip at the poker game. . .

Another memory of the poker game leaped into Jessie's mind. She whirled and trotted back to the Toyota. Walt's complaint about expensive repairs to the Toyota — he'd picked up the car on the way to the poker game, he'd had it in for a brake relining and carburetor work, plus routine maintenance. . .

Jessie yanked open the car door, knelt to scan the Union Oil sticker on the door frame, then compared the mileage figure written there by the service station to the mileage on the speedometer, jotting the numbers in her note pad. Velma Kennon watched from the kitchen window.

From the time Walt had picked up the car it had been driven two miles and whatever number of tenths that were unaccounted for. Gil's Union Oil Station was around the corner from the Kennon house; Walt had driven from there to Jessie's house for poker. Based on the time Velma had given as Walt's arrival home, he'd come directly here from the poker game. By marking off those distances in her own car she could tell if Walt's car had been driven after he'd arrived at his house. One thing she knew for sure: If this car *had* been driven, it hadn't been driven far.

Concealing her excitement, Jessie clumped back into the house. "Velma," she asked, "you drive that car after Walt got home last night?"

"Why . . . no. Of course not."

"I'm sealing it off, impounding it for the time being. I'll say goodbye to you for now."

Velma wiped her hands on her checked apron. "Something bad's happened to him," she said. "I know it."

I'll bet you do.

"I guarantee," Jessie said, her tone heavy and ominous, "I'll find out. One way or the other, I'll find out."

She had turned then and stalked out to her police car.

II

Jessie had taken Kate to an early dinner at the Sandpiper, a weathered clapboard restaurant on a steep hillside overlooking Seacliff and the Pacific. She restrained herself from supplying more details of Walt Kennon's disappearance while Kate gazed at a bank of fog drifting its way in over the horizon, over white-capped swells of gray-blue ocean.

"As good a career as you had in L.A.," Kate said musingly, "I can see what compelled you to come back here."

Jessie smiled, and realized that she had not smiled in the past three days. "Much as I don't understand it, Kate, I see that you belong where you are, too. They need the best cops they can find down there in that nether side of hell."

Smiling, Kate picked up her scotch. "You don't get lonely up here, Jess, away from any sort of . . . activity?"

"Gay women, you mean." Jessie refrained from pointing out that Kate herself was on vacation alone. "We do have gay people here — hell, we're everywhere. Seacliff has fourteen thousand population now, it's a fair-sized place. A few folks know about me . . . some of them have long memories. I was chasing after girls in this town from the time I was six."

She chuckled along with Kate. "I'm private about myself just naturally. But I can't say I'm all that careful, even though some people here would jump at any reason to see me gone. They can't abide the idea of a woman Sheriff, let alone—"

Jessie broke off to Kate's raised hand. Their first course, clam chowder, had arrived. Intoxicated by the aroma, Jessie dipped her spoon eagerly into the rich meaty creaminess, realizing that she had scarcely eaten since Saturday. As the waitress moved away Jessie continued, wolfing down the chowder as she spoke, "I'll tell you the truth. My time with Irene told me one thing plain as day — I'm cut out to be a bachelor. I'm still your perfectly normal queer," she added with an embarrassed grin, "I do love women, I drive up to San Francisco now and again and get in some girl chasing. But this town is my family, I've got roots here, and responsibility, good friends—" She broke off and put down her soup spoon. Walt's disappearance was again like an iron weight in her stomach, displacing further desire for food.

"Tell me about the Kennon car." Kate's voice was dry, businesslike. "I assume it checked out clean?"

Jessie's smile was inward. Kate had not changed much;

when her mind was locked into the details of a case, she spared limited attention for even such distractions as spectacular views of the Pacific or general conversation.

"No traces of blood," Jessie answered, "not in the car or on any of the tools. And Velma was made joint tenant on the savings account the week after Walt married her. Walt's the kind to do something like that."

Kate finished the last spoonful of her chowder, pushed the bowl away. She steepled her fingers and contemplated Jessie over them. "That's a point, Jess. If you're right about your gut feeling then the motive here figures to be money, pure and simple. Since she's joint tenant, why would she do anything to Walt? Why wouldn't she just clean out that account and take off?"

Jessie nodded. "It's a good point. But I've figured out a couple of reasons. Velma doesn't seem the type to run even if she knew how to cover her tracks, and that's a lot harder to do in these days of computers. She'd have to cover her tracks awfully well with Walt after her, him being an ex-cop. I think she'd figure he'd track her down, she wouldn't feel safe for a minute."

"And if she simply divorced him," Kate mused, "she probably wouldn't come out with much of a settlement, considering the length of their marriage."

Jessie moved her soup bowl aside and pulled a folded sheet from the Kennon case file, a real estate map of Seacliff. "I've measured mileage to the exact tenth, Kate. Drove from Gil's Union Station to my house, then back to Walt's. I've got to think he came as direct as he could to my place — Gil at the station said Walt picked the car up at six fifty-five, five minutes before the station closed. Walt arrived just after seven, like he usually did, and I've got four other witnesses to prove it."

"And afterward," Kate contributed, "aside from Velma's statement about when he arrived home, he wouldn't have reason to go anywhere. It was pouring rain—"

"And everything in town was closed, anyway," Jessie concluded. "So I got one and eight-tenths miles clicked off what Walt drove. That leaves an extra two tenths to account for, plus whatever other tenths were on there because the gas station only wrote down the whole number. Meaning Walt or Velma drove the car half of that distance, and Velma drove it back the other half."

Jessie extracted a pen from her uniform shirt pocket with the ease of habit. "Here's the Kennon house." She indicated a point on the map in the center of a circle inscribed in pencil. "I took a compass and measured and drew this circle around the Kennon house—"

Kate reached for the map, studied it closely. Jessie said, "Most of it's residential."

"True," Kate said, "but there's some vacant land in here, Jess, and part of a cemetery."

"Rolling Hills Cemetery," Jessie said with a nod. "Alice Kennon's buried just on the other side of my circle. The cemetery's all grass, kept perfect, just like a lawn. I checked it out Sunday. And all that vacant land, I walked every bit of it, Kate. I looked at every damn square inch."

"You said it rained hard Friday night," Kate pointed out. "Heavy rain could cover up traces of a grave."

Jessie looked at her soberly. "I'll tell you the truth. I don't expect to find a grave. I mean, how could a little thing like Velma Kennon dig a grave? Anybody who's ever put a shovel into the ground can tell you uncultivated earth is like digging into cement. Earth wet from rain is like lifting a pile of rocks."

Their food arrived. Jessie looked at her swordfish with indifference. Kate sprinkled lemon on her lobster, then cut off a piece and munched on it as she continued her study of the real estate map.

Jessie said, "Let me fill you in about the other leads I checked out."

❑

"Sheriff Graham," the young teller had said nervously, "I gave Mrs. Kennon just what she asked for—"

"I know you did, Sarah. Now just relax," Jessie said in her most reassuring tones. "There's no problem about it at all. Were any of the bills in series?"

Sarah nodded. "But that much money in cash, I had to take it from the PG&E payroll, and that's close onto a hundred fifty thousand dollars, so there's no telling which of those bills I gave her."

Disappointed, Jessie said, "Thank you, Sarah. You call me now if you see any transaction Mrs. Kennon makes that's unusual, all right? Confidential, you have my word."

Jessie interviewed Ms. Neville, the librarian, who had telephoned Saturday afternoon as word of Walter Kennon's disappearance spread around town.

"It was six weeks ago, Sheriff." Ms. Neville peered at Jessie over the narrow rectangles of her reading glasses. "She never did check anything out. Every day for a week she came in here. And hasn't been back since." Her words were a sibilant, penetrating whisper in the single-room cavern that was Seacliff's public library, crowded and murmurous at this mid-afternoon hour on the weekend. "Can't say what she was reading, either. And that's what seemed so suspicious. She'd just put her book right back up on the shelf and move off if I came anywhere near."

The librarian's reproachful frown deepened. "Why would anybody care if another person saw what she was reading?"

Maybe she just flat resented your nosiness, Jessie thought. But she said gently, "Ms. Neville, can you tell me what general section she spent her time in?"

"The sciences. Anatomy. Medicine."

❏

Jessie cut several pieces from her swordfish, moved them around on her plate. "I'll tell you what else I did. I talked to everybody in the Kennon neighborhood — nothing. I ran a check on Velma Kennon's background — nothing. I sent urgent inquiries to every doctor and pharmacy in Alta Vista county, all I've turned up so far is a Darvon prescription when Walt had dental surgery."

Jessie took a forkful of baked potato. "I'll tell you, Kate, I'm baffled. I can't figure what Velma did or how she did it. Right now my theory. . ." She thrust the forkful of potato down in recoil from the images. "I think maybe she's chopped him up and got a piece tucked here and there." She braced, expecting incredulous laughter.

But Kate said firmly, "Jess, put that nightmare out of your head. I'm not claiming this woman doesn't have the alligator mentality it takes to do such a thing, we both know better. But look at your own body, think about all those quarts of blood. Imagine anybody trying to cut through bone and muscle. Imagine the kidneys, the intestines. With all respect, Jess—"

Jessie nodded hurriedly, feeling both foolish and immensely relieved. "Got to be an answer to this, Kate. Got to be."

Kate said, "Why don't I take a few bites of that swordfish you don't want?"

Jessie cut a large section from her fish. "The rest of this'll be a nice treat for Damon, my cat."

Kate nodded absently, her eyes once more on the Pacific. "Before we go up to your place, I'd like you to drive me around the circle on this map. While it's still light."

III

Velma Kennon sat in her living room sipping tea, the day's *Courier* in her lap. But she was watching the patrol car, a black menace drifting along her street. Having passed the house twice, it would circle the block and come back once more. And a half hour from now, repeat the process. Velma knew the habits of Seacliff's Sheriff's Department well; she had been under its close surveillance for the past three days.

With an irritated shrug she unfolded the *Courier*. Her eyes were instantly drawn by a name in a small headline down the page:

Former D.A.R. Chapter Pres.
Margaret Paxton Dies Here

She shook the paper open and scanned the short article extolling the accomplishments of Margaret Paxton, sister to the recently deceased Grant Paxton, then turned to the obituary page. The notice was almost identical to the one six days ago which had branded itself into her memory. Chilled, she dropped the paper back into her lap, stared out at the black police car cruising back past the house.

Not much longer, she reassured herself, sipping the hot, bracing tea. Only a matter of days before Sheriff Jessie Graham could no longer justify detaining her in Seacliff, before the Sheriff would have to pursue her all the way to the coast of Florida if she wanted to continue her useless surveillance. A few years from now Velma Gardiner Kennon would be the stuff of memory and legend in this town, the suspected murderess who had somehow conjured away the body of her husband.

Soon . . . it would all happen soon, and exactly as she'd planned. She had a nice solid nest egg now, and the day would come when she'd have even more — when Walter was declared dead and his life insurance paid off, and the title to the house would clear as well. A few more days and she'd have her freedom. After two years of pure misery, she'd earned it.

Never again would she suffer the humiliations of facing the future without resources. She would be able to forget those months of paralysis after Johnny's heart attack and the stunning news of his insolvency, when all the security she'd taken for granted for nearly thirty years had been wiped out. And the bitter months afterward when she'd been forced to live on the proceeds from her few good pieces of jewelry, when she'd learned how friendships just melted away once you were in trouble. And the job she'd been forced to accept as cashier in the dining room of The Duquesne, a hotel frequented by traveling salesmen and the women who found its dining room and bar convenient for assignations with those salesmen.

Walter Kennon had been an anomaly in such surroundings, pure chance bringing him there for the ten days of his visit with his ill brother. His interest in her had been tentative, shy, and awkward; and she, having by this time taken cold-eyed stock of her situation, knew that marrying a man like the colorless, uninteresting Walter Kennon was probably about as well as she could do.

When he said she resembled his deeply mourned Alice, she had laid siege to Walter Kennon's affections by asking myriad questions about Alice, then pretending to be like her in every way she could devise. To her despair, Walter had returned to Seacliff after those ten days — but a month later reappeared to sheepishly propose marriage. That very same day she had resigned her detested job and, in triumph, traveled back with him to Seacliff.

But the town was slow-paced and quiet beyond all imagining. The spring and summer months of cloudy, foggy weather were depressing, unmitigated by the presence of the ocean; and the modest stucco or frame houses and their ordinary inhabitants were equally depressing. Her first husband had loved to socialize, to dance and drink; Walter Kennon sternly disapproved of alcohol, and looked forward only to his weekly poker game. Of all her pretense before their marriage, he was most unforgiving of the lie that she, like Alice, knew the game of poker and loved to play it.

But, deadly dull as Walter Kennon might be, he was, she conceded, kind and decent, and a good provider. She lived comfortably, if not agreeably.

In the first days of their marriage he had shown her the contents of the locked desk drawer. "So you can rest easy about everything," he told her. "There'll be plenty enough for you, but I've written out this will making it a condition my brother Ralph's taken care of, too. I've made Jessie Graham executor, I'm depending on you both."

She had agreed, of course. She seldom disagreed, argued even more rarely. As the waif taken under his wing, any wishes of hers were subordinate to his decisions, and in his house she could not so much as move a pillow from sofa to chair without him moving it back. The ghost of Alice Kennon pervaded every room including the bedroom: Walter was indifferent to her physically.

Every aspect of their marriage was a sham; and her status in the life of this man, her distinct inferior, added a fresh layer of gall to all her other humiliations. Walter Kennon had married her only to keep his memories alive, to serve as a reflection of his enshrined Alice.

Smothered by her life, without any acceptable alternative, she daydreamed of moving back to Los Angeles to flaunt economic independence under the noses of the "friends" who had deserted her; she yearned to live independently amid the bright lights and energy of a major city. She longed for freedom unencumbered by Walter Kennon.

Then the letter from Bergan Construction Company had arrived. The company was interested in the property in Santa Barbara, prepared to make an offer. There was a toll-free eight-hundred number to call.

Walter had crumpled the letter, thrown it into the trash. "Alice's parents left her that house. The Herreras, they've lived there for years, Alice promised they could stay so long as they pay the taxes and upkeep on the place. I'm bound to keep that promise."

She had fished out the letter and called the toll-free number the following day. And learned that the land was now re-zoned, and Bergan Construction would offer a quarter of a million dollars clear cash, the buyer paying all expenses of the sale. Stunned by the magnitude of the offer, she explained the situation. Perhaps, Jack Bergan suggested, with Mrs. Kennon's approval, and provided he had her cooperation in the matter of selling the property to him, he himself might talk to the tenants. Perhaps they could be persuaded to move out on their own. . .

Two weeks later a terse communication had arrived from Mr. and Mrs. Raul Herrera. At the end of the month they would be vacating the home they had lived in for nearly thirty years. The brevity of the note, its coldness, had bewildered, then hurt, then infuriated Walter.

At the height of his railing over the Herreras' lack of gratitude, Velma detailed the problems involved in refurbishing the house and finding suitable new tenants. When another letter from Jack Bergan fortuitously arrived in the next day's mail, Walter picked up the phone and called the eight-hundred number. Velma did not know how Jack Bergan had managed the Herreras' eviction, nor did she ever inquire.

She was now joint tenant on a bank account amounting to over two hundred and ninety thousand dollars, and heir to the house and Walter's life insurance and pensions besides. She could not simply take the money from the bank account — even if Walter's friends at the bank did not notify him moments after such a withdrawal, where could she run to that Walter would not find her? No, it would all be hers only when Walter died, and never mind that blood-sucking brother of his.

If only Walter would die.

The phrase echoing in her mind, she immediately told herself she meant nothing by it. Over the following days, as the thought further implanted itself, she argued that she was not truly contemplating murder, merely examining the possibility out of pure curiosity. And she continued to repeat this to herself during the months she spent seeking a method, a foolproof plan: she was merely searching out the solution to a difficult and fascinating puzzle, the only interesting thing she'd found to do since coming to this dreary town.

It was no easy matter, she learned, to safely rid oneself of a person. Modern crime detection was too highly sophisticated. And when the person was an ex-Sheriff who knew how to protect himself, who had strong ties to current law enforcement, the problem was immeasurably more thorny.

She dismissed the idea of a handgun: how did one go about finding an unregistered weapon and disposing of it properly afterward? Walter of course had a gun — his old service revolver — but the possibility of arranging an accident with that weapon seemed hopeless.

And how did one go about obtaining undetectable or untraceable poison? Stabbing was out of the question; it required expertise as well as a high degree of luck, and made a dreadful mess besides. Other methods — gassing, bludgeoning, pushing Walter from a height, arranging an accident with the car — presented their own problems. What if the result was not death but permanent injury? What could be worse than being condemned to caring for Walter Kennon, invalid, for the rest of her life or his? And if she was caught and convicted of murder, she would undoubtedly go to jail for the rest of her life, if not face a hideous death inhaling cyanide in California's gas chamber.

Given the fact that any method had to be absolutely foolproof, arranging Walter's death by other than natural causes seemed an impossibility. Yet there had to be some way. . .

IV

As Jessie traversed the circle she had drawn on the real estate map, Kate asked several times to stop. Once she got out of the car to look over a low bluff into a grassy ravine; then to tramp a weed-choked lot; then to scuff a jogging shoe in the dirt of another lot recently cleared of brush. As daylight faded to gray, she had Jessie stop at Rolling Hills Cemetery.

Jessie stood with Kate on the tar-surfaced road alongside the graveyard, its long green hillside extending all the way down to the fog-shrouded sea perhaps a quarter of a mile away. A hand extended over her eyes as if she were shading them from the sun, Kate looked out over the perfectly sodded graves with their embedded granite markers.

Realizing the memories undoubtedly triggered by this scene, Jessie offered gruffly, "My folks are buried here, you know." She gestured toward a distant green hill. "On the old side where Alice Kennon is. It doesn't have these flat headstones that all look alike." As Kate nodded in reply, Jessie reflected that she herself was getting just as cantankerous as Walt Kennon about every change in the world she knew and loved.

Kate lowered herself to a knee and ran a hand over the bent Bermuda grass of the hillside. "Tell me again what Walt was wearing Friday night."

"Gray corduroys, a blue plaid Pendleton shirt."

"A plastic raincoat, you said."

"That too. He arrived in it, left in it. A black one."

Kate stood, brushed her hands together to remove the dust of the grass. She walked slowly and for some distance along the hillside, stopping just beyond a white stake to examine a single tire track beside the paved road, any distinguishing features of the track obliterated by the recent rain.

"I have to tell you," Jessie muttered, staring down the smooth, steep hillside, "I considered the notion Velma might've rolled him down this hill and all the way to the ocean, I really did. I even walked it. But the land flattens out down there—" she gestured, "—a good hundred yards at the bottom of the hill. No way she could push or drag him to where the hill drops again. No way in hell."

Kate said, "I'd have considered the exact same idea, Jess."

Her hand once more across her eyes, Kate again surveyed the cemetery, a deepening gray shadow as nightfall approached. Jessie felt a renewed comfort that Kate was here and reviewing every detail of this investigation with her.

"Jess."

Alerted by the tone, Jessie looked sharply at Kate; but she was turned away from her.

"Anne told me once she wanted cremation." The tone was low, distant. "But I buried her, you know. Cremation was what her family wanted too, but they were good enough to leave me alone about it. The thing was, she burned to death. I couldn't bear to burn her again. Can you understand that?"

Jessie managed to find her voice. "I do understand. I do."

"But I think about her all the time there in the ground. And her not wanting to be where she is."

Jessie took Kate's arm. "I think she'd want exactly what you wanted," she said quietly, firmly. "I think she'd understand. I think she wouldn't mind."

Kate turned to Jessie, slid an arm around her waist, walked with Jessie toward the police car.

V

Velma could not remember the precise moment when she made the clear and irrevocable decision to kill Walter, but it was soon after that morning when she waited in the car as

Walter paid his weekly visit to Alice's grave. She observed the cemetery custodians rolling a freshly sodded grave, completing the interment process for a funeral held the day before, and she realized then that the true key lay not in foolproof method but in foolproof disposal of the body.

In the days afterward she deduced a method for ending Walter's life that would leave no evidence behind, deduced the exact circumstances that would allow her to handle more than a hundred and seventy pounds of dead weight. She decided that she would roil the waters of an investigation by withdrawing ten thousand dollars — any lesser amount seeming insufficient to confuse the issue of Walter's disappearance — and stash the money under the flower beds where it could remain until safe to remove; and if it was discovered in the meantime, what did that prove?

To validate her choice of weapon she made several trips to the library. Then she carefully fashioned her disposable, untraceable bludgeon from sand mixed with heavy steel bolts she found in Walter's tool chest, packing the material into one of Walter's thick wool socks until she was satisfied with the weight and heft. Knowing the act itself would take every ounce of strength, her every fibre of nerve, she waited in a state of feverish dread for ideal conditions.

Each morning she wrenched open the *Courier* to the obituary page. Over a period of the next five weeks there were seven burials at Rolling Hills — but either they were in the old section of the cemetery, or the weather was clear. Twelve times it rained — but there was no funeral.

Each morning as Walter ate his breakfast and prepared for a new day of golf or fishing or gardening, her anxiety grew. It was now March, and the prime rainy season along the

Pacific coast was waning. She might very well have to wait until late in the year before the rains returned — six more months at least of living with Walter in this dismal town before she had a likely opportunity.

Then she rose on a Friday morning to gathering black clouds over the ocean and a forecast of rain, occasionally heavy, throughout the day and night. She pulled from her apron pocket a two day old obituary:

Grant R. Paxton, 68, beloved husband of Margaret Paxton; loving father of John and Edward Paxton; devoted grandfather of Christopher and Julie Paxton. Services Friday, Mar. 7, 11:00 am at First Presbyterian Church; interment at Rolling Hills Cemetery.

She had already checked out the Paxton plot; it was located near the cemetery road and held two Paxtons already, with room for four more. Best of all, tonight was poker night; she would not need a pretext to lure Walter to the car at a late hour. Fearful as she was, just as well he would not be home until that late hour.

Pacing the living room, she heard his car pull into the detached garage just before midnight. She flung a raincoat over her shoulders and dashed from the house, her heart thudding, a hand clutching the crude truncheon weighting down her apron pocket.

Walter, his black plastic raincoat shiny with rain, emerged from the car and blinked at her in surprise.

Her voice raspy with strain, she gasped, "I just noticed I lost the diamond in my ring. I'm positive it's in the back of the car."

With a muffled exclamation he turned and yanked open the rear door. Her heart hammering against her ribs, she pushed the raincoat from her shoulders and stepped swiftly up beside him. Gripping the weapon in both hands she swung it behind her to give it the widest possible arc.

He bent down to climb into the car, then started to rise. "The car's been at Phil's station. How—"

She hit him squarely and with all of her strength just along the side and toward the back of the head, exactly where the medical and anatomy books said it was most dangerous to sustain a heavy blow.

There was a single sound from him, a grunted expulsion; then he pitched forward onto the back seat.

She stared, appalled at the concavity in his head, the gray matted hair welling with blood. What had she done wrong? There shouldn't be any blood — there *couldn't* be any stains on the car's upholstery. Panic-stricken, she stuffed the weapon into her apron pocket, hastily untied the apron and climbed over Walter's back to roughly, tightly bind his head.

She felt for the pulse in his wrist, his neck, as the books had said, as she'd practiced on herself. A second blow would not be necessary; there was no pulse. And she could see that the apron had staunched any flow of blood. Calmer now, she climbed out of the car and went around to the other door. Gripping his shoulders, she pulled and tugged at him, sliding him across the seat on his slick plastic raincoat until he was fully in the car. She closed both doors and retrieved her raincoat, and prepared for the rest of what needed to be done.

VI

Hands in the back pockets of her jeans, Kate stared out the huge windows of Jessie's living room, across the redwood deck at the fog-shrouded lights strung out along the ocean shoreline. As Barbra Streisand sang from Jessie's tape player, Kate prowled the room, looking over the record and tape collection, the bookshelves, poking at the fire, looking at the books again.

"Woman, what's bugging you," Jessie growled. "Sit down and relax, you're making Damon nervous." The marmalade-colored cat in her lap was stirring, its ears pricked.

Kate obediently lowered herself into the armchair beside the fire, picked up her scotch. "You sure I can't get you something, Jess?" She gestured to the wicker wine rack against the dining room wall. "You've got some nice reds over there."

Jessie shook her head. "Haven't had a thing to drink since this all began. It's enough trouble as it is to keep my head clear. I'm so tired, a glass of wine would put me out like a light."

"How about some coffee?" Kate's tone was solicitous. "Be glad to make it for you."

"Nope, that'll keep me wide awake and I hope to sleep a few hours tonight." She looked sharply at Kate, who was fidgeting with her scotch. She reiterated, "What's bugging you, woman?"

"Jess. . ." Kate put the scotch down on her coaster.

It was the same quiet use of her name as at the cemetery, and Jessie watched her uneasily.

"There was a funeral last week at Rolling Hills Cemetery," Kate said. It was a statement, not a question.

"Probably," Jessie answered, a prickling sensation along the back of her neck. "There's usually about one a week. I know for sure they buried Grant Paxton there. He ran Seacliff Realty, I knew him to say hello to."

"He was buried last Friday," Kate stated.

Jessie stared at her. "I don't know about that, but I can check it in a second."

She pulled herself out of her leather recliner and moved to the stack of papers on the brick hearth. "I haven't looked at a newspaper in days. . ." She sorted through the stack until she found last Friday's *Courier*, opened it to the obituary page.

Jessie dropped the paper back onto the stack, sat down on the hearth, and looked up at Kate. Her hands, all of her flesh was cold. "Like you said, Paxton was buried Friday. What are you telling me, Kate?"

Kate closed her eyes. "I'm sorry, Jess. Your gut feeling about Walter . . . is right."

Jessie rubbed her arms, edged closer to the fire. "I knew it." But still she had hoped. . .

"I'm sorry, Jess," Kate repeated.

"It's better I know. Just tell me how this was done."

VII

Driving slowly through the sheeting windblown rain, Velma pulled onto the road above Rolling Hills Cemetery and extinguished the car lights. The night was opaque in its blackness; and she drifted the car along until the fourth white roadside marker loomed by her side window. She pulled carefully over onto the grassy side of the road just beyond the marker and turned off the engine. She stripped off her raincoat; it would be useless in this downpour, and encumbering. She got out, opened the rear door of the Toyota.

Pulling, tugging Walter by his shoulders, her foot braced against the side of the car, she inched him across the seat until his head emerged from the car and struck the grass. Quickly she climbed into the car behind him and pushed his legs until he pitched fully out.

She closed the car doors, got the shovel out of the trunk. Again she pulled and tugged at Walter until he lay sideways on the hill. Bracing herself once more, she gave his body a mighty shove. He tumbled down the slope, his head flopping; she lost sight of him in the rain-filled blackness.

Carrying the shovel, wiping the pelting rain from her eyes, she staggered down the steep hill and nearly stumbled over his body. She slid the shovel down the hill knowing she could find it later, then pushed Walter, rolling him over and over in the spongy Bermuda grass, the apron coming off his head.

Standing between his legs as if she were pulling a plow, she dragged him farther, the wet slippery grass and Walter's slick plastic raincoat enabling her to maneuver him, as she had judged they would. She and her mother had once used a similar method — a quilt under a huge heavy chest to move it down into the basement. But she had been so much younger then. . .

Rain streaming from her hair into her blind eyes, she moaned with her straining effort. Would she ever get there? Then she tripped over the edge of the tarpaulin and pitched headlong onto the mound of the newly dug Paxton grave.

She sat on the tarpaulin and rested a few moments, her chest heaving. Then she climbed to her feet and used her tiny flashlight to locate the shovel as well as the apron which had come off Walter's head. She removed the rock-weighted tarpaulin, then the freshly laid strips of sod over Grant Paxton's grave, placing the strips with care on the tarpaulin to keep them intact.

Frenziedly, she began to dig, throwing shovel after shovel of the loose dirt onto the tarpaulin; the earth was becoming heavier as the teeming rain soaked it. When she reached a depth of several feet, she turned quickly to Walter.

Gritting her teeth, her arms quivering with the effort, she tugged and maneuvered him to the edge of the grave. Then gave him one final push. He thudded into the grave, face down. She threw in the apron, the weapon still in its pocket, and Walter's car keys.

She shoveled the earth back, grunting with the heaviness of each shovelful, her entire body trembling with this final exertion, and reshaped the mass of it into a mound, the surface a rapidly smoothing mud. Then she lay the strips of sod back, and reset the tarpaulin. And the rocks weighting the corners of the tarpaulin. Then she shook the muddy earth from the shovel, wiped it on grass.

Her legs giving way, her limbs jerking, she collapsed on the hillside in an agony of exhaustion, thinking she might die here herself. The rain picked up in fury, pelting her mercilessly and she lay unmoving, allowing it to slash the mud from her hands, her feet and legs, her clothes, her face.

As strength seeped back into her, she reviewed her next steps — no time now to make the slightest mistake. She would drive home, change into dry clothes. Destroy Walter's handwritten will in the fireplace and pulverize the ashes—

Abruptly she sat up. She had already made a mistake. The key to the desk was on Walter's keychain; she had buried it along with Walter. She lay back down again. It wasn't that much of a mistake. A sturdy kitchen knife would be sufficient to spring the desk drawer. After taking this much risk she *definitely* would not share any of her gains with anyone. It was now nearly one o'clock; at two she would call the Sheriff's office and report Walter missing, and then it would all be finished.

When her limbs finally ceased their trembling she struggled to her feet and switched on the small flashlight and inspected her handiwork. The Paxton grave looked untouched, the thundering rain continuing to wash away all traces of her presence. Even the shovel had been scoured clean of its evidence. Finally she summoned strength for the climb up the hill to the car, and to freedom. She had done it. And no one could possibly guess how.

VIII

Jessie moved away from the fire. She was warm, heated by anger, her mind seething with the image of the false grief on Velma Kennon's face that Saturday morning, scant hours after Velma had ruthlessly killed her own husband and Jessie's irreplaceable friend.

"I'm sorry," Kate said softly. "There was no good or gentle way to tell you any of this."

No one, Jessie thought, could have been more gentle than Kate. Not even Irene would be as good with her as this woman, with whom she shared an alien profession whose daily stock in trade was violence, who had herself been touched by the annihilating hand of death.

Kate said, "Of course you won't know if I'm right until. . . "

"I know it now." Jessie took a deep breath. "Everything you've theorized makes perfect sense. It does. To do what she did and then put him in someone else's grave—" She hissed, "It's *obscene.*"

Kate murmured, "Maybe I can get you some of that wine now?"

Jessie shook her head. She walked over to Kate, sat down

on the ottoman in front of her armchair. "I can't imagine how you figured this out."

"Anne told me," Kate said.

Jessie gaped at her.

"And then you told me the rest. The answers all came at Rolling Hills." Kate's eyes were fixed unseeingly on the fire; her voice was remote. "Looking over that place, I was remembering the day after Anne was buried. I drove out to the cemetery very early that next morning. I wanted to be with her. . . I wanted to dig with my bare hands till I could be in there with her . . ."

Jessie, her eyes stinging, kept her silence. Kate's renewed anguish over Anne was her fault. In sharing Jessie's sorrow, Kate had ripped the scar tissue from her own grief. . .

Kate's voice strengthened. "But you're the one who's responsible for solving this crime. How many investigating officers would have thought to check that Union Oil sticker? Velma Kennon would have gotten away with murder except for you. And your notion about Velma rolling him down the hill and all the way to the ocean — when I realized she wouldn't have to roll him far at all, it came together then, how a new grave as soon as it's rolled and sodded looks just like any other grave. And how Velma could use the rain, the slope of the cemetery and its bent Bermuda grass, Walt's slippery raincoat—" Fixing her somber eyes on Jessie, Kate shrugged. "And aside from all that, it seems after thirteen years in the cop business I'm beginning to think right along with the criminals."

Jessie sighed. She said softly, "You'd best get on to bed, Kate. Much as I want to, I can't lock Velma up tonight — not a thing to be done till morning and I get the search warrant to go in and get Walt. You've got only these few days of vacation, I want you out of here bright and early—"

"I'll stay up with you," Kate said firmly.

Jessie shook her head. "It's all on my shoulders now, Kate. I'd like to be alone with my thoughts."

Kate said quietly, "I do understand that, Jess."

With Kate settled in the guest bedroom, Jessie sat in her armchair and stared into the fire. But she did not yet think of Walt Kennon, or begin to mourn him; there was time enough for that. Instead she thought about Kate Delafield on vacation, making her solitary, lonely way up the California coast.

IX

The next morning, Velma again looked at the *Courier's* obituary page. Margaret Paxton would be buried today next to her dead husband — and Velma's. Velma swallowed the last of her tea and dismissed a brief impulse to attend. That would be foolish, would only arouse comment, if not suspicion. She had not realized that the bond of friendship between Walter Kennon and Jessie Graham ran as deep as it did — and she could not be too careful in these final days of the Sheriff's investigation.

Velma looked up, to see a patrol car coming up the block toward her house. Odd. This was out of pattern — another patrol car had already performed its half-hourly surveillance routine only fifteen minutes ago.

Then the patrol car was joined by Jessie Graham's car with its gold Sheriff's insignia. With a surge of alarm Velma watched both cars turn into her driveway as yet another police car came from the opposite direction to join them, screeching to a stop in front of the house.

Feeling the blood drain from her face, Velma watched Jessie Graham climb out of her car and adjust the gunbelt over her dark brown trousers. The Sheriff reached into her car to retrieve some sort of plastic sack; then marched toward the house at a purposeful pace, flanked by three deputies who drew their weapons as they approached the door.

What could this be? What had gone wrong? She had made no mistakes, *nothing* had gone wrong, there was no way on earth Jessie Graham could know *anything*.

Harassment, she decided. A last-ditch, desperation attempt to panic her, stampede her into making a mistake. Seeing the neighbors gather on their lawns and sidewalks to observe, Velma angrily threw open her front door. "What's the meaning of this . . . *circus?*"

"You're under arrest, Velma." The words were said with barely controlled rage; the dark eyes were implacably cold.

Holding the plastic sack by a corner, Sheriff Jessie Graham held it up to Velma's eyes.

A hand at her throat as if cyanide fumes were already choking her, Velma stared at her dirty, blood-stained apron.

PHIL ANDROS
Death and the Tattoo

For the second time in my life I was in the pokey. In Chicago. Accused of murder. It was, as a Brit might say, a deuced bit of inconvenience. But there I was, holed up in a cell about six by nine, a little barred window high up, a window just large enough to remind me of Oscar's line from his ballad — the "little tent of blue that prisoners call the sky." But I wasn't looking at it wistfully, you can bet. I was madder'n hell.

My first time in durance vile had been in Iowa when I was caught screwing a young guy in the washroom of a filling station. I got out of that one by a little judicious blackmail of the warden after I discovered that the warden's son was a cop, an M just itching to be slightly mistreated by a young and handsome Greek hustler. . .

But this time was a little different, a mite more serious, and twenty years later. The young and handsome Greek hustler I once was now had a bit of silver at the temples of his black curly hair, just enough perhaps to qualify him as a daddy instead of a cocky jocky $tud.

It had all begun in the time of plague when I decided to make a final swing around the country, a kind of sentimental journey to see some of my favorite people before everyone died. In the last year I'd lost a dozen friends, and furthermore — living as all of us do under a Damoclean sword — I kept wondering why the hell I hadn't come down with It myself, for no one had more reason to be fearful. Finally I decided to make the most of my good luck, and travel while I still could. Just how a hustler with thousands of tricks behind him could have escaped while thousands of young bucks with less experience were trapped was a mystery, a fluke I didn't want to examine too carefully.

So in Chicago I'd had a good evening with Art, the guy I'd once thought of as Apollo partnered with an ape, face like a gorilla's but the body of a demigod — very unlikely for a professor. That was the way he *had* looked, but now everything had slipped a little. His pecs had grown full and now pointed decidedly earthwards. I saw also that he'd ruined himself by acquiring a tattoo — a hideous black misshapen thing that might have been a panther, except that it had five legs. It must have been ten years old — blurred and heavy-lined, with a pale dot of red for the tongue. I shuddered, looking at it.

He saw me. "It's pretty bad," he said.

"You certainly didn't get that at Pete Swallow's place," I said.

"Nope," he said. "I got it at Lyle Longtree's."

"The young swabbies could never get his name right," I said. "They all used to call him Lily. Or Lila."

"Still do," he said. "Sometimes they even say Li-*lee*. But he promised he could fix it. Said he's got some mysterious new magical stuff probably made of moonbeams that he can inject to make it look like it had just been put on fresh. I'm to see him tomorrow to have him doctor it up."

"Bullshit," I said. "There ain't no such miracle — yet." But he looked so unhappy that I didn't say anything more. No one could ever have done ything to that black blob to make it look any better. The only cure for it would have been surgical removal.

Imagine the shock then that I felt when I saw his picture in the paper two days later, along with the story about his death. He had after all been a rather prominent professor in his university, and had for a time been a ghost-writer of speeches for the secretary of agriculture. He died from no apparent cause, except that his heart had stopped . . . a very sensible statement from a reporter. When the heart stops, death often is the result. Q.E.D. Very logical.

I felt unhappy for a while, but there had been so many gone. . .

At noon, three days after Art's death, I ran into another old trick of mine — Adam, the wild one who lived north near Edgewater, the guy who loved oiled bodies sliding around on an old black tarpaulin spread over the white shag rug in his elegantly furnished apartment.

"Imagine!" he said, twinkling. His face had slipped downwards even a little more than had Art's pecs and there were love-handles visible above his belt. "Ah was thinkin' about y'all, wonderin' whatever'd become of you-all." Twenty years in Chicago had not been able to change that soft southern drawl to the flat nasal midwestern rattle. I guess I wouldn't have had the nerve to charge him the regular hustler's rates now. It had been too much fun then, and after all this was a nostalgia trip mostly . . . wasn't it?

"How's about your comin' to my apartment tonight for a few drinkies?" he said, smiling with what I'm sure he considered a winning winsome expression.

"Sure," I said. "I got nuthin' on."

"You'll get into trouble if you travel around the north side naked," he said. He pulled a bunch of keys from his pocket and took one off the ring. "Just use it on the front door," he said, "and come on up. It also opens the apartment door. Make it about nine. I've got a kind of business appointment at eight, but I'll be through with that real quick."

"Hah!" I said. "Monkey business, I'll bet."

"No way," he said. "It's just — well, I'll tell you all about it tonight. I've gotta rush right now. Toodle-oo!" And he was gone with a small wave of his hand and a bigger wave of a ripe old musky cologne that smelled like cantaloupe.

I had a leisurely meal at a cafeteria in the loop, and then since it was a nice summer evening with a little breeze off the lake, I wandered over into the park to have a look at the big fountain. The small breeze fractured the rising pillars of water and pleasantly dampened everyone on the west side of the fountain.

The park was full of tourists and natives — many fat asses and fallen tits waddling around in T-shirts and pink slacks. There was something about Chicago — maybe the fumes, maybe the lake air, or who knows what? that always produced in me a kind of thoughtful attitude — or maybe I could even call it my Sophical-Phil mode — and when it hit me that evening I began to ruminate on the cause of all the sagging.

It was gravity, of course.

Ah, gravity! Mistress of the universe! It governs the fall of sparrows and parachutists, of brokers from Wall Street windows and Newtonian apples. It controls not only the rise and fall of tidewaters, but the loss of contact lenses and the drifting of a leaf from a tree top. It pulls down the eyelids and the breasts. It turns the impressive pectorals of weightlifters into the withered dugs of old women; it makes the stomach sag and the jowls draw earthwards. Under its power the nose lengthens and grows bulbous. It weakens the muscles that hold the belly firm, and flattens the rounded buttocks. It breaks the high arches of the feet and raddles the flesh of chin and neck. Under its sovereign power kings and athletes shrink and diminish, not only in power but in stature, and handsome lads turn into wizened pot-bellied monsters with spindly legs.

Dread mistress! She pulls you down as any mistress does — and just as fast!

A gaggle of teenage girls screamed and ran through the mist, chased by a coupla darkly handsome Latin studs in trousers so tight you could tell their religion. They, at least, were as yet free from gravity's pull. I watched the courtship antics with what I considered an amiable and generous avuncular eye, and when eight-fifteen arrived I started north on the elevated, screeching and bansheeing its noisy way around the curves.

Adam lived in the same building I'd visited a long time ago, a reasonably secure one without a lobby guard, so getting in with the key he had given me was easy enough. He lived on the eighteenth floor with a good view of the lake, as I remembered, and the elevator had the requisite music coming out of a hidden squawk box when you closed the door.

The cage eased itself to a slow stop and the doors opened on a softly lighted corridor. I started down towards the left, but then saw that Room 1869 lay the other direction, so I reversed and headed right. The door was solid — metal painted to resemble wood, I guessed, and the key opened the door.

"Hey!" I hollered. "Adam — I'm here!"

There was more soft music, and some rosy lights in the living room, off to the right. But there was no response from Adam.

Nor would there be. The sudden rush of adrenalin through my bloodstream set my ticker to pumping rapidly, and choked off a second call of "Ad—" after the first syllable. He lay on his side on the white shag rug, and beside him was the tarpaulin folded into a three-foot-square pile. He was wearing a dressing gown, striped blue and dark red; it was still tied around his waist, but his torso was bare. On the cap of his left shoulder which was turned uppermost was a black tattoo as formless as the one I had seen on Art, but this one seemed to be of just a panther's head, about three or four inches square. A malevolent green eye glared from it, and its fangs were bared on a dull red tongue.

I bent over his body, laying my hand against his forehead. The skin was already cooling — but still about room temperature.

I sat down heavily in a chair. My mouth was dry, and I swallowed noisily two or three times. The radio was playing a Strauss waltz. There was a muted tocking from the grandfather clock across the room, and some very faint street sounds from the Outer Drive far below.

Damnation, I thought. One of the last things I wanted at

any particular moment in my happily wasted life was any kind of involvement with the fuzz . . . unless of course it happened to be a stalwart handsome young stud giving me some kind of order about this or that — in the privacy of a bedroom or on a lonely sand dune along a neglected stretch of lake. And certainly I wanted no connection with a death of any kind — or maybe even a murder, although I could see no signs of any violence on him.

A loud banging on the door startled the hell out of me.

"Open up!" A gruff bass voice. "Police!"

If my heart had been giving me trouble before, this time it did a flip-flop that almost took me down. I panicked — and looked wildly around for an exit. None to be seen but the windows, eighteen floors up. Then I relaxed, because when you're trapped there's nothing else to do. I went to the door, took a deep breath, and opened it.

The muzzles of three .38s confronted me.

"Freeze!" Three shouts in unison.

I was so startled that my eyes tricked me — the gun muzzles suddenly increased in numbers so that I seemed to be looking at them with the hundred-lensed eyes of an insect. I saw a whole bouquet of round holes pointing at me. My hands went up — whether in response to a command I didn't hear, or from the conditioned response caused by seeing too many cop shows on television.

"W-wh-wh-at?" I stammered. "Sheez. . .!"

"Hold it right there!" a short plainclothes man said gruffly. "Up against the goddamned wall!"

❏

So that is why I sojourn here. [Alone and palely loitering. . .]
Where rust has gathered on the lock. [And no birds sing. . .]

I'd been questioned twice — at length. It seems that some-one had seen me coming out of Art's place — someone who'd known me way back when in my Chicago hustlin' days and had carried a grudge for twenty years — about what, I don't know. Perhaps he'd felt he hadn't got his money's worth. And some dumb cop said I'd been "surveilled" since coming out of Art's apartment. His use of the word made me laugh, and made a detective named McFadden laugh too. McFadden corrected him and said, "You mean we had our eye on him. There's no such word as surveilled." And then winked at me . . . and looked straight at my crotch. It's nice to know that there are friendly club-members everywhere.

I'd been properly Mirandized (another bastard expression) and allowed one phone call. I tried to locate Judge John Roberts, a name from my little black book in those days when I was making it with both him and his sailor son, but there was no answer — so I was waiting out my forty-eight hours. After that they'd either have to charge me or let me go — and there certainly wasn't much evidence against me. Moreover, I kept hollering for a lawyer and they finally sent a public defender who I think must have had difficulty graduating from grade school. So far no one had recognized me as a former Chicago cop — for which much thanks, and a fresh laurel wreath for Orpheus, keeper of secrets on Olympus.

And then — guess who showed up! Rudolf Dax, with whom I'd roomed during my brief fling as a Windy City fuzz. He still looked pretty good but his belly had slipped a little, and as he raised his cap to scratch his head, I noticed that he was nearly bald. But his profile still belonged on a Roman coin.

"Fuh chrissake, Phil," he said. "Wotcha doin' here? I saw

yer name on the bookin' sheet." He looked narrowly at me, his cornflower blue eyes lighting up just as they used to do. *Jesus, he was a handsome man . . . !* as e.e.cummings said of Buffalo Bill. . .

"I got some good news for yuh, ole buddy," he said. Then he paused and I could see, just as I used to, his little grey cells wrestling with some *big* problem. "Uh . . . well, it's good for *you*, I guess, but it sure ain't good fer who it happened to."

"What is it, Rudolf?" I said with the gentle inflection one uses sometimes with a slow child.

"Uh . . . well, there's been two more murders committed. Or at least two more dead guys. Except that one of 'em was a woman. They both had tattoos, lots of 'em. The woman also had a skin graft. One of 'em killed last night, and one the night before. Looks like they'll be processin' you outa here purty soon. Matter of fact, McFadden's workin' on it right now."

He lowered his voice and looked both ways, right and left. "You watch out fer dat guy," he said. "He's *queer!*"

That tickled me, and I had a momentary flashback to my view of the small bald spot on Rudolf's head as he bent over my crotch that first time. "Oh, well," I said. "Ain't everybody, one way or the other?"

He grinned. Happily. Innocently. "Sure t'ing," he said. "We's all got our problems, ain't we?"

Then he lowered his voice again. "Any chanct of us gettin' together again? While you're here? For old times' sake?"

"I sure as hell hope so, ole buddy," I said. I really meant it. "You still shave those broad beautiful pecs of yours?"

"Nah," he said, grinning. "I let it all grow out." He fingered a small triangle of his blue shirt open between buttons. A tuft of grey-blond hair spilled out. "See?" he said. "No more contests for me. But I still like what you and me usedta do. Specially what *you* did. You got a mighty talented tongue."

He reached his big callused hand through the bars and shook mine. "Gimme a call when you git out," he said. "I'm in th' book."

❏

It was late afternoon when they let me go and no daylight had ever seemed so beautiful. Even the gasoline fumes floating around the old jail on South State Street were fresh and stimulating. McFadden asked where I'd be staying in case 'we have to get in touch with you,' poking his tongue into his cheek and grinning. I told him the Y on Chicago Avenue. Then he asked me to sign a waiver promising not to sue them for false arrest — and I did, all too glad to extricate myself so simply from what could have turned real sticky if they had gone too deeply into my scarlet past. Little did they know that they had released the Great Whore of Babylon into their nice clean city. . .

It suddenly occurred to me that I was just five or six blocks south of where old Pete Swallow's tattoo shop used to be, and I decided to mosey up that way, past all the grimly bleak and dirty little shops and empty store-fronts. And then I saw Pete's tattoo sign hanging just where it always had, directly across from the Pacific Garden Mission.

The window still carried his elaborate neon display with his name curving above a rose in red and green, and the six elaborate sketches of handsome and hunky men illustrating the different styles of tattooing — Oriental, French, American Good and American Spotty, Maori, and S/M.

The bell tinkled when I opened the heavy door. The shop seemed much the same, even smelled the same — a not unpleasant blend of alcohol and piney disinfectant — clean and kitcheney. But who was that shrunken and diminished figure sitting in the old metal chair? A few sad last grey hairs streaked across his nearly bald head, and the hands holding a small orange box were like the dessicated claws of an ancient bird. If the years had been kind to some of the others I'd seen, they had been almost disastrous for Pete. He had always seemed a sort of young-old type, but now the young part had vanished. I did a little quick calculating in my head — and the reason for the change came clear. He must have been eighty-two or three. And with that figure in mind I ceased to be astonished. Matter of fact, he looked purty good . . . for his age.

He looked up at me. I saw the briefest possible flicker of recognition. And then he spoke, as if there had been no more than an hour's space between our last seeing each other — instead of twenty years.

"Y'know, Phil," he said, "technology's fine, and electricity the servant of man, but this time I think they've gone too far." He held up the small orange box and turned it slowly between his fingers.

"What now?" I said.

"This here's the I Ching," he said, opening the lid and pressing a button or two. Tiny red and green circles of light began to flash — randomly it seemed — in a circular design. "You get your main trend, with major and minor influences; then you look it up in this little book and that sends you to the major I Ching reference. No more yarrow sticks, no coins. Nuthin' but a goddamned gadget from Silicon Valley in Californiay. No more romance." He put the trinket aside and extended his hand. "How ya been?"

I shook it. "Dandy," I said. "If you don't ask for details."

"But that's what I like," he said.

"Okay," I said, and gave him a brief run-down on my first few days in Chicago, the whole schmear — beddings, pokey, tattoos and all — except Rudolf Dax.

"Good grief," he said when I'd finished. "Well, you were lucky they didn't dig any deeper into your scarlet past. Time was when they might have discovered you owed them about sixty thousand years in the pokey for your sexual exploits."

"Yah . . . lucky me," I said. "Just what the hell is going on in this town? Four people dead, and all of them tattooed? You been puttin' poison in your inks and colors?"

"You mean to say you think I put those tattoos on?" Pete said, bristling.

"No," I said. "They looked too old and black for your work."

Pete picked up a folded copy of a newspaper. "Here," he said. The tattoos had been reproduced — the panther with five legs, and the panther head on Adam, and the headline on the article about Adam had already labelled the murders to be the work of the "Tattoo Killer."

"See those two little dots?" Pete said. He pointed to the bottom edge of each of the pictured tattoos. "That's the way old Lily took to signing some of his early work."

"You mean Lyle Longtree?"

"Yeah," Pete said. "I used to work in a tiny letter S somewhere in every job I could — proud of my fine-line work, and with a beginner's enthusiasm. Old Lily copied everything I ever did. One year-end holiday I went to Paris and he offered to keep my shop open for me. So I let him. And what did he do? Found out later he had traced and copied every damn design on my walls — and used them from then on."

"Plagiarism," I said.

"Nothing so subtle," Pete said. "Outright thievery."

"What sort of work is he doing nowadays?" I asked.

Pete shrugged. "More of the same, I guess," he said. "I haven't seen much of it recently. I hear he's so hooked on speed that he's nearly bonkers. Someone was waiting in his shop in the outside room the other day, waiting for a tattoo, and heard the needles buzzin' away like mad. Pretty soon Lily opened the door and said 'Next,' and the guy went in. But there was no one inside and no other way out. Lily had just been buzzin' his needles and *thinkin'* he was working on someone."

"Tsk," I said.

"Cops came around asking if I put any of those tattoos on. I sent them up to see Lily. They were kinda surprised it was possible to identify his work."

"They find out anything?"

"I never heard," Pete said.

"I'm really getting interested in all this," I said.

"Whatever for?" Pete asked.

"Well, for starters — I really liked Art. And Adam too," I said.

Pete looked narrowly at me. "I thought whores never fell in love," he said.

"G'wan," I said. "An ole literary man like you? Even I could name a dozen cases, beginning with Messalina or Mary Magdalen or Camille. Anyway, I said I just *liked* them, not loved them. I'm interested just out of curiosity."

"Might get you in trouble," Pete said.

"Hah!" I said. "More so than I've already had in this town?"

"Maybe." Pete reached up to a shelf behind his chair and pulled down a notebook. "When I started in this business, I had all the customers sign a 'guest book,' names and addresses. Sent out about five hundred Christmas cards the first year. Made a design — a reindeer sitting on a chair tattooing 'Merry Christmas' across Santa Claus's chest. Of course, half of them came back. Phony names or addresses. But Lily even copied me in keeping a notebook too."

"I'm developing a kind of itch to see this Longtree person," I said.

"He's quite a salesman," Pete said. "Be careful, or you'll come away with another tattoo."

"Not too much chance," I said. "The phase of decoratin' this chassis is about over. I don't use it that much anymore. The ole dickybird I got from you way back when is all I need."

"How'd it hold up?" Pete asked.

"Just fine," I said, making a move to take off my jacket. "Wanna see it?"

"Lord no," said Pete. "Don't be so typical. Everybody wants me to see my old work. I'm not interested. Of course," he added slyly, "if showing it to me on your shoulder means I can have another look at your handsome torso, go right ahead."

I chuckled. "Another time, then," I said, hoisting my jacket back. "You haven't changed a bit. Still like to look at things, don't you?"

"One of the great pleasures," Pete said. "The church used to consider it a sin. Still does, I reckon. Called it *delectatio morosa.* Morose delectation. But what's so morose about it I never could figger out. I always enjoyed it."

I laughed. "I think I'll go on up and see this Lily person," I said. "Just nose around a little."

"Be careful," Pete called after me as I went out the door.

❑

Longtree's shop was close to the south end of the Loop, nearly under the elevated tracks on Van Buren Street. In its curved plate glass windows were large blow-ups of newspaper articles about Longtree, in which he spoke archly of his involvement with cosmetic tattooing, especially his work in tattooing "the pupils of the eyes to change their color." Odd, I thought; he must mean the irises. The pupils were black holes. But each story said "pupils." The framed enlargements were grouped in a semi-circle around a fake brown plastic skull with roses in its eye-holes. Painted on the plate-glass was his name, and underneath were the words "Tattoo Emporium." The shop was about a third the size of Pete Swallow's; the walls were white and covered with design boards, which Pete long ago had told me were called "flash."

I sauntered in. A three-panel screen decorated with palm trees concealed one corner of the small room, and from behind the palms came the buzz of working needles. I looked at the flash — it did in many cases resemble Pete's exactly, although there were some boards — mainly containing flowers and wreaths — that were new to me.

A thin face, a nose like the jib of a sailboat with huge tortoiseshell glasses riding astride it, thick ones like those that cataract victims have to wear, poked itself around the screen. The mouth was guarded by a scrawny grey needle-like mustache, waxed to preposterous points like a 1920

movie star's. A phony crazed half-smile like that of a televan-
gelist was pasted permanently on his puss.

"Be right with you," he said — a cracked old voice with
phlegm caught somewhere in it.

"Just lookin'," I said.

The palm screen did not completely cover a coupla
shelves on the wall above where his chair was. There were
several plastic bottles on the top one, labeled with the names
of the metallic colors he was using — mercuric oxide for the
red one, titanium for white, cobalt for blue, cadmium for
yellow, one called gifblaar, another "Encre de Chine" for the
India ink; and on the second shelf, several books, including
a coupla leatherette-bound notebooks. I wondered if those
were the address books for which he'd got the idea from
Pete.

I moved to a chair placed so that I could peek through one
of the vertical slots of the palm-tree screen, and saw that old
Lily was working on the deltoid cap of a good-looking young
black-haired stud. From what I could see of the design, it was
a Russian fire-bird — excellently colored with a long black
and red tail, folded wings of green and yellow, and a crowned
head with blue dots at the ends of several feathered spikes. It
certainly looked as good as some of Pete Swallow's best
work.

I was moderately surprised. This was not the all-black
stuff that Pete had said Longtree was producing all the time.

Lily was talking, a steady flow, to his customer. "Yeah," he
was saying, "I'm glad you came to me instead of some of the
jaggers you find here on Tattoo Row, because I've had more
experience than any of them."

Buzz-buzz. Dip-dip. "I've been in the business a damned

sight longer than anybody else here in town, and I know what I'm doing. . ."

Buzz, dip. "More than that, you're gonna have a tattoo done by someone who's tattooed a lot of notable people. Crowned heads of Europe. Like the King of Denmark. The Duke of Gloucester of England. The Prince of Wales, the one who married that Simpson woman. . ."

I listened as he went through, in rapid fire, the names of movie stars and rock stars, following those names with a list of improbable encounters and impossible accomplishments — from the pack of foxhounds chasing the fox down someone's back to vanish into a convenient aperture, of scaling snakes around dingdongs, of cosmetic tattoos — replacing torn eyebrows and female nipples to coloring lips and (of course) the pupils of many eyes.

A psychologist would have recognized his speech patterns and rapid delivery as caused by speed or crack or some stimulant designer drug, and would further have identified his ailment as confabulation — a lovely old word that ought to be used more. It meant filling in the gaps with fictitious events. . .

Was there time? Maybe I could check the notebooks to see if I could find the names of any of the well-known persons I'd heard him mention. I decided there was. I got up from the chair — careful to conceal my movement — reached for the nearest leather-bound notebook and flipped it open. Right! It was filled with names and addresses — just like Pete's. On the first page, dated about ten years before, were several names. Five or six were crossed out with blue pencil. But at the bottom, with a blue cross penciled beside it, was Art's name! And midway down the next page, below some more that were crossed out, was Adam's — with another blue X beside it! I shivered a little and the skin of my neck crawled a tiny bit westward.

Below that were two more crosses beside names I did not recognize, but two lines under those, one seemed familiar — Matthias Brown — and an address: 4941 Glenwood.

Where in hell had I known Matthias Brown? Or had I ever? Matthias was not a name easily forgotten; it somehow conjured up the Old Testament. . .

Then I had it! It was that guy in Milwaukee, the pedophile who'd been in the pokey down at Raiford in Florida — the schoolteacher who'd been in hot water for diddling around with kids! The address was in Chicago — had he finally moved from Milwaukee to the big city? Beside the name was a notation: "rose with Mom."

Perhaps it was time to . . . and then I heard old Lily say, "There you are, boy, as fine a tattoo as you'll get in these here United States." I put the book back on the shelf and peeked through the screen-slot again.

Lily tore off a piece of brown wrapping paper and slapped it over the tattoo, securing it with scotch tape top and bottom. "Take it off in two hours and wash it with cold water. Then keep it as dry as you can until it heals, and don't pick at it. That'll be forty dollars."

Wow! I should have been a tattoo artist! Those rates even surpassed my own! If you had a line of customers waiting, you'd make a mint!

Suddenly I began to feel a little uneasy. I had never been in the least psychic, never given to visions, weather predictions, ghostly visitations, or dreaming lucky lottery numbers, but at that moment I had a definite chill — maybe a better word might be antsy, whatever meaning attaches to that. I had a feeling that maybe I was putting myself somehow at risk — a vague disquiet or apprehension, an uncertain alarm going off somewhere deep inside.

The fresh-faced young stud came from behind the screen, grinning and sticking an arm down the sleeve of his leather jacket. "Chee, thanks, Mister Longtree," he said. "I like it a lot."

"Be sure to tell your friends where you got it," old Lily said. He was even smaller and more shrunken than Pete Swallow. His shoulders were rounded in what on a woman would be called the dowager's hump. On him you could call it the tattoodler's hump, I suppose — long years of hunching over the needles would bend anyone's spine.

His eyes slitted around in my direction, sort of snakelike. "What kin I do for you, boy?" he said.

At that moment I decided against it, not ever having been much for it. "Thought I might get another tattoo," I said, "but I reckon I've changed my mind. Have to think about it a little more. Truth is, I don't exactly know what I want."

"If you don't see what you like anywhere," he said, a certain oily tone creeping into his squeaky voice, "just gimme an idea and I'll draw up a new design for you. Absolutely no charge. Do it all the time. Even crazy ideas, doesn't matter, like to do it, no charge, glad to be of service, that's why everybody likes my work, they call me The Original Tattooist, do a lot of free-hand work, no designs at all, never have any complaints."

I didn't want to get into any discussion with him. His disjointed rapid speech indicated he was really high on something — speed, probably — and I had no wish to talk about his early black blobs that I'd seen on Adam and Art. I started to back out of his shop.

Every time I edged backwards he took a step forward, talking all the time. "You look like you need another tattoo," he said. "Got just the thing for you, how's about a nice dagger and skull, Death Before Dishonor? Or a motorcycle boot crushin' down a cop's cap? You got just the chassis needs a new tattoo. Give you bargain rates, best work, guaranteed, last you a lifetime plus six months."

I escaped, sweating, into the cool evening air. But instead of going back to Pete Swallow's shop I went downstairs into the subway, and took the train back to Chicago Avenue and the comparatively "normal" surroundings of my lodgings at the Y, where young men still soaped themselves with wild abandon in the showers and, with the same disregard for the future, still spread their legs wide on the thin sheets of the mean beds, awaiting the uncondomed entry.

❑

The next day, bright and early, I got up to check the phone books for the name of Matthias Brown. Yup, he was there — same address that I'd seen in Lily's book. I took the El northward and walked the two blocks to 4941 Glenwood. It was a dead-end street all right — it ended in the blank wall of a cemetery. His apartment was on the left side of a horseshoe-shaped complex.

I pushed his button. In a moment his voice came tinnily over the squawk-box. "Yes? Who is it?"

I told him and he buzzed me in — a little hesitantly, as if he didn't quite remember, and I suppose he didn't. But when he leaned over the top-floor railing and saw me, his face lighted up somewhat. Twenty years had not been good to him either. He was bald, and the perpetually red nose had turned bulbous and broken-veined. His face had an alcoholic flush and his teeth were too white and even to be real.

It was only eleven in the morning but he was already drunk, and that annoyed me considerably. We spent about a half hour re-establishing a kind of surface contact. He had shifted from the classroom to computers after being fired in Milwaukee because his prison record had been discovered. Now he worked at home, mostly, doing copy-work for a law firm, and sending his results back to the main office by modem. And gradually I brought him around to the reason for my visit.

"And what made you decide to get a tattoo?" I asked.

He tittered a little. "Y-you'd never be-believe me if I told you the shrink thought it might help me get over liking kids so much. Turn me into a man, more. H-help me have more c-courage, he said, 'on the battlefield of the bed.' Make me more able to c-confront a bed-partner my own age."

"And did it?"

He shook his head. ". . . Well, partly," he said, somewhat morosely.

"Who did the work?"

"Guy named L-longtree," he said.

"You heard from him recently?" I asked.

Matthias shook his head, looked blank for a moment, and then nodded. "Yes," he said, his voice slurring. "Now that you mention it, *real* recently. Yesterday. See — this rose I got, it's all faded. He called me up. Said he'd got a new process could make it look like new." He rolled up his sleeve on a disastrous looking job on his forearm — a rose that looked something like a five-leafed clover, hardly even pink, the green nearly gone from the leaves and stem, done in thick ugly lines, the "Mom" in the banner so heavy you could scarcely make out the letters. It was awful.

"Said he could make it look like new," he repeated.

"Hey, Matt," I said. "Now listen to me."

I don't know whether he understood the plan I outlined for him, or if he'd remember it. Lily Longtree had made a date with him for Thursday evening. That gave me two days to try to arrange the rest of the plan. But Matthias agreed to it, and I said I'd call to remind him on Thursday afternoon.

I started to leave. Matt laid a hand on my arm.

"Hey," he said, his big brown eyes as sad-looking as a spaniel's, "Phil — how's about a lil roll in the hay? Jus' a little one, for old times' sake?"

I disengaged myself gently. "Perhaps later," I said. "Afterwards. We'll see about it."

"Promise?" he said, rather plaintively. "You used to scold me because I liked kids too much. I've got over that . . . mostly."

"Glad to hear it," I said, and left.

I didn't really have a clear plan of action in my head at all. I went back to Pete Swallow's, but he wasn't much help.

I told him I'd watched Lily put a good-looking fire-bird on a young man's shoulder. "It was pretty good," I said. "Matter of fact — it was beautiful."

Pete snorted. "Yeah," he said. "He's picked up a lot of my tricks. Which is why he'd give a helluva lot to be able to correct his early tattoos." But he didn't really have any suggestions to make.

And finally I remembered Rudolf Dax, my old friendly fuzz. I phoned him at his home — number right in the book.

When I told him what I had in mind, he was dubious.

"Nuthin's gonna work unless you catch him red-handed," he said.

"That was my basic idea," I said.

"But you'd oughta have some legal person there to witness," he said.

"Just what I'd thought of," I said, faintly sarcastic. "Which is why I'm calling you right this minute. To ask you to be there too."

"Hey, I ain't no detec-a-tive," he said. "I'm just a patrolman."

"Wouldn't hurt you to catch a big fish, would it?"

"Uh... uh... no." I could see him scratching his head. "So ... when are you settin' this up for?"

"Thursday evening. Eight p.m." And I gave him the address again.

"Okay," he said finally. "I'll be there. It's my evenin' off anyway."

"Fine," I said, and arranged to meet him at the El station. "But you've gotta come in uniform, even if it's your day off."

"Why's that?"

I sighed to myself. I didn't know about Rudolf. There he was, still looking as if he'd just stepped down from the frieze on the Parthenon (when I'd first told him that's what he reminded me of, he'd looked blank and said 'The freeze on th' parkin' lot?' and I had greatly despaired of his little grey cells being able to rub against one another), and in all these years he hadn't improved. Still, I suppose he could rattle off who'd been Mr. Universe each of those past years without pausing in his recital.

"Because," I said. "We may catch a murderer and then again we may not. But if we really do apprehend a perpetrator, having him arrested by a cop is a lot easier than trying to make a civilian arrest, ain't it?"

"Yeah, it would be," he said.

"I'll see you tomorrow," I said patiently. "At eight."

"Okay," he said. We hung up.

❑

I didn't roll from bed to greet the rosy-fingered dawn the next morning until about ten o'clock. I had a Danish and a cuppa coffee in the cafeteria, and discovered — as I lifted the cup — that I was a little nervous already. My hand shook so much that I had to steady the cup with my other hand.

I bought a newspaper and there on the first page was an article about the four deaths. Seems that the forensics expert of the Chicago police department had sent blood samples to a nearby university with an electron microscope, and they'd had some puzzling results. They had discovered that the platelets in all four samples had coagulated, turned into a kind of red cheese, it seemed, which effectively stopped all circulation right away. They had also turned up a "proteolytic enzyme" in the blobs, and the presence of an as-yet-unknown organic substance that so far had everyone baffled because it was unlike anything on their identifying charts. They were now working on the theory that the victims had succumbed to the presence of some esoteric mixture of poisons. One expert thought that the coagulating substance had been ricin, notable as the "umbrella-tip" poison that had killed a British spy some years before — an almost undetectable "protoplasmic" substance. I began to think that the murders had been far beyond the poor talents of any unsophisticated State Street jagger like Lily Longtree. All those technical details made my head hurt.

I went to see Pete Swallow in the early afternoon. He had his screen up. Behind it, laid out on his slanted bench, was a young sailor with his pants down and his buns exposed. On the left cheek Pete had already put the imprint of a luscious pair of lips, done in brilliant scarlet as if they were partly opened, and on the other cheek he was engaged in writing "USDA Prime Cut" in a circular ring as if it had been a stenciled stamp on a roast of beef.

When Pete had finished and bandaged his work, the young sailor pulled up his pants, paid, and departed. I told Pete what I had arranged with my cop.

"But I think I'm on the wrong track," I said. "Old Lily sure doesn't seem to know enough to manage what the paper says may be the modus operandi."

"Yeah," Pete said. "Sounds far beyond that old boy's abilities. Besides — with his being on speed ... How'd he seem to you? Was he wired when you saw him?"

"With enough fiber optic to reach from here to California," I said. "He was really babblin'."

"Wouldn't be surprised you are barkin' up a wrong tree," Pete said. "Better let the fuzz handle things. Besides, you might get into a bit of trouble yourself. If anyone involved begins to notice you sniffin' around, you might end up with your own red cells all glommed together. No more sea pussy for you. Or any kind for that matter. Finis. Ended. Terminay. Kaput. Port after stormie seas, death after life, and all that Spenserian rot. Timor mortis."

"Same old classical Pete," I chuckled. "A regular storehouse."

"Keeps me happy," Pete said. "On the other hand—"

"Yeah — what?"

"Maybe he fell into all this without knowin' what really was going on," Pete said. "Maybe he really is the killer. But I doubt it."

"You know sumpin?" I said.

"What?"

"You ain't much help at all," I said, grinning. I punched him on the shoulder and left.

❑

The next day was Thursday. I found that I was not very enthusiastic about my plan after all. And Pete Swallow's remarks had added to my lack of conviction that my scheme would succeed.

The day wore on. I called Matthias to confirm that we would be there at seven forty-five. He seemed to be fairly sober, and I hoped he'd stay that way. And then I phoned Rudolf Dax at his station — or tried to, but some ladycunt put me on hold twice and forgot about me, so I finally called Rudolf's home number and left a message on his answering machine, reminding him that I'd be at the Argyle El station at 7:45, and hoped he would be too.

My nervousness increased and by late afternoon I was really jittery, a kind of jumpiness that I recognized could be cured only one way — and I hadn't indulged in that for a very long time indeed. So I retired to my cubicle at the Y, undressed, and lay down on the bed. I shut my eyes, and then in a session of sweet silent thought I summoned up remembrance of things past, until the room was peopled to overflowing with all the ghosts I could recall from the past years of beddings in Chicago — sailors and taxi- and truck-drivers, college students, judges and cops and swimmers and tennis-players and on and on and on. . .

When I was done, all traces of the frenetic had disappeared, and I was almost abnormally calm. I napped for an hour, and then went down to get something to eat. And gradually it was time to head north.

A genuine romantic thinks that nature — being sensitive to him — will always reflect his moods, instead of the other way around — which is the mindset of sentimental schoolboys. But this particular evening in Chicago played me completely false. It was as calm and serene as a custard, and in no wise mirrored the storm that was brewing in me. My afternoon with my remembered friends — and old lady Palm and her daughters — had by this time lost all its calming influence. When the train stopped at Argyle and I got off, I was even more nervous than I had been earlier.

At street level I lounged against one of the station pillars and watched the people passing — mostly hillbillies now, not the kind of persons — students, office workers, housewives — who had lived in this neighborhood twenty years ago.

Exactly at seven-forty a small black Thunderbird pulled up, and Rudolf Dax — resplendent in his black uniform — peered out at me.

"Goin' some place, fella?" he said, grinning broadly. "Hop in, I'll take you there."

His easy manner helped me a lot, and I felt my anxiety sliding away. It was just another routine police matter for him, evidently, and I picked up on his self-assurance and poise.

"What's that address again?" he asked.

I told him, and we drove there. He saw the blank wall of the cemetery.

"Quiet as the grave," he commented.

"Ouch," I said.

"How are we gonna handle this?" he said, getting out of the car. He put his cap back on, and I let out the half-breath I'd been unconsciously holding ever since I had seen how really bald he was. With his cap on, his profile in the growing dusk seemed just as handsome and breathtaking as it had been twenty years ago. Like a maiden's, my heart skipped a beat, tra-la, for Rudolf with cap on answered one of my all-time favorite cop fantasies.

"I really don't know," I said. "We'll just have to wing it. But I think you oughta be hidden when he arrives."

"I reckon you're right," he said.

"The uniform will probably scare Matthias out of his wits," I said. "Even though I told him I was bringing you."

"He got a guilty conscience?" Rudolf asked.

I didn't want to snitch on Matthias. "Hasn't everyone when they see a cop?"

Good old Matt didn't disappoint us. When he opened his door and saw Rudolf he let out a squawk and stepped back two feet.

"This here's Officer Dax," I said. "One of Chicago's finest."

Officer Dax put on his best smile and stuck out his hand to grab Matt's. "Name's Rudolf," he said. "Call me Rudolf." He pumped Matt's arm vigorously.

Matt was speechless. The beginning of a tentative smile twitched his thin lips a little. And then he managed to stutter, "G-g-glad to s-see you. C-come in." He stepped back out of the way and we went in.

"Djou guys l-like a d-drink?"

I remembered that once before a "drink" at his place meant iced tea or a coke. "Got any bourbon?" I said.

"Not for me," Rudolf said.

"I-I'll get it," Matt said, and disappeared into the kitchen.

"That's the place for you to hide when Lily comes," I said.

"*If* he comes," said Rudolf. "Ten to one he won't show."

"I think he will," I said. "But I won't betcha."

Matt came back with my bourbon. "You want some ice tea or lemonade?" he asked Rudolf.

"Naw," Rudolf said. "T'anks." He sat down in a wing chair and spread his legs wide. Matt and I both looked as if we'd been hypnotized by a cobra. Rudolf cupped his hand over his crotch and grinned at me.

"Hungry?" he said.

I was frozen. Behind me I heard Matthias gulp noisily. Damn — this was certainly a different Rudolf from the one I'd roomed with all those years ago. I might extend my Chicago stay longer than I'd first planned.

Just then the buzzer sounded. Any romantic dreams I was beginning to have popped like a balloon. Rudolf got to his feet.

"The kitchen," I said, flapping a hand at him. He moved quickly out of sight. Matthias stood uncertainly behind me.

"Push the buzzer, dummy," I said, and he did.

He turned to me. "Now what?" he asked.

"Just act natural," I said. "Tell him I'm an old friend."

A knock at the door. Matt moved to it rather awkwardly and opened it. It was Lily all right — dressed in a brown suede jacket and an Alpine style hat, complete with feather. He carried a small leather bag. His little slitted snake-eyes turned first to Matt.

"I'm here," he said. Then: "I've seen you before," he said to me. "Whatchew doin' here?"

"He's an old f-friend," Matt said nervously. "In town for a while."

"I generally do this kind of job alone," Lily said, scowling.

"I'm harmless," I said, putting on my best smile. "And I'll keep quiet."

He appeared to be thinking. Finally he said, "Okay, if you leave right after. He's gotta lie down for a while so's it'll take effect."

"All right," I said.

He put the bag on a table and opened it. All of his movements were jerky and uneven, almost spastic — a certain sign that he was well wired this evening. I couldn't check his pupils; they were hiding behind his blue-tinted glasses. He withdrew a bottle and a large hypodermic syringe.

I'd seen the bottle before. It was one of those on that shelf in his shop, the one with a name that I did not recognize, but which had seemed vaguely familiar. It had left a kind of small tickle in my brain, the sort that makes you feel you know something but can't quite recall what it was or is.

The old man took out the rubber stopper and inserted the hypo needle. He drew a good ten milliliters into the syringe.

"Now," he said to Matthias, "just take off your shirt. I put this directly into the tattoo — and that'll make it vanish. Then next week you come to my shop and I'll do the tattoo over, and you'll have a brand new one. This here comes from South Africa. It's called gifblaar."

I couldn't believe what I was hearing. There was no substance on earth that would make a tattoo vanish that way! And with that certainty there came another. From my reading of detective stories — either in Sayers or Christie or Carr — there came a sudden flashback, a memory so violent that I could feel it jump from the back-brain to the front. "Gifblaar — one of the most poisonous South African plants known.

Mixed with ricin. . ." and there the memory ended.

But that was enough. My muscles unlocked and I jumped forward, just as the needle-point was about to penetrate Matt's skin. I knocked Lily's hand backwards, but he held on to the needle.

"What the goddamned hell are you doing?" he screeched.

I seized his wrist, bending his arm backwards, and out of the side of my eye saw Rudolf emerge from the kitchen. But before he could intervene, a sudden twist by old Lily brought the hypo right to his own neck. The movement I had started continued in the arc of its direction with the force of my shove behind it. The needle stabbed into his carotid artery and I fell against him. His thumb was against the plunger, and my forehead knocked against his hand.

Rudolf seemed to be there, but all his movements were in slow motion. I was carried forward, and I stumbled against Lily. Rudolf caught him as he fell, but I sprawled on the floor.

"Damn!" I exploded, trying to scramble upright. Rudolf was holding Lily around the waist, but his body seemed limp as a rag doll, both halves drooping towards the floor.

"How is he?" I said, breathing hard.

"Feels like he's bought the farm," Rudolf said matter-of-factly.

"D-dead?" said Matthias, incredulous.

"Yup," said Rudolf. He eased the body to the floor. "Call 911," he said to Matthias. "I'll talk to 'em. We need an ambulance and a coroner."

Then he looked at me. "Sheez," he said. "What was that stuff anyway?"

❏

"That stuff" was gifblaar, all right. There were several articles in the newspapers for a few days after that, giving a history of the plant, its country of origin (South Africa), detailing its uses (not many!), saying also that it had been mixed with the coagulant "ricin" (accounting for the "blood like red cheese"), that its chemical name was fluoroacetic acid and that it was also known in a slightly different form as Compound 1080, a very potent rat-killer.

Rudolf had promised me he'd keep my name out of it — and he did. I heard a few weeks later that he'd been promoted to sergeant for finding the "Tattoo Killer." But before I left town I called him up and told him I really *was* hungry, reminding him that he'd asked me that question at Matt's place. He laughed, and invited me to his apartment and force fed me a spankin' good meal. And I also discovered that Matthias Brown really did have false teeth, which improved his lovemaking about two thousand percentage points.

On my way to New York I stopped to say goodbye to old Pete Swallow in his shop.

"Well, by damn," he said. "I hear through the telequeen network that you really did come up with the murderer. I never did like old Lyle, but that was a helluva way to go. Red cheese for blood."

"I guess his motive was partly jealousy," I said. "Of your work."

"Partly, I reckon," Pete said. "Who can tell what went on in that fried brain of his? He must have been really wild to destroy that bad early work."

"Speed'll twist the hell outa your little grey cells," I said. "You won't have so much competition now."

"Hell," said Pete. "That never bothered me. I'll really miss him. Don't have anyone to make fun of now."

"You can pick on Randy Webb or Oakland Jake," I said.

"T'ain't the same," said Pete.

He paused and lifted one eyebrow at me. "Say," he said, "by the way — any chance that we might have a . . . er . . . romantic encounter before you set sail?"

I chuckled. "What you got in mind?" I said.

"Well," said Pete, "I got this here drop-shipment of stuff from Hong Kong that I been dyin' to try out."

He opened the lid of a cardboard box behind his chair. I whistled. It was full of condoms — rolled and unrolled — all kinds, sizes, colors, and shapes — rooster heads, spiny ones, bubbly ones, barber-poles, black-and-gold striped, red ones, black ones, white and blue ones, glittery ones. He dipped a hand into the box and picked some up, letting them slide through his fingers. The sexual smell of them, a kind of latex gas, turned me on as it always had from childhood, back when I used to buy them in grade school to jack off in.

"Sheez!" I said.

"I give 'em out as souvenirs, one with each tattoodle," Pete said. "Take your choice."

I liked the black and gold one with the horizontal stripes, and picked it up. "Your back room still the same?" I asked.

"Yup," said Pete. He got up, locked the front door, and pulled aside the curtain to the darkened windowless room. I went ahead of him, and although I couldn't see him, I heard him unseat his teeth.

It was one of the finest farewells I'd ever had anywhere, anytime, from anyone.

IVY BURROWES
Terminal Anniversary

G od, Meggie, great party!" James — Jayme tonight — giggled, snagging me by the arm. He, she, was wearing a filmy crepe thing, peach, and seemed no less than delighted by my stunned reaction to her transformation from boy next door to flaming queen, so much so that she inadvertently jostled the tray of glasses I was carrying.

"Be careful, dear," she advised me, smiling an imperviously sinister smile. "One would think you'd never seen a butterfly emerge from her cocoon before."

"James, you look absolutely gorgeous," I said, winking. She really did.

"Jayme," she simpered, flushing appropriately.

"All right, Jayme," I agreed. "You should wander over and say hello to my sister. She won't even recognize you."

"Why would she? I've never even met her," Jayme laughed. "But you! I haven't even wished you a happy anniversary yet." She puckered glossy painted lips.

"Save it sweetie." I dismissed her. "Let me take these drinks around before the ice melts. I'll be back."

"You'd best be. I didn't come stag you know. I've a new beau around here somewhere. He's absolutely divine, despite a discouraging proclivity toward women," Jayme winced. "You've *got* to meet him."

"Hey, great," I grinned, genuinely happy for her. In drag or out of it, James was one of our dearest friends.

I carried on, sloshing drinks, wondering whatever had possessed me to insist upon a party. "Let's just go out, someplace nice, for a quiet evening with a few friends," Carol had proposed, bemoaning my suggestion that we hire a bartender, shaking her head at the lengthy guest list, but no. . .

"It's our anniversary," I had insisted. "Ten years! It's a momentous event, really something to celebrate." In my enthusiasm I'd forgotten that I couldn't function socially with more than a few people in a room. Everyone I'd invited showed up, except the bartender, and I didn't have time to stop and chat with anyone. And where was Carol, anyway?

"Oh there you are, Carol. Take this, will you?"

"Jesus, Meg, what are you doing delivering drinks?"

"Actually, just wandering around with them. Jeff promised to be here at 8:00 to tend bar. What time is it, anyway," I ran on, "after 9:00 I'll bet, and the cad hasn't even bothered to call. I shouldn't have paid him half salary in advance."

"Meggie, calm down," Carol chided me. "You've splashed something all over the front of your blouse. Put the damn tray down and let everyone mix their own drinks. There's plenty of everything at the bar and a couple of the fellas went out for another keg, just in case. Sit back and enjoy the party. Everyone looks to be having a wonderful time."

Carol sat and pulled me down beside her, clasping my hand. I smiled weakly.

"I can't believe you're doing this to yourself," she admonished me, wiping nervous sweat from my palm across the faded denim of her jeans. "You're a wreck. Now, cut it out. Everything's cool. Even I'm convinced that this party was a good idea."

Acquiescing to my better half, I saw that she was right. Jayme's roommate, Ralph, was a doing a stint behind the bar, and Jayme was swooning from lap to lap, lamenting her vanished beau. Several couples were dancing.

"So, who's this Chad?" Carol queried.

"Chad? Oh, Jayme's mysterious date? I haven't seen him. Jayme said he's 'divine' and bi, with that oh-my-I'm-in-love-again expression on her face, the one that precedes a broken heart." I waved at Jeanne and Jackie and pointed to another couple whom I didn't recognize immediately.

"Who's that?" I asked Carol.

"Who?"

"That woman dancing," I indicated.

"That's Chelsea's date, I guess. I don't know her name."

"Who invited Chelsea, pray?" I inquired stonily, Jayme's plight forgotten.

"Oh, Meggie, come on! I did, and why not?" She dismissed my suspicions with a careless wave of her hand. I watched Chelsea, Carol's ex-lover, dance to the music, her slender form pulsing sensuously to the beat. Her partner's movements were slightly more subdued, languishing in the residual motion of Chelsea's ebb and flow about the floor.

I spotted my sister through the doorway to the kitchen, chatting with Zeke, a really radical lesbian whom Carol had befriended at the clinic, while still in graduate school. Zeke was, as usual, ranting about something, but Leslie was smiling, apparently enjoying the conversation.

Inviting Leslie had been Carol's biggest reservation about the party. She had stiffened and turned from me, cold suddenly, changed, though to my mind including Leslie seemed an innocent suggestion.

"She can bring a friend, maybe," I persisted.

"Oh, can she?" Carol snapped. I resented her in silence for a moment, then let it go, determined to invite Leslie anyway. And she *had* come, dateless at that, demonstrating a rare acceptance of my relationship with Carol.

"I'd better go rescue Leslie," I exclaimed, rising suddenly.

"What?" Carol jerked as though she'd been dreaming and I'd awakened her.

"Leslie is over there with Zeke." I paused, wondering at the blank expression on Carol's face. "She appears in need of assistance." I liked Zeke, but couldn't quite manage to trust her.

Carol collected her wits immediately, though a dark cloud hovered over her head, and kissed me hastily. "Don't bother, Meg," she said, faintly. "I'll abduct Zeke. Relax and mingle, love. Enjoy the party."

"Happy anniversary, you monogamous wench," Zeke called as Carol approached, and I winced. Leslie paled a bit but said nothing, melting away at once into the colorful blur of the party.

Moments later, I was visiting with Alice Montoya, picking soggy broken fragments of chips from the mire of avocado dip, when a commotion encroached overhead and a shrill scream pierced through the drone of the music, crashing the party like a carload of cops. Carol charged up the stairs, and I gulped, willing myself to breathe and follow her through the labyrinth of stalled conversation and stilled dancing.

"Christ, Meggie, don't look," Carol whispered, closing the bathroom door just as I arrived. She stooped to comfort Jayme, who lay crumpled at her feet, her sobs echoing along the hallway, diminishing only as hysteria gave way to shock.

"What's going on?" I demanded, pushing past them to the ominous door. "Did someone get sick or something?"

"Someone's dead, Meggie," Carol cried, tears trembling miserably on her face.

"Who's dead? What's the matter with you two, did Zeke slip you some acid or something?"

I cracked the bathroom door, feeling heavy resistance from within the cubicle, and peeked hesitantly inside. The face of Jayme's divine lover grinned against the weight of the door, a rheumy film glowing white over his lifeless eyes. He appeared quite dead, clenching in one crippled hand my father's antiquated straight razor, a deep, jagged tear halfway across his throat. I felt for a pulse anyway and noted that he was still warm, gazing long at the thick petal of crimson that blossomed across the pale tile floor.

"Carol, you'd better claw the clops, call the cops," I tittered, unused to drinking and feeling a bit thready, but she had already gone.

By the time I found my way back downstairs Carol had tucked Jayme into bed, notified the police, and was in the process of reducing the festive mood of our guests to an atmosphere charged with the gloomy proximity of death, shivering condolences, and the general consensus that the party was over.

The sirens approached and the gathering dissipated as all but a few, who were for one reason or another envious of our unsavory plight, trickled out the door.

"Do you think the police will want everyone just to leave?" I asked Carol timorously. "I mean . . . if someone saw . . ." I trailed off.

"Shhh . . . ," she warned me. "No one saw anything."

"Carol, there's a corpse in our bathroom," I reminded her.

"I know. We'll talk about it later." She hushed me, taking my hand as the police and paramedics made their way up the walk, flanked by a useless stretcher, marching to the pulse of lights that signified an emergency though the crisis had already passed.

"What have you got there?" she whispered, unfolding my fist with her trembling hand.

I considered the object in my palm. "Oh, I forgot all about it. Leslie's earring."

"Let me hang on to it for her," Carol said, pocketing the earring. "You're likely to lose it all over again."

"Thanks. Leslie will appreciate that." I smiled half-heartedly, shrinking before the gaping doorway.

"Sergeant Reich," the leader of the procession introduced himself, extending a pudgy hand. After inquiring as to the whereabouts of the corpse, Reich disappeared with the officers upstairs to begin the physical investigation. Later, after the official confirmation of death, he returned to question Carol and me.

"What was your relationship to the deceased?" he asked.

"No relationship," Carol answered, gesturing toward a chair, which the sergeant declined. "We didn't even know him. We were having a party."

"And the other guests. . ."

"Have gone," I finished. The sergeant's demeanor confirmed my suspicion that the guests should have stayed.

Another officer, apparently Reich's junior, hastened into the room waving a wallet, presumably Chad's.

"We ran him through CII," the officer said. "No prior record."

Reich frowned as if dying was a crime Chad could have committed before. "What about next-of-kin?" he asked his subordinate.

"We're working on it," the young officer replied.

Reich returned his attention to us. Several other officers traipsed in and out of the room talking among themselves.

"So," he said accusingly, "a stranger walked into your house and ended up dead on your bathroom floor. Is that correct?"

Carol explained that Chad had come as the date of an invited guest. Now there seemed no choice but to let them interrogate Jayme.

Poor Jayme. Carol practically had to carry him down the stairs, though he tried to maintain his dignity and some composure, not that it mattered. His credibility as a witness was already compromised by the residue of cosmetic indulgence that ran in rivulets of black sorrow down his face, splotching indelible agony into the filmy fabric of his evening dress. It seemed to require every scrap of the sergeant's professional decorum, and a stern nudge that rippled among the uniforms, to keep the troops from laughing out loud.

James withstood the humiliation of the grilling that followed, tearing only slightly as he explained that he knew little more than we did about the identity of the mysterious man. "I met Chad at a bar. You know, the Blue Parrot?" They did. "He worked there, as a dancer, and he lived in an apartment on Logan. That's about all I know." And that's all he knew. They dismissed him as a bad joke and he stumbled out of the room.

The body was removed without ceremony or even the formality of a chalked reminder on the bathroom floor.

"Suicide," Reich informed us, some time later, "pure and simple. It isn't the first one I've seen in these, uh, circumstances." He grimaced sourly, as if his disgust with the matter was evidence enough to support his conclusion.

While Carol chafed at the callousness of his judgment, I felt grateful that he'd at least absolved us of any criminal responsibility, though I wasn't oblivious to the odious implications of his tone. He took his leave, telling us that the coroner would, of course, issue the final determination and admonishing us not to leave town.

After we'd cleaned up the bathroom, it was as if nothing had happened at all.

James stayed the night with us. Showered and snug, he called Ralph and insisted that he was fine and would be coming home in the morning. I wanted to call Leslie but it was late and I was afraid that Mother might answer the phone. I trusted that Leslie wouldn't say anything to her about what had happened. No point in telling her, not yet.

Leslie called early the next morning while Carol and James were still asleep.

"Have you seen today's paper?" she queried, obviously agitated.

"I'm reading it now," I replied. "I haven't even had coffee yet, but I don't see any mention of. . ."

"That's what I mean," Leslie cut in, "not one word about what happened. Not a thing."

"You sound disappointed," I retorted. She really did. For myself, I was pleased that I might be able to spare my mother this one awful thing.

"Do you want me to come over?" she demanded.

"No, I wish you wouldn't. It's been a rough time. I've been awake most of the night." I was curt. "James and Carol aren't even up."

"Okay then, bye." The line went dead.

James appeared, eyes red-rimmed but managing a weak smile as he dragged about in Carol's Levis and one of my t-shirts, a wan suggestion of his previous glory.

"Who was that you were talking to?" he asked, helping himself to coffee.

"No one," I said, hanging up, and signalled that I could use a cup of coffee as well. "There's nothing in the paper about last night," I offered, pushing the tabloid aside.

"That figures. Who cares if another fag bites the dust," he said bitterly. "Life goes on."

"Well, James," I eased in, "it's not as though. . ."

"I'm not buying the official suicide theory, Meggie," he cut in. "I just can't."

"What are you suggesting, James?" Carol asked, bursting into the kitchen.

"I'm not suggesting anything," he faltered. "I just don't believe that Chad was suicidal, that's all. I've been there. You two know that. He just wasn't the type." He considered our faces. "Besides," he joked feebly, "the prospect of an evening with me couldn't have been that repugnant."

"You think someone killed him?" I asked.

"One of our friends?" Carol added, indignantly.

"Look, ladies," James said, draining his cup, "I don't know what I think. I'd best be going home."

"Maybe so," Carol agreed, trailing him to the back door, shaking. "Are you sure you're all right?"

"Fine," he said, and started off across the lawn.

"Hey, James," Carol called after him, "who do you suspect?"

"I'll let you know," he hollered back and disappeared through the hedge.

"Chad couldn't have been murdered, do you think?" I nervously asked Carol, joining her on the porch.

"Heavens no," she replied, but didn't look all that convinced.

"Well, anyway, Chad won't be around to dump on anyone else."

"Megan, what do you mean by that?" Carol demanded.

"I was just thinking about James, I guess. You know how easily he falls in love and how often he gets crapped on. No reason to think Chad would be any different." She looked at me strangely. "It was a dumb thing to say. I'm sorry."

"No big deal," Carol said. " I thought you might suspect James." She laughed nervously. "I suppose shock entitles people to say dumb things."

"Let's go back in," I said. "It's chilly this morning." I shivered, feeling autumn in the air.

❑

In the weeks that followed, James proved right about one thing. Life went on. Carol's caseload increased at work, undaunted by the rumor and innuendo that reached a crescendo after the party and then dwindled to an unnatural hush whenever she stepped out of her office to greet a patient or walk about on rounds. My mother, apparently, was the only person in town who hadn't heard at least some version of what happened that night. Even Leslie surprised me by keeping her mouth shut.

The coroner's inquest confirmed the initial determination that the cause of death was suicide, and that was the extent of the official investigation. The weapon, after all, had been discovered still in his hands. The angle of the wound was consistent with self-inflicted injury.

Only James refused to abandon the notion that Chad had been murdered, but though his speculation was compelling, the conclusion was unthinkable. Who would have killed him, anyway? Why?

"I don't know," James admitted, "but even if he had intended to off himself, he wouldn't have done it that way. He was gay —well, mostly gay — a dancer, beautiful and remarkably vain. He wouldn't have mutilated his body. Can you imagine how much that must have hurt? He wasn't into pain."

Carol dismissed James's misgivings as obsession, grief, survival guilt, fantasy, and even wishful thinking, employing all the jargon of her profession to dissuade him. I, on the other hand, was impressed by the systematic vigor with which he employed his sleuthing and entered into his speculations enthusiastically, as if, I thought guiltily, they were a parlor game. I participated in one discussion after another, complimenting each dead-end lead, actually encouraging him without the least bit of condescension.

I provided him with the guest list from the party. He dissected it, comparing those names with others filtered through interviews with Chad's friends and associates at the Blue Parrot. He managed to locate several ex-lovers, both men and women, some communicative about Chad, others not, but none so bitter that they wished him dead. There was one woman who James couldn't run down. Though several regulars at the Blue Parrot remembered her, none could recall her name. She'd come in one night, months before, and made quite a scene, claiming that Chad had jilted her. No one had seen her since, nor had Chad mentioned her again. Though her identity tantalized him, James's queries were futile.

James had obtained entrance to Chad's apartment and sorted through everything, greedy for clues. He even contacted Chad's mother in Minnesota, who didn't seem to give a damn about her son one way or the other, and provided neither remorse nor information.

Finally one afternoon, Carol erupted, threatening to toss James out of the house, and angry at me for encouraging him.

"What's the matter with you?" I demanded of her. James fidgeted, embarrassed.

"He's upsetting you," she said.

"He is not," I insisted.

"Well, he's upsetting me . . . calling Chad's mother . . . rifling through his things . . . Chad's death on our anniversary was grim enough. I just can't stand him going on and on about it."

"Well, then, tell *him* to cut it out," James rose uncertainly, attempting to make light of it and tap dance out the door.

"Carol, calm down," I demanded. "James, sit down. Leslie always says. . ."

"I don't want to hear what Leslie always says," Carol retorted. "I'm sorry James, forgive me." She returned to me.

"I'm exhausted. I'm getting a headache, think I'll lay down for a while."

With that, she left, no kiss, no nothing. I could tell that James was wounded, too, in spite of her apology.

"I don't know what's wrong with her," I said wearily. "She's been so distant since the party. I'm really worried about her."

"She's just worn out," James offered.

"No doubt from expending her energies on common loons," I explained.

James couldn't help but laugh.

"Ah, James," I lamented, "will things ever be the same? Really the same?"

"I don't know, Meggie. The same as what?" he sighed. He slipped into his jacket and out of character, and I glimpsed past his facade for an instant and mourned the strain and anguish in his face. "I'm leaving," he announced.

"Maybe Carol is right about all this," I suggested gently.

"Maybe so," he smiled. "Oh, I almost forgot. Check out this snapshot I found at Chad's." He reached into his pocket and retrieved a photograph. "I freaked out when I saw this. Doesn't this woman in the shadows look a lot like you?" he asked, wonderingly, as he handed me the picture.

I appraised it summarily, noting only Chad with a woman at the park until I looked, really looked, at the woman's face. Though it could have been me, it wasn't. But there was no mistaking who it was, familiar in pigtails and her favorite faded blue denim jacket, with color bands of flowers embroidered down the front and around the soft, frayed sleeves.

"James, this is Leslie," I exclaimed, hearing the panic rising in my voice. "Chad and Leslie."

"Leslie," James stammered. "Your sister, Leslie?"

"She was here that night, at the party, but she couldn't . . . couldn't . . ." Something struck me. The memory of Leslie's misplaced earring throbbed in my head. She always wore clips, terrified of having her ears pierced. She lost the earring that night, at the party, and I had found it that same night, with Chad, in the bathroom. I gave it to Carol, didn't I? Carol had it. "Carol. . ." I screamed. I couldn't help it, couldn't stop screaming and screaming.

❏

Carol administered a shot to calm Meggie down and within minutes she was out. James apologized profusely and reluctantly explained everything, picking up the crumpled photograph which had fallen to the floor.

"Carol, I'm so sorry. I found the picture . . . curious. This was the woman who blasted Chad that night at the Blue Parrot, so I showed it to Meggie. I didn't mean to do this. . ." He shrugged sadly, lamenting the drugged mound on the sofa that was his friend.

Carol said nothing, settling on the arm of the couch contemplating the composite of features that comprised Meggie's sleeping face, far lovelier than any other face she had ever known.

Finally, she spoke. "It was Leslie. Leslie killed Chad."

"You knew," James stuttered, aghast.

"Not for sure. Suicide seemed a convenient explanation, plausible, reasonable, even, compared to the truth." She bummed a cigarette and lit it deftly, as if she'd not quit five years earlier. She plucked at her lover's hair, running slivers of light through her fingers, and went on. "Megan and Leslie grew up in a dysfunctional household. That's what we call them now, dysfunctional. There was incest, between Leslie and their father. Once, when Megan was ten or so, Leslie heard their father climb into bed with her. She wanted to protect Meg from what had happened to her and so she came up behind him with his own razor and slit his throat. Meggie never got over it. She always blamed herself."

"God, that's awful but what does it have to do with. . ."

"James," Carol said, putting out the cigarette, "has it occurred to you that you've never actually met Leslie?"

"So? I wouldn't introduce myself to my kid sister," James replied. "Hey, wait a minute, doesn't Meg call Leslie her little sister?"

"Now you're getting it. Leslie was seventeen when all this happened. In Megan's mind, Leslie's still seventeen. She couldn't be tried as an adult so she was sent to a camp for juveniles. While she was there, she killed herself." Hands shaking, Carol lit another cigarette.

"Then who's the woman in the picture?" he asked, watchful of his friend's face. "Meggie? Is it Meggie?"

"It didn't happen all at once," Carol replied. "Leslie overtook us slowly, biding her time. She was dormant for so long that I actually welcomed the mention of Leslie in one conversation or another. I thought it was a good thing, a glimmer of healing after so much time. I even encouraged Meg to remember Leslie, and the memory took hold." She smiled bitterly. "Megan *is* Leslie."

"Carol, this is crazy," James exclaimed.

Ignoring his outburst, she went on. "One night about a year ago, I woke up in bed alone. Meg was gone. The next morning she denied that she'd been out because she didn't *remember* going anywhere. It began happening often after that. I followed her once. She wandered from bar to bar, straight bars, aimlessly. Then she came home, crept back into bed, the same as before. After that, she started to talk about Leslie in the present tense." Carol tried to smile, but failed, painfully. "I know. Pretty scary, huh? It got so that every time I walked into a room, I felt I was interrupting a conversation, though Meggie was alone. She was talking to Leslie." James looked faint. "One day her mother called and wanted to know if Meggie had taken Leslie's old Levi jacket. I found it in a closet upstairs. When I asked Meg how it got there, she said Leslie must have left it. It goes on and on. . ."

"Carol," James said, to comfort her, but having breathed her name he didn't know what to say.

"I realized she was getting sicker, and I suppose that I couldn't deal with it myself, but I couldn't give her up!" She sobbed, revealing everything. "Even after I found her father's razor in the medicine cabinet. I couldn't let them lock her away."

"Who else knows about this?" James asked softly.

Carol's tears splashed her lover's sleeping face. "Her mother knows it, and I do, and now you. We know. Only Meggie doesn't know."

❏

They were right about one thing, Meggie doesn't know anything. I know, but I don't feel like telling them. Why should I tell them anything? They never tell me anything, like when we're getting out of here. (They never tell Meggie either, but then again, she never asks. She never says a word.)

Carol misses Meggie in the worst way. She comes to visit all the time, and she cries. Sometimes James comes. Meggie always liked him. (He really is the sweetest person. I'm glad

I rescued him from that awful Chad, just like I rescued Meggie once, from Father.) Of course Mother comes. She comes to see me, never minding that Meggie appears to have packed up and moved out. Mother always did like me best.

GERALD LEBONATI
Reunion

I f you don't take care of it now, you'll just have to come back and do it again later," Michael warned about the failing light switch.

"Fine, I'll do it later," Sam replied, screwing the plate back into the wall. He wiped his big hands on faded jeans, looked around the freshly painted room, and said, "This place is really shaping up."

"Yeah, I like it." He followed Sam's gaze to one of the moody, impressionistic paintings that seemed to flow so easily from Michael's palette. He sat in the middle of the living room on a floral couch flanked by a curvy *faux* Chippendale table.

Sam asked, "How about going out for something to eat?"

The thought of going out made Michael's stomach curdle. "I guess we could," he said unconvincingly.

"What do you have a taste for?"

"I'm not particular," Michael said, adding hastily, "but somewhere close."

"Close, huh? Well, there's Geno's." Sam looked thought-fully at Michael. "What's the matter?"

"I'm not really that hungry, actually."

Sam approached the couch. "Well, I'm famished. You can sit and drink coffee."

"Go without me."

"What's the problem?" Sam asked briskly.

"I'm nervous."

"About what?"

Michael shrugged his narrow shoulders and burrowed anxiously into the sofa.

Irritably Sam said, "What is it this time?"

"I told you, I don't know."

Sam looked away, as if to compose himself, then looked back at Michael. "Why is it that every time I want to go out somewhere, you get nervous? What is it, Michael? Are you seeing someone else? Is that why you don't want to be out with me?" His voice grew harsher. "'Cause if that's what it is, I'm going to find out, so you might as well tell me right now."

"I'm not seeing anyone," Michael replied, annoyed.

"What then?"

To make peace, Michael said, "Maybe if we took separate cars—"

Sam cut him off, "That's always your solution. Separate cars. What's with you?"

"It's just that, if we're out and I want to leave and can't, I feel trapped."

"Why would you want to leave?"

"I'm not saying I'd want to leave," Michael said, aware that he was contradicting himself, "but if something happens . . ."

"What something? What's going to happen?"

"I just don't like being in situations where I'm not in control, that's all."

"This is ridiculous," Sam snapped. "We've been living together for almost seven months now and it's always the same fucking thing. I don't understand why you're so afraid of me. What do you think I'm going to do, haul off and punch you or something? Goddammit, I love you."

"I'm not afraid of you." Michael was keenly aware, though, that the powerfully built Sam could easily overcome him if it came to that. But why would it come to that? he thought. This is crazy.

Sam now stood at the other end of the couch. "Yes, you *are* afraid of me. I keep hoping it'll get better, that you'll learn to at least trust me a little, but you don't. You don't fuckin' trust me. That's what it comes down to. And you know something, I'm sick of it. I really am, Michael. I want a normal relationship, not separate cars."

"Stop yelling at me," Michael said, pushing his fine black hair from his forehead.

"Why shouldn't I yell? I'm angry. I yell when I'm angry."

"Well, I don't like it."

"Tough shit! You don't like it, so what? I'm hungry and I'm gonna get something to eat. If you're still here when I get back, fine. If not, that's fine too." Sam grabbed his keys and left, slamming the door behind him.

Michael stared across the room at his own dim reflection in the blank TV screen, confused by the relief he felt that Sam had gone. He was afraid of Sam and it didn't make any sense. Sam was everything he'd ever looked for in a partner and Michael himself had always been outgoing and comfortable with people. At first, Michael blamed his feelings on the differences between Sam and him — Sam was blue collar, an electrician, while Michael worked at a big P.R. agency and painted. Later he thought his fears came from the stress of setting up house together, but he had slowly come to see that it was none of these things. It was as if he were rediscovering an old fear, from childhood or something, of which he had only the dimmest understanding. It was like looking into a mirror with the lights out.

❏

Cold night air seeped into the bedroom through a half-opened window, causing sheer curtains to flutter like a restless spirit. Sam slept curled up on his side, one knobby leg pulled up toward his stomach with only a sheet to cover him. Michael lay next to Sam, his naked torso exposed in a still, deep sleep. A patterned comforter lay unused at their feet, trailing onto the white carpet. The green and white glow from the stereo softly illuminated a corner of the room as Ella Fitzgerald whispered an old version of "When and Where."

As the music ended, Michael's fingers gently curled around the edge of the sheet. His smooth chest rose and fell with increasing speed like the spindly shadows of the trees on the wall behind him. His head fell to one side and then the other as beads of sweat slowly broke out on his forehead. His mouth quivered as if trying to speak, but could only groan. The shadows on the wall swayed wildly. His lips twitched more forcefully and then, in a voice higher than his own, he muttered, "No . . . don't go. Don't go," he sobbed, his voice breaking. A moment later, he spoke again, this time with rising panic. "Please, Marc, no." His body jerked convulsively across the bed and he screamed, waking himself and Sam.

Sam quickly turned on the bedside lamp. "Michael, are you okay?"

"The dream," Michael panted. "I had that dream again."

"I figured," Sam replied, rubbing Michael's back. "It's all right, crazy rabbit," he whispered into Michael's ear, "I'm here."

"I don't understand it."

Holding him, Sam said, "You called for Marc again."

"I did?"

"Who is he, Michael?"

"I don't know."

Sam looked at him skeptically and asked, "Michael, do you still love me?"

"Yes, of course I do. I'm just a little confused, that's all."

"Then maybe it's time to get some help."

"What do you mean?"

"This dream. The way you're afraid of me. Maybe you should talk to a therapist."

"Thanks," Michael said, rubbing his eyes. "Is that why you call me crazy rabbit?"

"No." Sam smiled affectionately. "Lots of people see therapists. It wouldn't hurt to talk to someone who's objective about this." He gripped Michael's hand. "I'm not and you sure as hell aren't." He pulled away and lay on his back.

"I guess I could talk to Laurie," Michael said, thoughtfully. "She's a psychologist."

"Laurie Bridges?" Sam sounded surprised. "She's also your friend. How objective is she going to be?"

"It's her job," Michael insisted. "Besides, she doesn't know anything about this."

"As long as you see someone," Sam sighed. "And soon."

"I'll see her tomorrow."

"Fine. Do that. Now let's get some sleep." He switched the light off.

Michael lay down next to Sam and touched him lightly. "Goodnight," he said and kissed his shoulder.

❏

First thing next morning he called Laurie's office for an appointment. Luckily, there'd been a cancellation and he was able to get in early, driving to her office which was in a small building just outside town. He stepped into an art-deco elevator that rattled as it took him up to the third floor. The silver doors parted and Michael clicked his way across the diamond-tiled hallway to her door. He entered a green waiting room, signed in for the receptionist, and sat down. Two magazines later, Laurie appeared.

"Hi, Michael, come on in."

She was the same height as he but a bit fleshier. Although sharp-featured and straight-nosed, her eyes were gray and gentle and peered out from behind thin wire glasses that seemed to belong to another, more romantic time. In contrast, her thick dark hair was fashionably short, threaded with gray. She led Michael into a small office that resembled someone's living room. Two big leather chairs separated by a round glass-topped table dominated the room. One wall was full of books while another held a painting Michael had done of a man adrift on a lifeboat. Her small oak desk, like an afterthought, stood cluttered in a corner, the brass lamp turned on.

They sat down in the two chairs.

"How's Linda?" Michael asked, awkwardly, not knowing how to begin the conversation.

"She's fine. She's excited about a business class that she's taking at night school." Laurie smiled. "So, how are you doing? I saw your name on the schedule this morning and I was wondering what was up."

Slowly, Michael told her about the problems he'd been having with Sam and the irrational fear he seemed unable to shake. She listened intently, as if he were giving instructions. "And every time we get into an argument," he concluded, "I have this dream."

"The same dream?"

"Yes, it's always the same."

"That's interesting. Tell me more about it," she said encouragingly.

"Well, I'm in a small room. I think it's a kitchen or something and it's dark out."

"Is it dark inside as well?"

"No, but it's hazy and indistinct."

"Okay, go on."

"I'm aware that I'm not alone. Someone else is there but I can't see him very well. I know his name is Marc."

"He tells you his name?"

"No, I just know it."

"Any connection between the word *mark* and Sam that you can think of?" she asked. "Is Marc his middle name by any chance?"

Michael shook his head slowly. "No, he doesn't have a middle name."

"Is there something he does as an electrician, like mark wires or something like that?"

"I don't really know."

"Okay, go on."

"Anyway, this guy, Marc, is going out the door and that

somehow makes me very sad. I'm just overwhelmed by this great sadness, but I don't know why, and I beg him not to go. Then he stops and I walk toward him. He turns around and his face is distorted, like an animal. He's not hazy anymore but very clear and he attacks me."

"Does he look like anyone you know?"

"It's hard to tell what he looks like because of how distorted his face is," Michael replied.

"Who does he feel like?"

"Feel like?"

"Yes, who do you think of when you see him in the dream? Who does he remind you of?"

"I can't say."

"What happens then?"

"I scream and wake up. It's always the same thing."

"And this dream happens every time you have an argument with Sam?"

"Yes."

"Do you argue a lot?" she asked gently.

"Not really," he lied. "I've only had this dream maybe three or four times. I'm not sure exactly." He worried about what she would say if she knew the dreams — and the arguments — were more frequent.

"Well, it's not unusual to have your emotions pop up in dreams, especially if you're not facing them consciously or if your feelings are in conflict."

"You think that's normal."

"I think it's not unusual, given the circumstances. You have some very strong feelings for Sam. You obviously want this relationship to work out and when it's threatened, as in an argument, your anxiety level goes up and you react by having bad dreams, that's all." She leaned back in her chair and fell silent for a moment. "I think we should try some relaxation techniques, perhaps recreate the dream to see more clearly how it might relate to you and Sam."

"I'm not sure I want to do that," Michael said nervously. "It's pretty scary."

"You'll be in complete control. Hypnosis isn't as mysterious as it's cracked up to be."

"Hypnosis?"

"I'm simply going to give you some suggestions to help you remember. You'll be doing all the work. Would you like to try?" She smiled. "I promise not to seduce you."

He laughed. "All right."

"One last thing," she said. "I usually tape these sessions, to go back over them with my clients. That okay?"

"Sure."

"Good," she said, getting up and dimming the lights. "This is just to help you to relax." Returning to her chair, she said, "I want you to get comfortable, take a deep breath, and listen to me." In a low, steady voice she directed Michael to think about and relax each part of his body, from his feet to his scalp. When she thought he was ready, she asked him to recreate the dream. He tried to visualize the scene and talk about the room and the man and the door but, in the end, he could remember nothing more than he had already told her.

"Sorry," he said, when she brought him out of the twilight state.

"That's all right, you were a little resistant. I think we should try it again."

"You think that's really necessary?"

"I'd like to see you connect with your dream at a more

conscious level. At least you'll feel that you have more control that way. You see what I'm saying?"

"Yes. Okay," he said, getting up, "I'll make an appointment on my way out."

"Good."

"Say hello to Linda for me."

"Will do. Say hello to Sam."

❏

That weekend Sam took Michael out for dinner at a restaurant with rough stuccoed walls, white tablecloths, and tall candles. After they ordered, Sam raised his glass: "To quiet dinners and crazy rabbits."

Michael smiled and took a sip. "You'd better be nice to me."

"Why's that?"

"'Cause of what my horoscope said."

"You and horoscopes."

Still smiling, Michael said, "It says I'm going to have a reunion with an old flame."

"Oh, yeah? Anyone I know?"

"That's not the response I was hoping for." He took another sip.

Sam also drank, set his glass down on the table, and said, "You know, I didn't think I'd get you out of the house. Those sessions with Laurie must've helped."

"I've only had one so far."

"Well, it worked. You're here with me."

"That's true," Michael replied. He didn't add that he knew the subway was only a block away.

Sam leaned forward. "I really love your eyes in the firelight."

"I really love looking at you, too."

Sam smiled.

Michael said, "I know that sometimes you don't feel secure with me, but I want you to know that I really do love you. If I seem distant at times, that's just the way I am. I haven't seen anyone else since we started living together."

"Neither have I."

"I wasn't fishing for that, I'm..."

"I know."

"I just want to reassure you, that's all. You seem to have this idea that I'm going to run out on you and I'm not."

Sam's eyes were shiny with affection as the waiter brought their food.

❏

On Friday, a week after his first appointment, Michael returned to Laurie's office. He wasn't as apprehensive as he sank into the well-worn leather chair. Laurie sat across from him and asked how he was.

"It was a good week. Things went well with Sam and me. I wanted to tell you that I didn't have the dream again."

"I was going to ask about that."

"Sam says it's because I talked to you," he said.

Laurie smiled. "I'm glad to hear that. Are you ready?"

"I guess so," he replied, adjusting his position.

The lights were dimmed and the tape recorder switched on. Soothingly, she directed him to clear his mind and relax specific parts of his body. Eyes shut, he listened to her steady voice. It was as if he were no longer in the office but, rather, in a familiar inner space of daydreams and fantasy. He did as Laurie directed and felt the tension drain from his body.

"Now I want you to see the kitchen that you told me about in your dream. Do you have that image?"

He paused and answered. "Yes."

"Can you describe it for me?"

He swallowed. "It's hazy."

"Tell me as much as you can about what you do see. As you speak, it will become clearer," she said, confidently.

"There's a yellow counter with a sink in it. I see a doorway that goes to the rest of the house, I think, and another door, to the outside. It has windows in it. Pretty little windows," he said dreamily, his voice weakening. "It's dark outside and I'm. . ."

"Yes," Laurie said sharply. "You're what?"

"I'm. . . ," There was silence for a moment. "Where am I?"

"You're in my office," Laurie said, perplexed. "Michael?"

"Why did you call me that?"

"What?"

"You called me Michael."

"That's your name," she replied. "Your name is Michael Edwards."

He paused, then said, "No, it isn't."

"What do you think your name is?"

Michael's breathing quickened and he squeezed the armrests on the chair. "My name is," he said, licking his lips and then sitting motionless. "Name. It's. . ." Suddenly, the expression on his face changed and when he spoke his voice was different, higher. "It's Vincent and I am weary of your incessant harping. I am not so stricken with grief that I cannot remember my own name. Good God, you'd think my own sister would leave me in peace."

The silence that followed was as heavy as the air in the aftermath of a summer storm. Startled, Laurie gazed at the man in the chair.

"And stop staring at me like a horse without a wagon."

"Uh," she stammered, "who are you?"

"I've already told you that. Weren't you listening?"

"You said you were Vincent."

"Well, at least your memory's still intact," he said, examining his fingernails.

"Where is Michael?" she demanded.

"Why do you insist on calling me by that dreadful name?"

Calmly, she said, "Your name is Michael Edwards, and you are under hypnosis in my office remembering a dream that takes place in a kitchen."

He laughed, "I assure you, madam, whenever I have the occasion to dream, it is not about kitchens."

"All right. Where do you think you are . . . Vincent?"

"At home. Where do you think you are?"

"Let me ask the questions, please."

"Just trying to help." *Sotto voce* he added, "Testy."

"Is there a kitchen in your house?"

"Most houses have them now," he replied dryly.

"Does it have a yellow counter and a back door with a window in it?"

"You already know that."

"Where is your house?"

"Why?"

"Just tell me, Vincent."

"On Oak Avenue, where it's always been."

"What number?" She moved closer.

"Seven twenty-four."

"What town?"

"Riverdale."

"What state?"

"New Jersey," he snapped. "Are you done?"

Laurie fell back in her chair, exhausted. A stillness descended in the room. Catching her second wind, she leaned toward him again to try another approach. "Vincent?"

"Yes?"

"I want you to tell me a little about Michael if you can."

"I told you I don't know any Michael."

"But you're here in his body," she said, quietly. "Where is he?"

"I don't know," he said, confused.

"Have you come to him before?"

"Why are you asking me this? I'm getting tired."

"Because I don't want you to bother Michael any more."

"What are you going to do?"

"You're going to go to sleep again and when you awaken, Michael will return. Do you understand?"

"Am I going to die?" he asked helplessly.

Strangely moved, she was unable to answer for a moment. "Relax now," she said. "In a moment I will count from one to five and when I reach five you will awaken and feel fine. One, two — coming around slowly now. Three, more and more awake and feeling good. Four. Five. Open your eyes." When he did their eyes met in a painfully long gaze.

He spoke first. "So?"

"Michael?"

"Laurie."

"Thank God."

"I fell asleep, didn't I?" When she didn't respond, he asked, "Are you okay?"

"Do you remember what happened?" she asked slowly.

"No, what happened?"

She sighed. "I'm not sure,"

"You're starting to worry me."

"I'm sorry. I don't mean to." She put her hand on the recorder and rewound the tape. Hitting the play button, she said, "Listen."

Afterwards, he sat stunned, unable to believe that it was his voice he heard, but it was all there, the kitchen, the yellow counter, the door with four small window panes, exactly as it was in the dream.

"What does it mean, Laurie?"

"I really don't know. At first, I thought it might be another part of you."

"You mean like a split personality?"

"Michael, you're not a split personality," she said reassuringly. "You're a very sensitive, imaginative human being. Sometimes when we have emotional conflicts we create dream stories to help us cope with them. They act as a way to let off steam and they express feelings that we are unwilling to express consciously. You may be stuffing some things that you don't want to face so, clever as you are, you create Vincent to face them for you. It's part of what makes you so creative."

"And what if it's something else?" he asked, emphasizing the last phrase.

"Like what?"

"Do you believe in spirits?"

"No," she said firmly. "I don't believe in ghosts."

"Wait a minute. What about the house, the one in the dream? He gave you an address."

"So?"

"I've never been to New Jersey in my life."

"Michael, there may not even be such a place."

"You wouldn't have a map, would you?"

Rising slowly, she went over to the bookshelf. "Better than that," she said and pulled out an atlas, opening it on her desk. Michael joined her as she thumbed through to a map of New Jersey spread over two pages. They moved their fingers and eyes across the pages.

"I can't believe we're doing this," she said.

"We're just covering all the possibilities," he retorted. "Riverdale, it must be by a river."

A few moments later, Laurie said, "Here it is, over here. No river."

"It's real." He looked at her.

"Michael, you might have picked this up somewhere, maybe when you were looking at a map."

"Maps of New Jersey have never been my favorite reading," he replied. "I'm going out there. I'm going to find that house."

"What if it's not there?"

"I won't know unless I look."

She walked away. "Even if there is a house, what do you expect to find?"

"A clue about these dreams," he said, following her back to the two chairs. "Who knows, maybe some guy over there is having dreams about me and my place."

"Michael, you're blowing this thing way out of proportion. I think the dream has more to do with conflicts closer to home."

"Why don't you come with me?"

She looked surprised, as if the answer were obvious. "Because it's a wild goose chase."

"Come on, Laurie, I could really use your support."

"Boy, talk about service above and beyond the call of duty."

He smiled. "You're not afraid, are you?"

"Of course not."

"Then come." He tapped her playfully. "If nothing else, it'll be a nice trip in the country."

"Well, I suppose if you put it that way," she replied. "Linda's been a megabitch lately, so a day away might be good for us."

"Absence makes the heart grow fonder."

"When do you want to go?"

"As soon as possible. Right now."

"Are you serious? I've got appointments all afternoon."

"Tomorrow's Saturday. How about then?"

"Great. You drive." She glanced at her watch. "And your hour is up."

Michael pointed at the tape recorder. "I'd like to borrow that tape and listen to it later."

She popped the cassette and gave it to him.

"See you in the morning," he said. "Eight o'clock?"

"Nine."

❏

Sam worked late to finish up a project so that he wouldn't have to work the weekend. Michael was waiting for him in the peach-colored living room, having just listened to the tape of his session with Laurie again.

"Hi," Sam said as he came in and tossed his coat on a chair.

"Hey, there." Michael kissed him eagerly. "You look tired."

"I am. I'll be glad when this job is over," he replied, walking into the bedroom.

Michael followed him in and talked as Sam undressed. "Think of the money."

"That's the only reason I put up with it, but at least I'm free tomorrow."

"Oh, I wanted to talk to you about that."

Sam turned, stripping off his shirt. "What's the matter?"

"I saw Laurie again today," Michael began.

"Oh, yeah. How did it go?" He tossed the shirt.

"Something interesting happened."

"What?"

"It seems the dream is set in a little town in New Jersey."

"Oh, yeah?" Sam grinned, putting on a clean pair of 501s. "No wonder you wake up screaming."

Michael laughed. "Yeah, but the thing is, we looked it up and there really is such a place."

"That's weird," Sam said. "So what about the nightmares? Are they over?"

"Well that's just it," Michael replied. "We're going tomorrow to see what's there."

"Who?" Sam asked, walking out of the bedroom.

"Laurie and me," Michael shouted after him, picking up the clothes Sam had thrown across the floor. He joined him in the kitchen.

"I thought we were going to work on the house tomorrow," Sam said, beer in hand.

"I know, but I think this is important to me."

Sam let out his breath, slowly. "That's great. I mean, we planned to do this all week, and then at the last minute you decide to go trekking off to God knows where to follow some stupid dream."

"I'd hoped you'd understand," Michael said.

"Well, I don't." He slammed the beer can on the table, spilling some. Michael stepped back. "You go off the deep end sometimes, and everything else falls to the wayside. Fixing up this place was something that we were going to do together. Evidently, it doesn't mean all that much to you, 'cause as soon as something else comes along you're onto it without even asking me or anything. That's what pisses me off. You're not even asking me to go along with you."

"Well, you could if you'd like. I just didn't think you'd enjoy running around, that's all."

"Oh, right. Don't do me any favors." He looked at the beer can and said, "I need a real drink." He reached up and took a bottle of J&B off the top of the refrigerator.

"You're making a big thing out of this, Sam."

"Yeah, I know. It's my fault," he said, pouring whiskey into a tumbler.

"Sam, something important happened at the session today."

"You already told me," he said, taking a swig.

Michael looked at him, "Not just about the town. Something else."

"I'm not interested," Sam said, cutting him off. He finished his drink and walked out of the kitchen to the hall closet. He got out his windbreaker.

"Sam, where are you going?"

"Not to fucking New Jersey," he said, and left the house.

❏

Michael drove to Laurie's house the next morning, leaving Sam still asleep on the couch where he'd spent the night.

"You're early," she protested, getting into his car. Holding up a thermos of coffee and two cups, she asked, "Want some?"

"Mm, smells good." He pulled away from the curb.

"Fresh-perked and mountain-grown."

They headed for the Jersey Turnpike and turned north. Near Perth Amboy they took the Garden State Parkway toward Passaic before turning west into the tree-covered countryside of north Jersey.

"There's something about this old road," Michael said pensively.

"Pretty, isn't it," Laurie observed.

"I meant, something familiar. Something about the way the hills sit by the road, and the overhanging trees."

"Have you dreamt about this, too?"

"No, but I feel a sense of déjà-vu, you know?"

"Yes, I've had those, too," she said. "There's a sign ahead. Slow down." As they passed the marker, she read, "Riverdale."

"Well, this is it," he said, swallowing hard. Clapboard houses began to appear as did stop signs and traffic.

"How do you feel?" Laurie asked, touching his hand as he downshifted.

"Nervous as hell. What am I going to say to this guy?"

"If he exists," she reminded him.

"C'mon, help me out."

Playing along, she said, "Just tell him what happened."

"Oh, yeah, right." They were stopped by a traffic light suspended above the street.

"Well, what else did you come all this way for?"

"The truth?" he answered softly. "I don't know. I haven't got the slightest idea."

The light flashed green. "Does any of this seem familar to you?" Laurie asked.

"Not really. It sort of comes in bits and pieces." Then, glancing at her, he said, "God, I just had a creepy thought."

"What's that?"

"What if he's expecting us? What if he planned the whole thing?"

"Stop scaring yourself. There's got to be a logical explanation for this and it probably has to do with your own memories. Memories you don't even know are there. Who knows, your parents may have driven you through here when you were a kid. Did you ever think of that?"

"Maybe," he said, uncertainly.

They pulled into a gas station, filled the tank, and asked the attendant where Oak Avenue was. He adjusted his cap and rubbed the back of his head.

"Well, let's see. If you take this street into town, you could turn left at Chestnut, then go for about two miles and that'll run you into Oak. What's the address?"

"Seven twenty-four," Michael said.

"North or south?"

"Not sure."

"Well, I don't know which way to tell you to turn. You'll just have to check both ways, I guess."

"No problem," he said. "Thanks."

They headed into town and Michael squinted hard as they passed an old bank and a 5 & 10.

"What's wrong?" Laurie asked.

"I know this," he replied.

"Maybe I'd better drive."

"Good idea." He pulled over and they changed places. In a minute they were back on the street again, Laurie behind the wheel, approaching an intersection.

"Anderson Street," Michael said. "Wait a minute. Turn left at the next street. It'll be Main. There's a circle with a fountain in the middle of the road."

"The guy at the station said to go to Chestnut."

"He was wrong," Michael said, firmly. "All the tree names intersect Main."

When they reached the intersection, Laurie turned left onto Main and saw the white fountain in the middle of the street, two blocks down, just as Michael had said. She circled around it and parked.

"How did you know?" she demanded.

"I just did." He looked at her. "I'm sure I've been here before."

"You're giving me the creeps," she said.

"Let's find the house."

"Right." She started up and drove off, following the road. As they passed each corner she called out the street names, "Maple, Cherry, Elm, Oak. Here it is. She turned left and proceeded for seven blocks. When they got to 724 they found an old stone church that faced the street with a big stained-glass window depicting Jesus talking to Nicodemus.

"Damn," Michael said. "It's the other way."

"So much for ESP," Laurie joked, edgily.

They turned around and backtracked, crossing Main again and going seven blocks north. The neighborhood was an old residential area that had seen better days. Some of the larger houses were now apartments and sat on wide, weedy lawns, shaded by sprawling oak trees and bordered by broken sidewalks. They drove slowly, looking at the addresses, coming finally to 724. Laurie brought the car to a stop and they peered out the window at a vacant lot.

"And that's the end of that," Laurie said.

"I don't know whether to be happy or sad."

"Well, there's no house, no kitchen, and no Vincent. I'm afraid we've just been chasing a fantasy. You probably pulled the address out of your head. Maybe you heard the numbers somewhere and remembered them under hypnosis. That happens sometimes." She read the disappointment on his face. "We were prepared for this, Michael. We knew it was a possibility, remember?"

"What about the town?" he insisted, stubbornly.

"Same thing. You know, the mind is incredible. You might have seen a map and subconsciously picked up Riverdale because, I don't know, maybe you have a thing for rivers."

"But I knew there was an Oak Avenue in this particular town," he said, ignoring her attempt to joke him out of his mood.

"Michael, there's an Oak Avenue in hundreds of little towns around here."

He sighed. "Maybe you're right."

"Sometimes these things. . ."

"The fountain," he said excitedly. "How do you explain the fountain?"

She shrugged. "Michael, I'm just saying there is an explanation, not that I know what it is. I just don't want you to be disappointed."

He rapped the dash with his fingers.

"What are you thinking?" she asked, hesitantly.

"How do we find out who owns the lot?"

"You're not serious," she said. When she saw he was, she said, "The city tax assessor, probably."

"Let's go."

"First, you're going to buy me lunch," she said, "for chauffeuring you around."

"Right."

Michael insisted that they stop at the first coffee shop they saw. Inside, they sat at a formica-covered table next to a window that looked out on the parking lot. On the juke box, Barbra Streisand sang "The Way We Were." From the kitchen counter a black cook yelled the names of the aging white waitresses as their orders came up. Their own waitress, a strawberry blonde, sauntered over to the table, put the food down, ripped a check off her pad, and placed it on the table in what seemed like a single motion. "Enjoy," she said. Michael chewed nervously at his ham and cheese sandwich while Laurie dawdled over vegetable soup.

"I think we're on to something here," Michael said, taking a french fry from the plate and popping it into his mouth.

"Like what?" Laurie asked, blowing over a spoon of soup to cool it.

"The more I see of this place the more familiar it seems."

Laurie stole a french fry and pointed it at him. "When I was in college I planned a trip to San Francisco," she said, nibbling the fry. "It was something I'd always wanted to do, you know?"

"Yeah," he said, wondering where she was leading.

She finished the fry. "When I finally arrived, it was exactly what I thought it would be. It was like I'd always lived there."

"It's not the same."

"The point is, any place you feel strongly about visiting is going to seem somewhat familiar because you want it to. Do you understand what I'm trying to say here?"

"You're not going to discourage me, Laurie," he said, beating her to the last fry.

"I'm not trying to discourage you. I just want you to consider some other options, all right?"

"Sure, fine. As long as we check it out, and talk to the owner of that lot, you can say anything you want. I'm not making this up."

"Okay," she said, to make peace. "Whatever you say."

"Laurie, just bear with me on this — as a friend. Forget the psychology bit for a while."

"All right, Michael. I'm sorry. Why don't we get going then?"

"Thanks."

As they pulled up to City Hall, Michael said, "Shit. It's Saturday. They're not open."

"Now what?" Laurie asked. "I can't stay the weekend. I've got too much to do."

"Let's try the neighbors," he said, after a moment's thought.

"The people next door to the lot?"

"Can you think of anything better?"

"Yeah, going home."

"Please, we've come this far."

"All right," she grumbled. "Let's go bother the neighbors."

He put the car in gear and they sped back to the over-grown trees and aging houses, parking in front of the lot that had been 724. They walked back to the neighboring house and up the narrow walk to a door in need of painting.

As they stood there, Laurie said, "I want you to know I haven't done this since I worked for Avon when I was sixteen."

"Then it should still be fresh in your memory."

"Flatterer."

He rang the bell. Almost at once it was opened by a teen-age girl wearing a black t-shirt adorned with a picture of Bruce Springsteen. "Yeah?"

"Hi," Michael said, "we were wondering if you could tell us who owns the lot next door."

She turned away from them and brayed, "Ma, this guy wants to know who owns the lot next door."

An older woman appeared, wiping her hands on her apron. "You want to know about the lot next door?"

"Yes, ma'am," Laurie said.

"That belongs to Marion Danelli. You need to talk to her?"

"Yes, if we could," Michael said.

She looked at them appraisingly for a minute and then said, "Well, you look all right, I guess. She lives on the edge of town, now. It's a senior-citizen apartment house up on Montridge."

"How do we get there?" Michael asked.

She gave them directions and they were off again.

❑

They found the building exactly as the woman had described it, plain, brown-brick, square with a small parking lot in front. Entering through glass doors, they went to apartment nine and knocked several times.

The door was finally opened by a small white-haired woman who stood looking them over.

"Yes?"

Laurie spoke first, "Mrs. Danelli?"

"Who wants to know?" she asked gruffly.

"My name is Laurie Bridges and this is my friend Michael Edwards."

"How do you do," Michael said.

She grunted an acknowledgement.

"We're sorry to disturb you," Laurie said. "We were interested in the lot on Oak Street and the lady next door told us it belonged to you."

"That's right," she said, "but I don't know that I've ever thought about selling it."

"Oh, no," Michael said. "We don't want to buy it."

"You don't?" She sounded disappointed.

"We just want to know about its history."

She eyed him curiously. "Are you some kind of reporter or somethin'?"

"No."

"I gotta tell you," she said, cutting him off, "you look awful familiar." She narrowed her eyes. "You sure I ain't seen you on TV? I watch all the news programs at the same time. Remote control!"

"Could we ask you some questions?"

"Questions, huh?" She looked back and forth at them suspiciously, and then over their shoulders as if for TV cameras.

"Please," Michael said.

She seemed to favor him. "Oh, okay. Come on inside." She waved them in and led them into her parlor, hands flapping at her sides as she walked.

They sat on an old green velvet sofa whose back arched gracefully and curved down into wooden armrests. Next to the sofa was a small table supporting a lamp with tassels hanging from a yellow shade. Mrs. Danelli sat across from them on a chair cushioned in the same material as the sofa. Michael's eye wandered to the painting on the wall behind her. It was early impressionism, but somehow distinctly

American. He looked back at the old lady. "Now what is it you kids wants to know?"

"Was that lot always vacant?" Michael asked, smelling cloves in the air.

"It has been for the last ten years or so. That's when they tore the house down. Oh, it was old and in need of repair. Not the kind of house you'd want to live in any more."

"So there was a house on it."

"Oh, yes. There was a house all right. I grew up in that house. Lived there until I was sixteen. You two married?" the old woman asked hopefully.

"No," they said in unison.

"I guess you wouldn't be, with different names and all. You want some tea or somethin'?"

"No thank you," Michael said. "Now this may sound crazy but the kitchen. . ."

"Wait a minute," Laurie interrupted. "Mrs. Danelli, could you describe the kitchen for us?"

"Well, it was an ordinary kitchen as kitchens go. I mean, except it was small because we had a separate dining room. Had an icebox and a little table in the corner." She shrugged. "It was just a kitchen."

"Back door?" Michael asked.

"Yes, there was a back door. Most of those houses had back doors in the kitchen."

"Do you remember what color the counters were?" he asked, feeling foolish.

"Yes, I can remember because I hated them. They were this awful yellow."

Michael felt a chill. "Who else lived there?"

"Just me, my mother, and my uncle."

"No other men?" Michael asked, disappointed. "Someone younger maybe? A tenant?"

She shook her head. "My mother, me, and Uncle Vincent." Laurie looked at him.

"Mrs. Danelli, this is very important," he said slowly. "We'd like to know whatever you can tell us about your uncle."

"Now why would you want to know about my uncle?"

Looking over her shoulder again, at the painting, Michael noticed the artist's signature — Vincent Bello. He looked at the old woman. "He was a painter, wasn't he?"

She looked startled. "How did you know that?"

"The painting on the wall behind you."

She turned her head to look at it. "Oh, yes. Vincent painted that all right." Turning back to them, she added, "But if you ask me, it's best to let the dead rest in peace." She fell silent as if remembering, then said, "Yes, he was an artist, and a good one, too. But he was, you know, an odd duck."

Laurie said, "I beg your pardon?"

She looked at them nervously as if considering something important. "Well," she said, finally, "he was an artist. Artists are supposed to be a little strange." She lowered her voice. "He didn't go much for the ladies, if you know what I mean. Had himself a friend, too, used to come by all the time. Everybody knew they was more than just friends."

"You mean they were lovers," Michael said.

The old woman winced. "Yes, but at that time nobody talked about that sort of thing. Not like today, no. But Vincent was a good man and folks round here took to him. Not like his friend."

"What do you mean?" Laurie asked.

"It was a real shame, I gotta tell you. Nobody liked that one, and for good reason. The way he treated my uncle was shameful, just shameful." She shook her head angrily.

"How's that?" Michael asked.

"He used to drink a good bit, that for one. He'd get drunk and beat that poor man like nothin' you ever saw. It was terrible. Went on for years. I can remember being in my bedroom and hearing Vincent screaming in the night. I was just a little girl then but I still shudder to think about it."

Michael asked, "Why didn't Vincent throw him out?"

"Oh, my mother told him to and so did everyone else that knew him and cared for him, but he refused." She shook her head in bewilderment. "I gotta tell you, he loved that man as much as any wife could love a husband. He'd throw him out for a while but then he'd take him back. Just never learned. As it happened, one night that animal beat Vincent near close to death and left him there." She looked at Michael. "Left him in the kitchen, now that I think about it, and off he went never to be heard from again. Folks say he had someone else on the side, if you know what I mean. Course, Vincent was heartbroken. Always kind of sullen after that."

"Whatever became of Vincent?"

"Oh, he stayed in the house, but he was never the same. My mother remarried in the meantime, so we moved out. Vincent lived there by himself until he died."

"When was that?" Michael whispered.

"During the war," she said. "'Forty. 'Forty-one. Something like that. Long before you were born."

"Do you have any photos of your uncle?" Michael asked.

"Well, yes, I have my family pictures. I keep them in a

special place. Wait a minute." She went into the next room and returned with a large heart-shaped candy box, trimmed in yellowing lace, and opened the lid. Rummaging through a sheaf of old photos, she pulled out a large brown one. "Now there's my uncle standing in front of the fountain he designed over on Main. I'd say he's in his forties there." She passed the photo.

Michael looked at it and moved his fingers over its surface. "We were there," he said.

"There?" the woman asked.

"I mean we saw the fountain earlier."

"Oh, how nice."

Laurie took the photo and scrutinized it. "There's something about the eyes," she said, looking up at Michael.

"Yes," Mrs. Danelli said, "Vincent had lovely eyes, just like yours, young fella."

"Thank you." He smiled briefly, intent on the photo, and wondered what the connection could be between the skinny little man in the photo and the strange voice on the tape recorder.

"Oh, now here's something you might be interested in," Mrs. Danelli said, frowning. "A picture of his friend, Marcos."

"Marcos," Michael said, reaching out for the photo. "The Marc in the dream."

"Now that was taken quite a bit earlier because they were the same age."

Michael's hands trembled. "Oh, my God."

"What's wrong?" Laurie asked, but Michael couldn't speak. She took the photo out of his hand and looked at the image there. "Sam!" she exclaimed. "But that's impossible. This picture must be fifty years old."

"I gotta get some air," Michael said, suddenly, bolting for the door.

A moment later Laurie got up and put the photo back on the coffee table. "Thank you for your help, Mrs. Danelli."

"Is he going to be all right?" she shouted after Laurie.

"Yes, thank you," she replied quickly and hurried out to the parking lot where she found Michael supporting himself against the car.

"Michael, are you okay?"

"Yeah, but can we go now?"

"Of course. Let me drive."

He got into the car as Laurie went around to the driver's side. As she started it up, he said, "Now it all makes sense."

"What makes sense, Michael?"

"You saw the picture. It was Sam."

"It was a photo of someone who looked like Sam."

"Laurie, don't you get it?"

"Get what?"

"Sam was Marcos."

"What do you mean — reincarnation?"

"Yes, yes, Vincent wasn't speaking through me under hypnosis — he *was* me. I lived and died in this town," he said, scanning the road as they drove out of Riverdale. "Sam was with me and I'm afraid of him now because of what he did to me then, don't you see? It all fits together. Look at me, I'm still shaking." He held out a trembling hand.

"Calm down, Michael. It's true the photo looked like Sam but you're jumping to conclusions here."

As if he hadn't heard her, he said, "I was always . . . Vincent was always afraid that Marcos would leave him, but now it's Sam who's jealous and afraid that I'll walk out." He turned to Laurie. "It's like a karmic payback."

"Maybe it wasn't such a good idea to come up here."

"I'm glad we did. I feel good about this. At least I know I'm not crazy."

Laurie rolled her eyes. "No, of course not. You're simply telling me that you used to live in another body and that we just had a chat with you 77-year-old niece."

Michael suddenly started laughing. "I know how it must sound."

"Well, I'm glad you're laughing again. What do you think Sam is going to say about all this?"

The smile drained from his face. "Sam," he said. "We've got to get back. I want to tell him."

"Tell him what?" she asked, disturbed at the swings in his mood. "Maybe you shouldn't tell him anything."

He stared at her, incredulously. "Wasn't that the point of this whole thing, Laurie, to get it out in the open so the dreams will stop? I have to talk to him." Suddenly, his face colored and he erupted, "That bastard! I can't believe what he did to me."

"Michael, this *is* crazy."

He shook his head and stared out the window. "Just get me home."

It was early when they finally pulled up in front of Laurie's house. She let herself out of the car while he moved across the front to the driver's seat.

"Are you going to be all right?"

"Yes," he said automatically.

"I'll call you later."

"Okay," he answered and sped off.

It seemed that he hit every red light in the city, making the drive home interminable. At each light, his rage mounted as he recalled, clearly now, the brutal scene in the kitchen between Vincent and Marcos. It was as if he could feel Marcos's blows again. Arriving at his house, he hurried out of the car and up to the front entrance. Fumbling with the keys, he unlocked the door and pushed it open, to find himself in a darkened room.

"Sam," he yelled and looked around. "Sam!"

He rushed through the living room into the bedroom, switching on the light. The room was dishevelled, bureau drawers open and clothes scattered on the floor. He looked in the closet and saw that all of Sam's clothes were gone.

He stood motionless, unable to absorb what it was he saw. He heard a noise, listened, but the house was silent. Slowly, he retraced his steps back into the living room. The pale glow of a street light angled across the wall, casting shadows of branches thrashing in the wind. Out of the corner of his eye, he saw something move. A man stood silhouetted against an open window in the kitchen. Michael stood frozen until the sound of shattering glass made him jump.

"Shit," the man said.

Michael moved toward the kitchen, hitting his foot against something in the doorway. He turned on the light. Sam stood near the sink, a bottle of scotch in his hand, glass and ice at his feet. A suitcase partly blocked the doorway.

"Turn the light off," Sam commanded. Michael hit the switch.

"Sam, didn't you hear me calling you?"

"Yeah, I heard." He realized Sam was drunk.

"Where are you going?"

"To my brother's, until I can find a place of my own."

Helplessly, Michael asked, "Why?"

"You know why . . . Vincent," he replied.

The hatred in his voice sent a shiver down Michael's spine.

"I loved you," he said. "I loved you more than anything. We could have done it this time, you know."

"We still can," Michael said quickly. He reached out and touched Sam's arm. "Please don't go."

"Don't touch me," he shrieked. He raised the bottle and swung it wildly, smashing it against Michael's chest. He grabbed the suitcase and dashed out of the room.

Michael fell back against the wall. He heard the door slam and the sound of a car starting up. After a long time, he stumbled to his feet and checked himself for damage. Finding none, he made his way into the living room and turned on a lamp. It was then that he noticed the stereo receiver was lighted. He walked over to it and saw there was a cassette in the tape deck. Pushing the play button, he heard someone breathing, and then Vincent's voice, asking, "Am I going to die?"

ALAN IRWIN
Skip

We'd met in April of '84. My company in L.A. had sent me to Washington D.C. for a week. The week was over, and I was staying through the weekend to catch the sights. But it was Friday night, and I had something besides sightseeing on my mind. It was a little past eleven when I stood in line clutching my Club Baths card. How long had it been? Two weeks? A month? Too long, anyhow.

Once inside, I took my clothes off and sized myself up in the mirror; a lanky man, light brown hair, ordinary features, but nicely muscled. Times like this I was glad I pumped iron. I wandered around the place, sizing up the night's pickings.

He was lying on his side in his room, and he fell into the My Type category: lean and dark-haired, with a moustache and a good set of pecs. He indicated by a nod that I met his approval, and I walked inside and dropped my towel. We commenced with an experienced efficiency that needed no words.

We had a half hour of good, safe sex. He was good — he was very good. Stomachs crusted with semen, we both passed out.

A lot later I woke up and found his head on my chest and his arm around my neck. He snored slightly. I tried gently to untangle myself. He woke with a start.

"Thanks," I whispered. "That was great."

But the arm stayed around my neck.

"You take it easy," I said.

"What's your name?"

"Alan."

"I'm Skip."

❏

Slits of morning sunlight came through the louvered glass doors in his apartment when I woke up for the second time that morning. He was sitting up in bed with a cup of coffee in his hand. For an instant we looked at each other. His skin was ruddy, his eyes were sharp blue. He held up well in daylight. I hoped I did too.

"Morning, Alan."

"Morning."

"Coffee?"

"Sure."

He slipped on his robe and disappeared. What was his name now?

I got up, stretched, and looked around. There was a Picasso-esque print on the wall opposite me, a bookcase filled with rows of high-brow books, the kind no one ever really read, like the *Aeneid* and Dante's *Inferno*. On the top shelf was a high school yearbook from Holyoke High School. Holyoke, Virginia, circa 1972. On a roll-top desk in the corner was a group of framed photographs. Three or four were of him and another young man, a thin, dark-haired fellow with horn-rimmed glasses and a shy smile. There was also a picture of a middle-aged couple standing in front of a two-story brick house. Mom and Dad? Probably. Beside that was a pile of letters addressed to Skipford Helm, Jr. I got back into bed.

He returned with my coffee. I took a few sips and tried to think of something to say.

"You must be quite a reader," I pointed at the bookcase. "I tried to make it through some of these in college. Thank God for Cliff Notes."

"Nah, I didn't read them either," he replied. "Someone gave them to me."

He opened the sliding glass door and walked out onto the balcony. Pulling on my Levis, I followed. We were three stories up, and the view was of an open wood filled with willow trees, other apartment buildings, then, in the distance, D.C. and the Potomac.

"Where are we?" I asked, standing beside him.

"Fairfax, Virginia."

"Great view."

"Thanks." He turned toward me smiling. His robe was open to his navel.

"What's the mark on your stomach?" I asked.

"Knife wound."

"Hope it wasn't serious."

"Not for me. High school punk tried to knife me as I left a bar once. I put him in the hospital. Preacher's kid, real mixed up."

I did as much sightseeing as I could squeeze into two days. Skip was my guide. He was one of those people who never seem to get tired. Then, too soon, it was Sunday evening. I grabbed my bag and we piled into Skip's red Subaru pickup for the drive to the airport. It started to hit: I didn't want to go home. It was more than facing Monday morning. I was starting to like this man.

We got to the airport. "Thanks for everything," I said.

"No problem."

"I had a great time."

"Me too."

It ran through my mind to mention I could cancel my flight and stay a couple more days. Instead I said, "Hope you can visit me in L.A. sometime."

"Love to."

Then there was a quick kiss. I grabbed my suitcase, hopped out, watched him drive away. And wondered if I'd ever see him again.

A week later, I came home from work and found a message on my answering machine from Skip. He'd made tentative plans to come out to L.A. the weekend after next. Was that a good time, he wondered, and could he stay with me?

I had two roommates at the time, Ed and Jim. They were lovers. The three of us lived in Ed's ranch-style house in North Hollywood.

Ed and I went way back. Ten years ago, he'd been the older man with the knockout body that I fantasized over. We'd gone from boyfriends to best friends, and now he was turning from best friend to old acquaintance. Jim was the reason.

Ed and Jim were sitting in front of the tube that night. They were on their second bottle of wine, and Ed had a bowl of popcorn in his lap. He'd recently passed the forty mark, and he was letting himself go to fat.

"Got a friend visiting weekend after next. Okay if he stays here?" I asked Ed. Asking was a formality. Ed was generosity personified.

"Sure. Anyone I know?"

"His name's Skip. Met him in D.C."

"He's coming all the way from Washington D.C. to see you?" He grinned impishly.

"Yeah."

"Sounds serious."

"Nah."

Jim piped up. "Hope he's better looking than most of the bums you drag home."

Jim was a slim, curly-headed blond, nineteen going on thirty-five, an actor/singer/dancer/waiter who'd worked few days in his life and been sober even fewer. He was still waiting around for his Big Break in show business. Barring that, he was waiting for the sucker who'd pick up the bills. In the meantime, he had Ed.

Skip arrived, and for three days we did the rounds of Southern California tourist spots. Jim found an excuse to run around in a pair of jockey shorts, an obligatory performance for all my boyfriends.

The next six months were a blur of traveling cross country squished in an airplane seat, weekends that went by too damned fast, and godawful phone bills. Twice a month I'd leave the office at four on Friday, fight traffic to LAX, catch the flight for D.C., and land at National Airport in the early morning. Skip would be waiting there, tired-eyed but smiling, and I collapsed into his embrace. Arm in arm we'd walk out of the airport and to his pickup, ignoring any hostile stares. Back at his apartment we'd drop our clothes in a heap on the floor, climb into his bed, and make love. Then I was up at two on Monday morning, out to National Airport to catch the four a.m. flight back to L.A. to be there in time for work.

It was a lot of hassle and expense, but it was worth it. Those weekends with Skip were the most important times of my life. I still looked at other men, but I compared them all to Skip, and they didn't measure up.

And then it was October, and I was again at National Airport. I'd taken off work Thursday at noon. We had three days to explore two-lane country roads, browse the Smithsonian, and mull over whether I was going to move out there or he was going to move to California.

Skip was waiting at the airport. He gave me a quick embrace, mumbling, "Too many people here." We drove home in silence. I looked over at him and wondered why I couldn't think of anything to say.

We entered his apartment, and I grabbed him in a bear hug. He pushed my hand away when I started to unbutton his shirt. "I'm tired tonight. Okay?"

"Sure. It can wait till morning."

He walked into the kitchen. "I need a drink. You want a drink?"

"No," I said, and looked around the room. "Looks like you did some redecorating. What happened to all your books?"

"Gave them to the Goodwill."

The Picasso print was gone, as were the photographs on top of the roll-top desk. The only picture left was of Skip and the other man.

"I always wondered who the other guy in the picture was. An ex?"

He handed me my drink. "Just a friend." He went over and snapped on the TV set.

"You eaten?" I asked.

Skip nodded. "There's leftover roast beef in the fridge if you're hungry."

"Nah," I said, and lay down on the bed beside him.

Skip had the cable box in his hand and was thumbing through the TV channels. "He's dead now."

"Who?" I asked.

"Guy in the picture."

"Sorry. AIDS?"

He nodded. "We never went to bed together. Just friends." He took a swallow from his glass.

"Skip, is something wrong?"

"No. Just kinda tired. Okay?"

I let it go.

On Saturday we drove to the Blue Ridge Mountains. It was getting dark when we headed home. Skip had been driving all day, so I volunteered to take over. I was a Southern California driver; speedometers had a habit of creeping past seventy on me. As we bolted down a two-lane highway, I saw a red light flashing in my rearview mirror.

"Uh-oh," I said.

"Pull over," Skip said. "I'll handle this."

I slowed down and pulled off on the shoulder, and brought the truck to a stop. In the side mirror I saw the black and white stop behind me.

"Change places," Skip ordered.

"What the hell—"

"Do it!"

He slipped his body over mine as I got into the passenger

seat. Over my shoulder I saw a uniformed figure get out of the car and take a few steps toward us.

"Here goes," said Skip.

With a screech of burning rubber, he lurched back onto the highway. Soon we were passing cars at speeds around a hundred, hotly pursued by an angry siren and flashing red lights. We rounded a curve. Skip leapfrogged past five cars at once, snapped off the headlights, and pulled onto a side road. Without our lights I couldn't see anything. He was driving by intuition.

After a mile or two, he brought the truck to a stop by the side of the road.

"What the hell were you doing?" I demanded.

"I don't like cops."

"You could have killed us."

"I didn't."

"That's crazy."

"Drop it." He snapped the lights back on and continued down that road.

"No, I won't. I want an explanation."

"I don't like cops."

"For Christ's sake, they don't haul you off to jail for speeding."

He pulled the truck to a stop again, turned to me and said, "Listen, how'd you like to fly home tonight instead of tomorrow? We can be at the airport in less than an hour."

He started driving again. I fought off emotions and said, matter of factly, "If that's what you want."

When he didn't say anything, I continued. "If it's over, it's over. Better this way than to pretend."

The truck ambled down that lonely country road. The

engine started to lug, but he didn't shift. He pulled over to the side of the road again and snapped, "Christ, I don't know where the fuck we are."

"It's up to you, Skip. You want to end it now?"

He put his hand over mine. "Sorry. I didn't mean it." He reached in the glove compartment and thumbed through till he found an envelope. Opening it, he got out a stick of marijuana and lit it.

Five minutes later we were rolling down the road in God-knows-where, Virginia, passing the joint between us. I started giggling. Weed sometimes has that effect on me.

"We got to do that again sometime," I said. "That was better than an E ticket at Disneyland."

We spent Sunday in front of the movie channel in his bedroom. Evening came, and we set the alarm for two so I could make my four-o'clock flight the next morning. He placed his head on my chest. I relaxed into sleep.

I was in the middle of a dream when I felt someone nudging me.

"Al," Skip was saying, "wake up."

"Huh? Is it time already?"

"No," he said. "Sorry I been acting funny."

"Forget it." I shut my eyes and rolled over on my side.

He put an arm across my body. "I've been thinking."

"About what?"

"I'll move out to L.A." He paused. "You still want me to?"

"Sure."

I had almost fallen asleep again when he nudged me again.

"Only first I got to tell you something."

"What?"

"In the morning."

I was over the Mississippi before I was awake enough to wonder what it was he was going to tell me, and hadn't.

❏

I called him a few times the next week and got his answering machine. Finally a week later he returned my calls.

"Well," I said, "the mystery man. You're hard to reach these days."

"Am I?" There was a pause. "There's some things happening."

"Like what?"

"We gotta talk about it."

"Let's talk."

"Not right now. Listen, I'm sorry I didn't call back sooner."

"Forget it."

"I got some time off for Thanksgiving in a couple of weeks. Can I come out then?"

"That'd be great. Ed's having some people over. You'd be more than welcome."

He left a message on my machine the next day that he'd be arriving at 10:05 on Thanksgiving morning on a United flight. I wrote it down on the calendar.

The Monday before Thanksgiving, I called Skip to confirm our plans and told his answering machine, "Hi, Skip. Missing you. Looking forward to Thursday." I was a little concerned when I couldn't reach him either Tuesday or Wednesday, but I kept thinking I'd meet him at the airport on Thursday and things would work out fine.

I left for LAX at nine that morning. The Santa Ana winds had blown through the city the day before, and the sky was a clear blue. I parked my car and walked to the terminal. Checking the monitor for arriving flights, I saw his flight was

– 169 –

right on schedule, 10:05, and due at Gate 25. With fifteen minutes to spare, I walked to Gate 25, sat down, and waited. Exactly at 10:05, the gate was opened and passengers started filing off the plane.

I was still sitting there when the last passenger got off the plane and the stewardess closed the doors behind him. I found a phone and dialed Skip's number. His machine answered. That must mean he was on his way, I thought. He missed his plane, that's all. D.C. to L.A. was a well-traveled path. He'd catch another. I'd just wait till he got here.

Three hours later I was still waiting. And understanding.

I need a drink, I told myself, and went into the first bar I found. A man in a bow tie and a handlebar moustache handed me a scotch and water. Just one, I told myself. I'm already late. What's ten minutes more going to matter?

But one drink led to another, and that still wasn't enough. I wasn't going home to face Ed and Jim and everyone else with their questions about where Skip was.

I have clouded pictures of the rest of the day. I was at the Eagle on Santa Monica Boulevard. The place was empty but for me and the bartender, and I was telling him my problems. By early evening he had me on coffee. "I'll call you a cab," he kept saying. "Go home and sleep it off."

The next place I remember being is 8709, that monumental bathhouse on Third Street. The last place was jail, busted on a 502, drunk driving. It was five in the morning when Ed came to get me. He asked no questions, but put a steadying arm around my shoulder and walked me to the car.

I waited for a few days for a call from Skip, thinking that he'd better have one hell of an explanation. The call never came.

Finally I broke down and dialed his number. The recording I got wasn't his. Instead, a woman's voice said, "Ah'm sorry, you've reached a numba' that is disconnected and no longa' in suhvice."

So I sat down and wrote a letter. A week passed without an answer. Finally I packed my duffle bag and stuffed an airline ticket for D.C. into my pocket. I made it as far as the garage, and then it hit me. There was no mystery about what happened. I'd been dropped. I took the ticket from my pocket and tore it up.

Back inside, I called up a friend who had a friend who was a dope dealer. He dropped by later with a bag of Columbian. I got out my rolling papers and prepared to forget everything.

I was well on my way to being wasted when Jim came in singing "The Man that Got Away." When I didn't respond he said, "I knew it'd never last first time I saw you two together."

"You're skating on thin ice," I replied, looking up from the table.

"He gave me the eye when he was here."

"I'm warning you."

"It's the truth," he said, grinning. "We all saw it but you."

Good thing I was stoned. Sober I wouldn't have had the nerve to knock him to the floor the way I did and get in a few good kicks to his ass before he got away, screaming.

The next day I started looking for an apartment of my own.

The letter I wrote Skip finally came back, and Ed passed it along to me. It was unopened and marked, "Moved, return to sender." I tossed it in the trash can. There's too many other men, I told myself. Forget him.

A year passed. I was still forgetting him.

Then my company needed someone to go to Washington D.C. for a week and asked if I'd be interested. I was. I left on Friday to give myself the weekend to look for Skip.

Saturday morning I rented a car and drove over the river to Fairfax to the apartment complex where Skip had lived.

I knocked at his door. A young woman in a bathrobe with a towel wrapped around her head opened it and looked at me suspiciously.

"I'm looking for Skip Helm," I said.

"Who?" Her look got more suspicious.

"Skip Helm. He used to live here."

"He don't live here no more." She shut the door in my face.

I knocked on other doors. Only one neighbor, a middle-aged woman, even remembered him, and she had no idea where he'd gone to.

I wandered through the complex until I found the office labeled "Rental Information." There I asked a Kate Smith-ish woman with arms like a Sumo wrestler if she had a forwarding address for him.

"Skip Helm? Just a second," she said. She opened a drawer in a file cabinet. "I show a Skipford Helm that lived here, moved out last November."

"Any idea where he left?"

"Didn't leave no forwarding address. Didn't even bother to get his deposit back. Musta been in a hurry."

It was time for Plan B. I remembered the high school yearbook in Skip's apartment. It was from someplace called Holyoke, Virginia. I got a road map of Virginia. Holyoke was about a hundred and fifty miles away.

It took three hours to get there. It was a quiet little town of magnolia trees, large brick houses with American flags hanging in front, and a church on every block.

I stopped at a gas station, filled the tank, and checked the phone book. There was a Skipford Helm listed on 657 East Third Street. Skip's dad, I figured. The gas station attendant gave me directions, and I was there in ten minutes.

I drove by the place. It was the same house that had been in the picture, all right, a big, two-story brick house with a white picket fence in front surrounding a well-kept lawn and neatly trimmed bushes. The Helms weren't sharecroppers.

I went around the block and drove past the house again. Yeah, this is the place, I thought. Are you really going to do this?

I pulled the car to the curb, walked up to the door, and rang the bell.

She was several years older than the picture, but it was the same woman. Her steel-gray hair was neatly styled, and her face was in transition from middle to old age.

"Mrs. Helm," I said quickly. "How are you? You probably don't remember me, it's been several years. I was a friend of Skip's in high school."

She stared at me.

"I lost track of him," I hurried on, "and I was just passing through and I said to myself I bet his folks still live in the same place and they can tell me what's become of him."

She continued staring, as if she wasn't understanding a word of it.

"I hope I didn't come at a bad time," I said, losing my nerve. "I can come back some other time."

She opened her mouth and said in a voice I could barely hear, "Come in."

"My name's Alan Johnson," I said, stepping into the entrance hall. "I doubt you'd remember me, though. We only lived here six months or so, then Dad moved out to California."

"No, I'm afraid I don't." She smiled faintly. "But do have a seat, Alan. So nice of you to drop by." Now she was a Southern lady. "May I get you something? Coffee?"

"Please."

There wasn't a speck of dust on the hardwood floors, and the mahogany coffee table was so brightly polished I could see my reflection on its surface. There was a fire going in the fireplace.

"I hope I'm not inconveniencing you, ma'am," I said.

"Oh, heavens no," she replied, and disappeared into another room, returning a minute later with two steaming cups that she placed on the coffee table.

She sat down opposite me and said, "So you were friends with Skip."

"Yes. I live in L.A. now, but we kept up a correspondence, and I'd see him when my company sent me out this way. It's been a year since my last letter got returned by the post office. I figured since I was driving through town anyway, I'd stop and see if his folks still lived here, hoping maybe you could tell me where he is now."

"Did Skip ever write and say he wasn't feeling well?" she asked slowly.

"No, ma'am. Nothing serious, I hope."

"It was rather," she replied.

"Is he all right now?" I asked.

"He'd been sick for a while before we found out. He had a bad case of — pneumonia."

"Pneumonia?" I echoed.

She looked away from me and went on, as if to herself.

"We didn't know about it until afterwards." Her voice became so faint that I strained to hear her. "We had drifted apart, you see, and we hadn't heard from him in quite a while. He was sick and he wouldn't even call and tell us." She reached into her pocket for a handkerchief and dabbed beneath her eyes. "Then finally we did get a call. In the middle of the night. From the hospital. They wanted to know what to do with our son's body." She looked at me. "That's why your letter came back."

My insides turned to jelly. "I'm so sorry."

"I'm sorry too," she said, composing herself. "Skip was a good boy. There were things about him we couldn't accept. It seems silly now."

"He seemed so alive last I saw him."

"I wish I could have him back alive just for five more minutes. There's so much I'd like to say to him."

"I'm sure he knows, ma'am."

"You think so?" She looked at me like she really wanted to believe.

"I do."

"Thank you for being Skip's friend. He never had many. He was a shy boy."

"He outgrew it."

"Did he?"

"Sure."

I picked up my coffee and swallowed it down. I was about to excuse myself and leave when I heard the footsteps coming up the front steps. The door burst open and two men came in. I recognized the first as Skip's father.

"Hardware store said they'd have to order the part for the stove," said Mr. Helm, then noticed me. "Howdy."

"Hi." I stood up.

Mrs. Helm said, "This is Alan. He was a friend of Skip's. This is my husband and my son Buck."

Mr. Helm gave me a hearty handshake and said, "Pleased to meet you," with a good-ole-boy smile.

Buck said, "Howdy." He was a skinny man, with a nose too big for his face. He touched his fingers to my outstretched hand and took a step back, looking me over. "One of Skip's friends, huh?"

I said, "I'm terribly sorry about Skip."

"It was too bad, wasn't it?" said Buck, grinning like a preacher about to ask for money. "Tell me, whereabout you know my brother from?"

"He's known Skip since high school," said Mrs. Helm.

"That so?"

"Yes. My family lived here for a few months back in the early seventies till we moved to California. Skip and I wrote to each other after I left, and we kept in touch over the years."

"Skip and I were only a year apart. I don't remember you at all." Buck still kept up that inane grin, but his voice had an accusing tone.

"It was ten years ago. I'd be surprised if you did remember me."

"You know about my brother?"

"I'm not sure what you mean."

"You know he was queer?"

Mrs. Helm said, "Buck!"

I tried the coward's way out. "Well, it's funny, I never knew, but my wife met him once, and later she says to me, 'I'd bet that guy is gay.' Now, I don't know if it was so or not, but it wouldn't have made any difference."

Buck looked me in the eye. "You know how he died?"

I had a good idea, but I wasn't about to blurt it out. "I believe your mother said it was pneumonia."

Buck snorted contemptuously. "That's what Mom tells everyone. Skip died from AIDS, the queer disease."

I turned to Mr. and Mrs. Helm. "I've got to go. I'm so sorry about Skip."

"Real nice of you to stop by." Buck moved in front of the doorway, blocking my exit. "I still think it's real funny I don't remember you at all. Skip never mentioned he had someone in California that he was writing to."

I shrugged. "I'm sure I don't know why."

"You sure you didn't meet him after high school? After he turned queer?"

This time it was Mr. Helm who said, "That's enough, Buck."

Buck took a step forward. "Who the hell are you, and what do you want?"

"I was a friend of Skip's."

"You queer too? You the one that gave him AIDS?"

Mr. Helm's voice snapped, "Buck, shut up."

"No, I won't. You know how they took advantage of him. Now tell us who the hell you really are."

"I was Skip's lover."

There was a silence. Then Buck said, "You come into our house lying, upsetting my mom, pretending to be somebody you aren't. I want to know why you're here, what you came for. Better yet, I'll call the police and they'll find out."

He reached for the telephone on the table in the hallway. His mother got up, came over, and yanked the phone out of his hand. Her voice was angry.

"Alan is our guest and you'll treat him with respect or get the hell out."

"Mom, don't you know what they did to Skip?"

Mr. Helm yelled, "Buck, get lost! Get outa here!"

Buck glared for an instant, then walked down a hallway and slammed a door.

"I'm sorry for all this," I said. "I better go." I walked out the door and hurried down the walkway.

There was a voice behind me. "Hold on a second." It was Mr. Helm. He looked uncomfortable as he walked up to me. "Buck's still bitter. He misses his brother a lot. He took it hard."

"Sure," I said. We started walking toward my car.

"It was hard on all of us, what happened." He hesitated. "Sometimes I get up in the morning thinking Skip's going to be there at the breakfast table. Then I remember it isn't so. You understand?"

"Yeah," I said. "I do."

"And I start thinking about all those years we wouldn't talk to him and he wouldn't talk to us." Anger flashed across his face. "God damn it to hell, if we'd only known."

"But you didn't."

"No, we didn't."

I fumbled in my pocket for the car keys. He said, "Skip's buried in the cemetery right outside of town, next to his grandma and grandpa. Just in case you want to stop by."

"Yeah. I'd like to."

We shook hands, and he gave me his ole-boy smile and said, "You take it easy now, hear?"

I watched him as he walked away and thought, at least his wife could cry.

❏

It was an old country cemetery surrounded by an eight-foot wrought iron fence. There were tombstones dating back to the Civil War. The Helms had their own section in a corner of the graveyard. I found Skip's tombstone, already covered with lichen and moss.

I stayed there only long enough to recite a prayer. Graveyards make me nervous.

It was a lonely drive back to my hotel in D.C. At least I knew now what had happened to Skip. We'd had only safe sex so I wasn't particularly concerned he'd infected me. But it slowly started to hit me that he was gone. It seemed impossible that this man who had been so alive a year ago now lay in that little graveyard in Virginia.

And the more I thought about it, the harder it was to believe. But I'd seen the grave, so there was nothing to do but believe.

I lived in L.A. a few more months, until a position opened in my company's Santa Rosa office, sixty miles north of San Francisco. I was asked if I wanted to take it. I decided I'd had enough of L.A., took the job, and found a house near the Russian River.

"Who's that?" people occasionally asked about the picture of Skip I kept on the mantel.

"A friend who died," I'd say. There were other boyfriends, and life went on. It had seemed so right with Skip. I wondered if I'd ever find that again.

I'd been in my new home almost two years. One Tuesday night, feeling a little lonely, I walked down the hill to one of the local bars, a noisy and popular place called the Bayou. It was September, the tail end of vacation season, and the bar was wall-to-wall men in various stages of intoxication, swaying to jackhammer disco music.

Sitting at the bar I saw a drunk and familiar face. I debated whether to ignore him, but finally went over. "Hi, Jim."

"My God," he yelled — it was the only way to be heard over the music — "we thought you died."

I yelled back, "How are you doing?"

"Great. Wonderful."

It had been three years since I'd seen him, but it could have been twenty by the way he looked. His boyishness was gone, and his thinness gave him a shriveled look.

"How's Ed doing?"

"We broke up."

"Sorry to hear it." But not very. "Gin and tonic," I told the bartender in a red tanktop.

"He'd gotten real difficult," Jim yelled, and emptied his glass.

"We all do. What you drinking?"

"Screwdriver."

"And a screwdriver," I yelled at the bartender.

"We wondered what the hell happened to you," Jim told me.

The bartender brought our drinks and I placed a five on the counter.

"I needed a change of scenery. Live up here now. Down the street as a matter of fact."

I took a long swallow from my drink. This seemed like a good night to get wasted.

Jim yelled something to me. "Huh?" I said.

He yelled it again. "You just vanished. We didn't know what to tell your boyfriend."

"So what did you tell him?"

"That you disappeared off the face of the earth."

I took another swallow from my drink. "Which boyfriend was that?"

"Your boyfriends all looked alike." His drink was disappearing rapidly, too. "How long you been up here?"

"Couple years."

The music pounded in my ears and I felt an alcoholic-induced mellowness. I didn't even dislike Jim any more. He'd be a good drinking buddy tonight.

"Now I remember," he yelled.

"Remember what?"

"Which boyfriend."

"Which one was it?"

"That one from back East."

It took a second to register. My first thought was Jim was playing some gross practical joke. But there was no smirk around the tired mouth.

"Jim, let's go outside to the patio where we can talk."

"It's cold outside."

I ordered another set of drinks and waited for them to be delivered. "Now let's go outside," I said. I grabbed Jim's arm and half pushed him, half held him up as he staggered along.

"It's fucking cold out here," he whined. He was in shirtsleeves, so I took off my jacket and put it over his shoulders. We sat down at a table.

"Now tell me, who came by?"

His voice was slurred. "I don't know. One of your boyfriends."

"When was this?"

He shrugged. "Year ago, maybe."

"How'd you know he was from back East?"

He paused and looked around him. "Huh?" he said.

"You said he was from back East."

"Did I?"

"Yes."

Jim thought this over. "He said he was. I guess."

"What did he look like?"

He lifted his glass and finished his drink in a few swallows. "I told you, your boyfriends all look alike." Then he giggled.

I sprang up and grabbed him by the collar. "Tell me!" I could see by his face this wasn't the way to get answers, and I released my grip.

"I'm not your social secretary."

I tried again. "Did he have dark hair? About your height?"

"Sure."

"Trace of a Southern accent?"

"Sure. I'm cold." He slowly stood up on wobbly legs.

"Was it Skip? Did he say his name was Skip?"

"Sure. Whatever you say."

"Think. Did he say his name was Skip?"

He shrugged. "It's cold out here. Thanks for the drink." He handed my jacket to me and staggered back inside.

I set my drink down, got up, and left the bar. I ran most of the way home. It was past one in the morning, but this wouldn't wait. I dug out my old phone book, looked up Ed's number, and dialed. The phone rang five times before a sleepy voice answered, "Hello."

"Ed, it's me, Alan."

A pause. "Long time. What's up?"

"I got to talk to you. You awake?"

"Half."

"Someone came by your house looking for me about a year ago. Remember?"

"There's been a few people by."

"Was one of them named Skip?"

Silence. "I don't remember."

"Try and think. I dated this guy when I lived with you and Jim. He lived in Virginia, but he came out and visited a few times. You remember him?"

"I remember you were flying back East an awful lot for a while."

"It's real important to me, Ed. His name was Skip. The guy that came by a year ago, was that Skip?"

"Could be. Listen, I got to work tomorrow."

"Ed, don't hang up. Not just yet. He had dark hair, medium height, blue eyes, slight Southern accent."

"Maybe."

"Ed, would you recognize him? Would you recognize his picture?"

"Maybe."

I looked at my watch. It was 1:30. L.A. was a nine-hour drive. "Where will you be at 10:30?"

"10:30 when?"

"Tomorrow morning."

"At the office."

"What's the address?"

He gave it to me. "I'll meet you there," I said. I hung up the phone, grabbed the picture of Skip off the mantel, and went to my car.

Two large cups of coffee from an all-night truck stop guaranteed I'd stay awake at the wheel. I hit Interstate 5, put the accelerator to the floorboard, and went ninety. I made it into L.A. the next morning just after rush-hour traffic had subsided. Ed's office was in a high-rise on Wilshire. The receptionist buzzed him.

"Jeeze, you look terrible," he said, stepping into the reception room.

"And you look great." He'd lost his spare tire and his muscles showed through his shirt.

"Thanks. Started back at the gym. Let's go to my office." I followed him down a noisy corridor. He sat behind his desk and motioned for me to sit in the chair opposite him.

"So tell me, what happened? You just disappeared, and we didn't know where you'd gone."

"Moved up north. Russian River area." I showed him Skip's picture. "Was this the guy that came by?"

"Could be."

"It's real important to me."

He shut his eyes for several seconds, opened them, looked at the picture, shut them briefly and said, "Can't be sure. Looks like him." He took out his keychain and fumbled with it till he'd taken one key off. "Hey, listen, you better get some sleep. Go over to my place and crash. I'll try and get off work early."

"Thanks," I said.

"Sorry we lost touch," he said, as I stood up to go.

"Me too."

I slept for an hour on his couch. When I woke up, I knew I wouldn't sleep any more.

I called United Airlines and learned they had a flight for D.C. leaving in an hour. I wrote Ed a quick note, got in my car, and headed for LAX. When I got there, I grabbed my briefcase from my trunk and stuck the picture of Skip and a flashlight into it. I managed to buy a ticket and get to the gate just as the last passengers were boarding.

Six hours later we got to D.C. It was just getting dark. Within a half hour I had rented a car and was on my way to Holyoke.

After a while, the road began to blur. Glancing at my watch, I realized I'd been driving on it for a couple hours. Up ahead a sign welcomed me to Pennsylvania. "God damn it," I said aloud. I'd made a wrong turn someplace. For Christ's sake, I thought, get a hotel room and grab some sleep. Instead I stopped at a truck stop for coffee and directions.

It was one in the morning by the time I made it to Holyoke. I drove around a little bit before I found the cemetery. The gate was locked, but that wasn't going to stop me. I stuck the flashlight in my back pocket and climbed the fence.

A freezing wind was blowing. Inside it was pitch black. I was still dressed for California. Shivering, I turned on the flashlight and walked through the cemetery shining my light on gravestones, looking for Skip's. A pair of headlights appeared in the distance. I snapped off the light and stood in darkness till the car had passed, then resumed the search. "Shit!" I said, tripping and banging my knee against a gravestone.

Finally I found the Helms' corner and the stone that read, "Skipford Helm, Jr." I knelt down beside it and wiped away the damp moss and lichen. It was like ice.

"Beloved son," I read aloud. "1954–1983." I kept repeating the full inscription, "Skipford Helm, Jr., Beloved son, 1954–1983."

All the way from L.A. I'd been remembering everything I knew about Skip from the first day I met him. The first day was April 14, 1984. On that date, whoever lay beneath this stone was already here.

Suddenly I looked around and realized I was in an old graveyard on a very black night. I got out of there and back to my car. I started the engine and didn't stop driving till I was back in town, under the awning of a well-lit all-night gas station, where I filled the tank.

I spent the night at a roadside motel. When I woke my first thought was, what do I do now? All I had was a photograph, a memory, and a name that didn't belong to either.

On my way out of town, I stopped by Holyoke High School. At my request, a harried secretary went searching for the high school yearbook for 1972, and returned with it in a few minutes. I thumbed through it till I found the name "Skipford Helm" and a picture above it.

"What the hell," I mumbled, remembering where I'd seen the face before.

On my way back to D.C. a plan came to me — a crazy plan, but one I had to try.

I had a couple of credit cards in my wallet. That afternoon I went into a bank and walked out with credit card advances totalling $3,000, all in twenties. Then I got a Bob Damron's. That night I went to the bathhouse where I'd met Skip.

I asked the attendant, "How long you worked here?"

"Three months."

I showed him the picture of Skip. "Ever see this man before?"

He shook his head.

From my pocket I produced two twenty-dollar bills. "Sure?"

He shrugged. "We get lots of people in here."

The bills went into my pocket. "Bring the other guys that work here to the window. I want to ask them."

"I don't know if I can."

I slipped him a twenty. He looked at it for a few seconds, then stuffed it in his pocket.

"Just a minute," he said. He disappeared and returned with three rather scrawny-looking specimens. None of them recognized the picture.

After three weeks, I'd driven to every major city on the east coast north of D.C., checking out bars in the day and bathhouses at night, and wiping out most of my savings account in the process. I didn't care. With the money I had left, I started working my way south. Eventually I made it to the Club Baths in Atlanta. I presented the picture to the attendant at the window.

"Ever seen this guy before?"

I got the same blank stare I'd seen for the past weeks. I set two twenties out on the counter and slid them under his hand. "Let me see the other guys who work here."

The three other attendants looked like men who had never seen the sun. I put the picture on the counter. "Any of you guys recognize him?" Two of them picked up the picture and looked at it without a flicker of recognition.

The third man, a little guy with a punk crewcut, grabbed the picture, looked at me, and said, "Buzz this guy in. I wanta talk to him."

I pushed the door open and followed him to a tiny cubicle with a desk. He sat on the desk and I remained standing.

"What business you got with him?" the punk asked.

"It's personal. All I need to know is does he come in here."

"You from the police?"

"No."

He snickered. "You got vice written all over you."

"If you think that, you're not too smart."

"What's this guy done?"

"Nothing."

"Why you after him?"

"I told you it was personal. You know him, don't you?"

"Maybe."

I took five twenties out and set them on the desk beside him.

"What if he don't want to see you?"

"Then he can tell me that."

He looked at the bills for a second, then grabbed them. "What's your name?" he asked.

"Alan."

"Where you staying?"

"Just passing through."

"There's a bar in town, Demetrio's. Maybe I seen him in there once or twice. Maybe I didn't. Maybe if he wants to see you, he'll show up there tomorrow night. Maybe he won't."

"What time is he gonna show?"

"Is who gonna show?"

"Him. The guy in the picture."

"Never saw him before in my life."

❑

Demetrio's was dark and dingy, a throwback to the time when we had to hide. Though I'd come in from dusk, it still took a few minutes for my eyes to adjust.

I sized the place up. It was a Levis and leather crowd. "Gin and tonic," I said to the bartender.

It was a common failing to assume that if you loved someone, if you kept his picture on your mantel and carried a torch for him, he had to feel something in return. But life didn't work out that way. So why was I here, I wondered.

The door opened and let in a shaft of light. I turned and saw a huge black man in full leather enter.

I promised myself to go easy on the drinks. If he did show up, I didn't want to be drunk.

The door opened again. A group of bikers came in, middle-aged, bearded, and paunchy. The bartender brought me another drink, and I waited.

And waited. My promise to stay sober went to hell. At a quarter of eleven I decided it was about time to go. I'd give him till eleven.

The door opened again. Another biker came in, in Levis and leather jacket. He had a bleached blond crewcut, goggles, and a wooly beard.

I asked for a cup of coffee. The biker came to the bar, sat next to me, and put his hand on my thigh. "Not interested," I said, and pulled my knee away. He grinned and grabbed my crotch.

I could use a good fight now, I thought, as I reached and grabbed him by the collar and said, "Keep your fucking hands to yourself."

That's when he took the goggles off.

I let go of him. We stared at each other.

"Well, well," I said.

We stared at each other some more.

"Your hair used to be brown," I said at last.

He leaned toward me, kissed me on the temple, and said, "Let's get out of here. We've got a lot of catching up to do."

I followed him out. "You eaten?" he asked.

"No."

"I know just the place," he said. "You got a car?"

I handed him the keys, and he drove through town. Neither of us spoke. We got to where we were going, an almost ridiculously romantic place with candles on the table and checkered red-and-white tablecloths.

After we'd been seated he said, "I guess you got some questions about what happened."

"Most of it I figured out."

"That so?"

"A punk finds some poor sucker dying of AIDS. The punk has some reason for disappearing. Maybe the police are after him, or maybe he's just never had anything and he sees his big chance. Anyway, he worms his way into this guy's good graces. After the guy kicks off, the punk takes over the dead man's identity, lives in his apartment, spends his money. Only someone finds out. So pretty soon this punk has to run from the law again." I looked at him. "Am I right?"

"Some of it," he said. "Nobody would hire me after I got out of prison."

"What were you in prison for?"

"ADW. Assault with a deadly weapon."

"Who'd you do that to?"

"The guy came at me with a knife because he didn't like queers. I broke a beer bottle over his head. They put me on trial for attacking him. I was a fag and he was a clean-cut all-American. Guess who the jury believed?"

The waiter beside us cleared his throat. We ordered wine just to get rid of him.

He continued. "After I got out, I did things I'm not proud of."

"Such as?"

"Dealt drugs till I got busted. They let me out on bail, and I got lost real fast. I was still on probation for the ADW. It would have meant going back to prison. That's when I met Skip. He was dying all by himself. He didn't have anyone, I didn't have anyone." He shrugged. "I nursed him, cleaned his puke, emptied his bedpan, the works. He left me everything when he died. His family had deserted him. His folks took his body, but they weren't interested in his stuff. So I became Skip. I looked enough like him I could get away with it. I took over his apartment, his driver's license, his credit cards, his bank accounts." He smiled. "It worked real good for a while."

"So what happened?"

"His brother showed up. I didn't even know he had a brother, and this guy was telling me to clear out, that everything of Skip's was his now. I told him to fuck himself. A week later he came back. Somehow he'd found out all about me. He knew I was on the lam. I threw him out. He came back with the cops. I climbed down the back stairs and ran as fast as I could. I went down to Mexico and stayed there a couple of years."

The waiter brought our wine and made a production of uncorking the bottle and pouring it.

"Finally I decided it'd blown over. I came back to the States, went to L.A., and looked for you. You'd moved, then you'd moved again, and nobody knew where."

"You could have called. You could have written," I said.

"I could have done a lot of things, but I didn't. Now I want to make up for it."

I shrugged.

"I want to start up where we left off."

"What's your name?" I asked. "Your real name?"

"George."

"George. Well, George, I'm glad to see you and I'm glad you're all right. I was curious, and I've satisfied my curiosity." I looked over at him again. "You really think it's worth giving it a try again?"

He nodded.

In my best matter-of-fact tone I said, "I don't know. I'll have to think about it."

"Bullshit," he said, and smiled. I felt myself smiling back.

We picked up our wine glasses and touched them together. "Here's to whatever happens," I said.

MICHAEL NAVA
Street People

The first time Ben saw the boy was at a 7-11 on Santa Monica Boulevard where Ben had stopped to buy rubbers. The boy was no more than eight or nine, scrawny, brown-haired, dark-eyed, Mexican maybe, dressed in old, dirty clothes. Standing behind the kid at the cash register, Ben watched him carefully place his purchases on the counter: a bag of Doritos, two pre-wrapped ham and cheese sandwiches, a carton of milk, and a Hostess cupcake.

The clerk's nametag identified him as Ahmed. Through thick glasses he peered at the boy and said, "Five dollars and thirty-two cents."

From inside his worn jeans, the boy brought up a handful of crumpled bills and some change, dumping it on the counter.

Patiently, Ahmed counted it. "This is only four-fifty," he said in a kind voice. "You have to put something back."

The boy stared at him.

Ahmed picked up one of the sandwiches. "Take this one back, ok?"

Mouth quivering, the kid took the sandwich and stepped back, bumping into Ben. "Sorry," he whispered.

"Wait a second," Ben said, laying a hand on the boy's thin shoulder. "I'll cover it, and give me a pack of Merits."

Ben put a ten-dollar bill and the rubbers on the counter. Ahmed tossed him the Merits, rang everything up on the register, and bagged the boy's groceries. The boy grabbed the bag and threw Ben a look of startled gratitude as he hurried out of the store.

"Kind of late to be grocery shopping."

"He's just a street kid," Ahmed said. "He eats when he's got the money. You need matches?"

"Sure," Ben said. "You think he hustles?"

"Could be," Ahmed said. "I never seen him out there, though."

Ben pocketed the matches. "You must see a lot working here."

Ahmed laughed. "Yeah, they don't call it the graveyard shift for nothing." Ben moved toward the door. "Take care, my friend."

Out in the parking lot, a panhandler leaned drunkenly against Ben's car. Ben smelled him before he reached him.

"Hey, is this your car, man?"

"Yeah, do you mind?"

The drunk staggered out of his way. "Can I wash it or something, for a little bread?"

"You plan to give it a spit shine?"

The drunk pulled a soiled handkerchief out his coat pocket. "I'll clean the windshield for a buck."

Ben laughed. "What's your name?"

It took the drunk a minute to remember. "Ron."

Ben handed him a buck. "Go have one on me, Ron. For protecting my car."

"Hey, thanks," Ron said. "Thanks a lot."

Driving away Ben saw the kid from the store on the other side of the street lugging his little sack of groceries. He was trying to look tough but when Ben honked at him and waved, the boy jumped. He stared after Ben as if he'd seen Santa Claus and waved wildly with his free hand. For a second, Ben felt like turning around and giving the kid a ride but he was already late and the boy was no longer visible in his rearview mirror.

❏

Ben woke at the first light and made his way through the dark rooms of the hillside house to the bathroom, leaving the owner of the house asleep in her canopied bed. Coming back, he stepped out onto the terrace from the living room for a cigarette. Across a small valley were other hills and other houses. The air was cool, damp, and fragrant. In the thick brush below something moved. Leaning over the railing, he was amazed to see a deer.

"Hello," he said, quietly.

The deer lifted its head, watched him for a moment, then went on grazing. Ben thought back dreamily to a morning long ago, at one of the prep schools where he'd spent his childhood, awakening to the first snow and a family of deer huddled beneath shaggy branches of pine. Just as then, he wished he had someone to show this to. He remembered the boy from the night before. He would have liked the boy to have seen this.

❑

Wade was in the hallway, stalled in his walker, when Ben came up the stairs of the apartment house. The old man smiled, or grimaced, it was hard to tell which. Since he'd broken his hip the summer before he was always more or less in pain.

At seventy-nine, Wade believed that he was entitled to certain liberties in the matter of attire. Today he wore an old Pendleton shirt and a loose garment that could only be called a skirt. His skin was as fly-specked as the pages of an old book and the years had made it hard to discern his features, but his eyes were still bright and he missed nothing.

"Just getting home, baby?" he wheezed.

"Yeah. How about some coffee?"

"Come on in and make us some," Wade said.

The door to Wade's apartment was open, as it always was unless he was sleeping. He spent most of the day in a rocker snaring passersby into his room. The other tenants avoided him because once he got started it was hard to shut him up. Ben didn't mind; there were days when Wade was the only person who talked to him.

Wade's room smelled faintly of bird shit. The source of the smell was an empty bamboo bird cage. Wade had had a pair of canaries, Goneril and Regan. Opening the cage door to change the water, he'd moved too slowly and the birds had flown out and through an open window.

Ben helped Wade into his rocker.

"God, being old is fucked," Wade said. "It's the most depressing thing in the world."

Ben smiled. "Yesterday you said bad drag was the most depressing thing in the world."

"This is worse." Wade rocked morosely.

From the doorway of the little kitchen, Ben asked, "Did you eat today?"

"Yeah, yeah."

Inside the refrigerator was a can of Folgers, yoghurt, wheat germ, and something green in a Tupperware container.

"I'll go shopping later on," Ben said and set about making coffee.

"So, what was it last night," Wade asked when Ben brought him a mug of coffee. "Scrumptious dick or disgusting cooze?"

Ben sat on the floor, back against Wade's narrow bed, and smiled. "A woman."

Wade pretended to shudder.

"Your doctor's a woman. You like her."

"I've liked many women in my time," Wade replied, "above the waist." He blew across the surface of his coffee.

"You ever fall in love with any of your tricks?"

"People who pay for sex aren't romantic."

"You're pretty smart for a whore."

"Give me a break."

"You don't even know if you like boys or girls."

"Money doesn't have a gender."

"Get *her*."

Restlessly, Ben's gaze swept across the room. Over a dusty desk was a framed photograph of the young Wade at the gates of M-G-M, proof of his claim that centuries earlier he'd been an actor. Wade had told him that the night Ben stumbled drunkenly into the old man's room. Ben's only friend had died that day, and he'd been a mess. Wade was the only person in the building Ben knew well enough even to say hello to. Wade had been good to him that night.

He told Wade about the kid he'd seen at the store the night before. "He must've been around eight. Where does a kid like that live?"

"The queen who used to manage this place rented to a couple of street kids. I think he took the rent in trade. Filthy little things."

"Not this one," Ben said. "He was just a little guy. I felt really bad for him."

"Life's a bitch, and then you die."

"You've been reading too many tee-shirts," Ben replied. "What do you want from the store?"

❑

A few days later, Ben was on the boardwalk at Venice, walking back from the beach. He'd had a couple of beers and was woozy from the heat and the alcohol. Someone clamped a hand on his shoulder. Ben shook it off and spun around. The hand belonged to a man in a black tank-top and cut-off jeans that revealed a pale, bloated body. There was something vaguely familiar about the man's bleary face.

"You remember me?" he asked hopefully. It was the drunk to whom Ben had given money outside the 7-11.

"Sure," Ben said. "Ron, right?"

Ron nodded. "I saw you walking and wanted to say hi."

"You get around."

"You don't need money to come to the beach," he said, hostility creeping into his voice. Catching himself, he smiled nervously and added, "I take the bus."

"Yeah, well, enjoy," Ben said, moving away.

"The thing is," Ron said, "I need bus fare back into town. Could you maybe help me out?"

"Sure." Ben stopped and got his wallet out. "Will a couple

of bucks do it?"

Ron grabbed the wallet and started running.

"Shit." Ben started after him, but the heat, the beers, and the crowd slowed him down. Ron ducked down one of the alleys off the boardwalk. By the time Ben reached it, he was gone.

"Fuck." He stopped and looked around for the police who patrolled the boardwalk in walking shorts and patent leather shoes. Seeing none, he stood irresolutely for a moment and then headed to his car.

At the Venice substation, a harried cop took a report from Ben between phone calls. He didn't offer Ben much hope of recovering the wallet and so Ben spent the rest of the day at DMV obtaining a new license and cancelling credit cards over the phone.

❏

A couple of weeks later, Ben was doing laundry at the West Hollywood Wash-n-Dry. The regulars were out in full force, divided into two groups, Mexican women and gay men. The women brought their laundry in pillow cases and grocery bags carried in from big rusted-out cars. The gay men came in carting wicker baskets and paperback novels, cruising each other listlessly beneath the harsh lights. The two groups could have been on different planets for all the contact between them.

Sitting in his car, Ben drank a Corona and listened to Tracy Chapman while he waited for his clothes to finish washing. Though it was a warm night, he was wearing a leather jacket. It had belonged to his father, who had died when Ben was eight. His mother had given him the jacket when he turned sixteen.

He had only seen her a half-dozen times since then and each time she was younger, thinner, and blonder, until it hardly seemed possible to him that she was his mother. She insisted that he call her by her first name. Ben remembered the time when she had been "Mom" instead of "Martha," and there'd been a "Dad" instead of whatever the first name of his current stepfather was. They'd lived in Santa Monica, then, six blocks from the ocean.

After his father's death, Ben and mother returned to Chicago and her wealthy parents. She had eloped with his father at nineteen and her parents were appalled at having a half-Jewish grandson. They persuaded her to send him off to a prep school, the first of many. At seventeen, he ran away from the last one and made his way back to L.A. where he'd now lived for eight years.

Once, when he was drunk, Ben went looking for the house he'd lived in as a child. A black family'd bought it. They'd sobered him up and let him have his cry, and then sent him on his way. Now, when anyone asked him, he said he was an orphan.

A siren's wail broke through "Fast Car." On the street an ambulance was stuck in traffic, lights flashing, siren blaring. Ben finished his beer. His wash would be about done.

Inside, he spotted an empty dryer at the far end of the room. Piling his clothes into a cart, he headed toward the dryer. Just before he got there a boy stepped out, his back to Ben, and opened the dryer door.

"Are you using this dryer?" Ben asked.

The boy jumped and turned around. It was the kid he'd seen at the 7-11 almost two months earlier. Without a word, the boy slipped away to a tall, thin man folding pillow cases at the end of a long table nearby. The man was grizzled, stooped, and nearly bald. He wore a cheap plaid shirt, black 501s, and orange construction boots. The boy looked at Ben, who smiled. The boy smiled back for a second, then backed up, brushing against the man's legs.

Sourly, the man looked down at the boy and then up at Ben. Smiling resolutely, Ben approached them.

"Hi," he said. "I asked your friend here if he needed that dryer."

"No, we're finished," the man said, and went back to his folding.

"Your son?"

"That's right." His eyes were bleary and suspicious. Something about him hit a note that wasn't close to paternal.

"You know, we met before," Ben said to the man, and then to the boy. "Remember?"

Slowly, the boy nodded.

"It was at a store," Ben explained, then interrupted himself. "My name's Ben."

"Frank," the man said. "And Bobby."

"Hi," Ben said to Bobby.

Bobby whispered, "Hi."

"How old are you, eight, nine?"

"He's eight," Frank said.

"I'm eight-and-a-half," Bobby said huskily.

"I guess six months means a lot when you're eight," Ben said. "When's your birthday?"

"In six months," Frank said abruptly. "That's his birthday. You want that dryer?"

A big woman carrying a basket of sopping clothes waddled toward the dryer where Ben'd left his cart. He got there just before she did and stuffed his clothes into the machine. She grunted and turned away. He put a couple of quarters into the dryer and pushed in the slot. Nothing happened.

"Shit," he said, turning back toward Frank and Bobby, "these things never. . ." But they were gone.

When he finished his wash, he drove back to the 7-11 where he'd first seen the boy. He'd gotten into the habit of visiting Ahmed on nights he couldn't sleep. The door buzzer yelped as he stepped inside. Ahmed looked up from his *Playgirl* and smiled.

"My friend," he said. "Pack of Merits?"

"Yeah, thanks," Ben said, taking the cigarettes. He opened the pack and offered one to Ahmed. "Business is slow."

Ahmed lit their cigarettes. "It's early," he said with a thin smile. "The boys have to turn their first tricks before they can buy."

"Ahmed, do you remember that kid who was here the first time I came in?"

"Yes," Ahmed said agreeably.

Ben exhaled a stream of smoke. "No you don't."

Ahmed shrugged. "There are so many." He narrowed his eyes. "The little Mexican," he said finally. "You paid for him."

"That's the one. Have you ever seen him in here with a guy named Frank?"

"I haven't seen him for a long time," Ahmed replied, "and when he came in he was always alone. He put his dirty dollar bills on the counter." He touched the counter with a long finger. "Sometimes they were enough, sometimes not. You helped him that time, maybe this man is helping him now."

"I know a john when I see one," Ben said.

"Around here, Ben, everyone is someone's john."

"Jesus, Ahmed, the kid is eight years old."

"Did he look healthy?" Ahmed asked. "Well fed? Did he have shoes?" Ahmed crushed his cigarette in a green foil ashtray. "Sex is all these kids have to bargain with. They're lucky someone wants them." He tapped the magazine. "Me, I like Mr. September."

"You've been at this job too long — my friend. How much are the smokes?"

"On the house."

"I'll see you around." Ben said, starting out the door.

"Ben."

He turned. "What?"

"Stick around. I'll show you ten kids who need your help more than your little friend does."

❑

"That's it. Slide it in all the way," the man whispered, rolling his head on the pillow beneath Ben.

Ben pushed his cock into the yielding flesh as the man's legs tightened around his neck. The man closed his eyes and pursed his lips, making little sucking noises. Ben turned his face to the big window that framed the city's grids of light below.

"Don't stop," the man said.

Ben looked back at him. "Sorry."

"Try to be a little more into it."

Ben closed his eyes and tried to concentrate but the smell of cologne and shit that hung above the bed repelled him. He felt his cock retracting. He tried thinking of something sexy but the satin sheets and the man's enveloping softness soiled his imagination. Instead, involuntarily, he began to remember the first time he'd been fucked.

He was twelve years old. He had gone to see the school chaplain because he was troubled about the feelings he had been having for another boy. Reverend Paul told him the feelings were normal and would pass. He encouraged Ben to visit him as often as he needed and Ben became a regular visitor to the chaplain's bachelor quarters. Over Christmas vacation, knowing that Ben had nowhere else to go, Reverend Paul had invited Ben to stay with him.

The first night Ben was there he had awakened to find Reverend Paul in bed with him, naked. He remembered how enormous the chaplain's body had seemed, forcing Ben against the wall. He could still feel the cool plaster at his back and the chaplain's stubby fingers pulling down Ben's shorts. Once he got them off, he raped Ben without much ceremony.

"That's right, that's right," the man beneath him moaned as Ben, in a rage, pounded into him.

Surging toward orgasm, Ben muttered, "You asshole, you filthy queer, I'm going to kill you."

"Kill me, baby. Kill me."

"I'm gonna fucking kill you. I'll kill you."

"Kill me, kill me, kill me. . ."

"Shut the fuck up." Ben closed his eyes as the rush overtook him, blanking out everything. As soon as he came, he jerked himself free.

The man masturbated himself into his own frenzied orgasm, groping Ben with his free hand. When he finished, he said, "You're really something, baby."

Ben slapped his hand away. "Don't touch me."

"Hey, I'm paying for this, honey."

Head pounding, Ben snapped, "Fuck you."

❏

He awoke the next morning to a hangover and the click of his answering machine recording a message. He pulled himself out of bed and stumbled into the bathroom where he drank tap water from cupped hands and swallowed aspirin and a couple of valium. Back into bed, he listened to a police officer on his answering machine tell him to call Detective Gomez at the Venice substation. Ben tried to go back to sleep but he couldn't close his eyes without wanting to throw up, so he picked up the phone and dialed.

"Did you find my wallet?" he asked Gomez after identifying himself.

"Yes, we did."

"Where was it?" Ben asked, burrowing into the blankets as the valium kicked in.

"The guy still had it on him," Gomez replied.

Ben asked through a yawn, "Is he in jail?"

"He's dead, Mr. Weiss. Someone killed him, maybe to get to your wallet."

"You're kidding. Where?"

"They found him in an alley behind the boardwalk."

"Are you sure it's the same guy?"

"No, the only I.D. he had was your wallet and there wasn't much left in that but an address book and a couple of credit card receipts. It would help a lot if you came down and took a look at him."

Ben shivered. "You want me to what?"

"Take a look at him. If it's the same guy who stole your wallet that gives us something to work with."

"You want me look at the body?"

"Look, Mr. Weiss," he heard papers rustling. "Uh, Ben, look, this is more serious than a stolen wallet now. This is the third killing this month of one of these street people in Venice."

"I just woke up," Ben muttered, as if this would excuse him.

"I'll be here 'til five."

"Okay, okay. Give me an hour."

❑

Gomez's first name was Ed. He was a big man, half a head taller than Ben, who was nearly six feet, and easily fifty pounds heavier, all of it muscle. He had a stony handsomeness and looked at Ben in a way that made him wish he hadn't popped another valium in the car.

He led Ben to a small windowless room across from a couple of cells. Gomez explained it was the drunk tank. A green body bag lay on one of the two bunks.

"It's a good thing I caught you," Gomez said, conversationally. "He's going downtown to the coroner in about an hour."

"For what?"

"Autopsy," Gomez said. "You ready?" Without waiting for an answer, he unzipped the body bag, filling the room with the man's stench. "This Ron?"

Ben looked quickly. The guy still wore the black tank-top. "Yes."

"You're going to have to look closely," Gomez said, patiently. "I know it's not easy but we want to be sure."

Ben looked again at the bloated, ash-colored face. "That's him. I'm sure." He looked at Gomez. "I'm going to be sick."

"There's a toilet behind you."

Ben staggered to the toilet and threw up.

Back at Gomez's desk, the cop took Ben's statement and apologized for not being able to release his wallet.

Holding a big styrofoam container of coffee between shaky hands, Ben said, "The only thing I need is my address book. Can I get that back?"

"I'm afraid I have to keep it," Gomez said. "For evidence."

Ben wasn't up to arguing the point. "Who would want to kill a guy like that? He was just a drunk."

"That's why," Gomez said. "He was an easy target, like most of these street people. A lot of them are too nuts to protect themselves. And a lot of them are women and kids."

Ben thought of Bobby. "Can I ask you about something?"

"What?" Gomez pulled a cigarette out of a pack of Winstons and lit it.

"I've seen this kid around where I live. He's about eight, I guess. The first time he was by himself. The second time he was with this old guy who said he was the kid's father. I know he wasn't the kid's father. I think he just picked the kid up off the street and he's getting it on with him. You know what I mean?"

"Yeah, why do you think that?"

"I talked to this friend who used to see the kid around. He was always alone, and suddenly he's got a daddy." He shrugged. "I saw them together and it didn't look right."

Gomez tapped ash into his trash can. "There's not much we can do about things that don't look right."

"The guy's a child molester."

"You don't know that," Gomez replied. "We don't investigate suspicions around here. We're busy enough with crimes."

"Kidnapping," Ben said.

"Come on, Ben."

"What if I found out more?"

Gomez shook his head. "You don't want to be getting into

other people's business."

"What if the kid shows up in that room back there?"

Gomez dropped his cigarette to the floor and crushed it with the toe of a scuffed shoe. "I don't blame you for being upset, Ben. Go home. Do something relaxing."

Ben got up. "Just tell me I can call you if something comes up."

Reluctantly, Gomez said, "Yeah, sure."

❑

A few nights later, Ben got caught in a traffic jam on Santa Monica just past Fairfax. Approaching the intersection, he saw that there'd been an accident. Flares were out, roadblocks were up, and a cop was directing traffic around a crushed motorcycle and a sheeted body. Ben looked around for a detour and wheeled into the parking lot of a fast-food drive-in looking for an exit onto Fairfax.

As he swung behind the building, he heard a racket near the dumpster. A kid was trying to climb the metal wall but couldn't get a foothold. He dropped down and stumbled to his knees. Getting up, he glanced over at Ben. Ben recognized him immediately and stopped. He got out of the car and walked toward the dumpster.

"Bobby? Do you remember me?"

Dully, the boy looked up. His eyes were rheumy. Slowly, he nodded.

"Where's Frank?"

"Sick," the boy squeaked. His clothes were shabbier and dirtier than when Ben has last seen him. He gave off a thin, rancid smell and his hair was matted to his skull.

Pointing to the dumpster, Ben asked, "What were you looking for in there?"

The boy began to cry. "I'm hungry."

"Come on," Ben said, taking him by the arm and leading him toward his car.

The boy struggled weakly to get away. "Frank said—"

"Forget about what Frank said," Ben replied. "Let's get you something to eat."

The boy gave up and Ben half-dragged, half-carried him to the car.

Once at his apartment, Ben put together a meal from the odds and ends in his refrigerator. Bobby ate everything, his attention riveted to the plate as if he was afraid to look at Ben. When he finished eating, Ben brewed him a cup of tea and gave it to him with a shot glass of brandy. The boy sipped the brandy, shuddered, and pushed it aside.

"Drink it slow," Ben said, pushing it back toward him. "It'll help you sleep."

The boy looked at him nervously, picked up the glass, and drained it. He coughed violently. Ben rushed to get him a glass of water.

"I said slow. Drink some water."

He held the glass to the boy's lips. The boy gulped water until it ran down the sides of his mouth. He jerked his head away from the glass.

"Are you okay?"

The boy nodded, leaning as far back in his chair, and away from Ben, as he could.

Ben sat down. "I'm not going to hurt you, Bobby."

"I want to go home."

"Where do you live?" Ben asked.

In a sing-song voice, he recited, "8900 Sunset Boulevard. Room 221."

"Is that where Frank is?"

Bobby nodded, and started crying. "He stopped talking."

"Who, Frank?"

He nodded again, snot running down his nose. Ben handed him a paper napkin and told him to blow.

"Frank's dead," the boy sniffled.

"That's all right," Ben said stupidly. "You can sleep here tonight. You want to watch some TV?"

"Okay," Bobby said, and began to cry again.

❑

The boy fell asleep in front of the TV and Ben carried him into his bed. Returning to the living room, he lit a cigarette and shut the TV off. It was a little before eleven. He thought about what Bobby had said, that Frank was dead, and knew he should do something but was afraid to leave the boy alone. He went next door. Wade, in a voluminous nightgown, sat in his rocker like Whistler's mother reading a biography of Elizabeth Taylor.

"Hello, honey," he said to Ben. "Early night? "

"Can you do me a favor, Wade?"

"That's why I'm here, baby."

"There's someone in my apartment. Could you keep an eye on him?"

Wade cocked a shaggy eyebrow. "I thought you were out-call only."

"It's not a trick. It's the kid I told you about, the one I saw at 7-11 a couple of months back." Quickly, he sketched for Wade the night's events.

"I don't mean to sound like *Dragnet*, honey, but isn't this a job for the police?"

Thinking bitterly of Gomez, he said, "If the police gave a

shit, he wouldn't have been on the streets in the first place."

"Ben, he could be a runaway or something. His parents might be looking for him."

"I'll figure that out later. Right now he needs to sleep. Could you watch him for a little while?"

"Where are you going?"

"To that place on Sunset."

"Help me up," Wade said, "and I'll come and babysit for you."

❑

The address the boy had given him was to a decayed motel at the end of Sunset Strip in a corner that Ben had never noticed before. A driveway led down to a parking lot. Ben pulled into a space and got out of his car. From the edge of the lot was a panorama of the city from downtown to Century City, the lights scattered like confetti in the cold November night. Ben made his way up to the second floor past closed doors and the squall of TVs and radios and voices.

There was no sound from 221. He tried the door and found it unlocked. Pushing it in, he reached for a light switch without luck. Keeping the door ajar he stepped into the shadowy room. The stench forced him back out.

Breathing through his mouth, he re-entered and stood still, accustoming his eyes to the darkness. Across the room was a door, and behind it, a light was shining. Heart pounding, he took cautious steps toward the light.

"Frank?" he whispered, tapping at the door.

He waited for a response. Hearing nothing, he pushed the door open and crossed the threshold.

"Jesus."

In lamplight, Frank lay in a filthy bed. His bare body was

skeletal and gray. Next to the bed was a plastic bucket. Shit ran down its sides. Strewn nearby were hamburger containers from McDonalds, some with half-eaten food still in them. Frank's eyes were closed and his mouth hung open.

Stumbling through the darkness, Ben hurried out of the room and back to his car. Back on Sunset, he saw a bar and skidded to a stop in front of it. Inside, he found the pay phone. Hands shaking, he dialed 911. The phone rang and rang.

"Answer the fucking phone," he said.

"Police emergency," a woman droned.

"There's a dead guy," he said, all in a rush. "He's in a motel room on Sunset. You got to send someone."

"Sir, sir," the woman interrupted. "Slow down."

"It's at 8900 Sunset, room 221," he said.

"Are you sure he's—"

"He's dead," Ben snapped and clanged down the receiver. He went into the bar and ordered a double bourbon. A few minutes later, he heard sirens passing on the street outside. When he went out to his car, he saw an ambulance turn off Sunset where the motel was. He drove home.

❏

Entering his apartment, Ben was startled to find Wade's doctor, Iris Wong, emerging from his bedroom with her black bag in hand. Wade was sitting on the sofa, looking frail and tired.

"What happened?" Ben asked him.

Wade said, "He woke up, and wandered out here, delirious or something. When he saw me, he got hysterical. I didn't know what else to do, so I called Iris."

"Is he okay?" Ben asked her.

"He has a fever," she said coolly, "and it looks like he's suffering from malnutrition. Do you want to explain what's going on here, Ben?"

"Yeah, I'd like to tell someone, but you better sit down. It'll take a while."

When he finished, Iris asked, "Do you want to call the police, or should I?"

"What do you mean?" Ben asked.

"State law requires physicians to report kids who they think have been abused to the police," she said. "It's a criminal offense if I don't."

"Can't you just forget you were here?"

She shook her head. "No. Who's going to take care of him, Ben?"

"I will."

"He has parents somewhere," she said. "He belongs with them." She got up. "I'll try to stop by this afternoon. In the meantime, give him baby aspirin and feed him something decent. And call the police."

"Does it have to be today?"

"The sooner, the better," she said. "Good-night."

After she left, Wade said, "I'm sorry, baby, but I couldn't handle him."

"That's okay, Wade. Thanks."

Wade left and Ben went into the bedroom. The boy was a small lump beneath the blankets, his face upturned, eyes screwed shut, scowling. Ben sat at the edge of the bed and touched the boy's forehead. He stirred and muttered something.

Exhausted, Ben lay down beside him. Listening to the boy's noisy breathing, he fell asleep.

❏

After the first few days, Ben decided that Bobby wasn't so much afraid of him as just generally afraid. Ben treated him as gently as he could, not asking about Frank or anything that had happened to him. He bought Bobby toys and clothes and cooked his favorite foods for him. They rented *E.T.* and went to see a circus in Santa Monica. The boy accepted all this impassively, as if he had no ability to be a kid. Then one night after finishing his macaroni and cheese, he said, "I want chocolate ice cream." It was the first time he'd ever asked for anything. He talked more easily after that, but never about Frank. It was as if Frank no longer existed for him except in the nightmares from which he awoke, screaming Frank's name.

One morning, a couple of weeks after he'd brought Bobby home, Ben sat down beside him as he ate his Cap'n Crunch and watched Bugs Bunny. "What are you watching?"

"Cartoons," he said softly. He spooned some cereal into his mouth. On the screen, Bugs appeared in drag on the back of a plump white horse.

"The night I brought you home with me I went to see Frank."

Without looking up at him, Bobby said, "I want more juice."

Ben took the boy's glass into the kitchen and filled it with apple juice. Returning, he set it on the tray and said, "Bobby, did Frank ever hurt you?"

Eyes fastened to the screen, the boy shook his head.

"Look at me, Bobby," Ben said gently. The boy looked. "It's okay to tell me," he continued. "How come you were staying with Frank?"

"Georgie told me to."

"Who's Georgie?"

The boy's breath got shallow. "Georgie's my brother. He told me to stay with Frank."

Ben wondered if Georgie had been the boy's pimp or just another street kid who made some change by turning Bobby over to Frank. "Georgie gave you to Frank?"

The boy seemed to curl into himself and nodded. Ben backed off. "It's okay, Bobby. We don't have to talk about Frank."

"I want to stay here," Bobby said.

"Don't worry about that," Ben replied.

❑

When Iris Wong found out that Ben hadn't yet called the police she gave him twenty-four hours to do it before she called them herself. Grudgingly, he phoned Gomez.

"Hold the line please," he was told when he reached the station.

"Okay."

From the kitchen table, Ben could hear Bobby quietly talking to himself in the living room. He craned his neck around the doorway. Bobby was playing with the Masters of the Universe dolls that Ben had bought the day before. He-Man was pounding Skeletor to a pulp while Bobby provided sound effects. He seemed just like a normal eight-year-old, Ben thought, except for the nightmares, bed-wetting, and crying jags.

"This is Gomez."

"This is Ben Weiss. You remember me? My wallet was stolen by the guy that got killed in Venice and I came down—"

"Yeah, sure, Ben. I'm afraid we can't release the wallet yet."

"That's not why I'm calling you," Ben said, lowering his voice. "Do you remember that I told you about the kid I'd seen on the streets?"

There was a dubious pause. "A kid on the streets?"

"Yeah. I told you he was being molested by a guy who said he was the kid's dad."

"Okay, I remember. What about it?"

Ben paused, torn between going on and hanging up. Recalling Iris's threat he decided it was better to tell Gomez, who'd seemed halfway decent, than have her go to a cop he didn't know.

"I found him a few nights ago going through the garbage behind that hot dog stand on Santa Monica and Fairfax. The guy who had him is dead."

When Gomez spoke again, his voice was alert and impersonal. "How do you know that?'

Ben explained how he'd gone to the motel.

Gomez said, "I think you better come down here."

"I don't want to leave him by himself. Can you come here?"

"What's the address?"

Ben gave him the address to his apartment. Gomez said he would be there in a half-hour.

❑

An hour later, there was knock at the door. Ben opened it to Gomez who stepped into the room diminishing it with his bulk. Bobby looked at him and then at his He-Man doll.

"Are you He-Man?" Bobby asked.

Gomez smiled briefly and shook his head.

"This is Detective Gomez," Ben said. "This is Bobby."

"Hi, Bobby."

"Hi."

To Ben, Gomez said, "Can we go somewhere private to talk?"

"The kitchen," Ben said. "You want a cup of coffee?"

They went through a pot of coffee while Ben told his story to Gomez. The cop listened with the same cool attentiveness that he'd shown the day Ben identified Ron's body in the drunk tank. When Ben finished, Gomez got up and stretched, walking to the window, through which the Hollywood sign was visible through the sludgy winter air.

He said, "You probably expect me to tell you what a good guy you are, Ben, but it's not going to work that way. You should've done what that doctor told you and called me the day you found the kid."

"He was sick."

"We have doctors."

"Look, the kid's happy here. No one else cares about him."

"His parents?"

"What parents? He was living on the streets."

"I'm going to have to take him with me," Gomez said.

Ben shook his head. "No."

The two man stared at each other. Finally, Gomez said, "What do you do for a living, Ben?"

"I work as a waiter for a catering company."

Gomez smiled, grimly. "You're a hustler." He reached into his pocket and extracted the thin address book Ben carried in his wallet. "Remember this?" He opened it, flipping through the pages. "Adonis — Adonis Escorts, right? GQ Escorts. For Ladies Only. I worked vice for a long time, Ben, I know all about these escort services. I wouldn't have to dig very hard to find something on you. Like drugs, maybe. You were stoned out of your mind the day you came down to the station. I bet I could walk into your bathroom and find enough of something to arrest you on the spot. Don't make me do that."

"You fucking asshole," Ben said softly, so that Bobby wouldn't hear.

"If you say so," he said, flipping the book across the table to Ben. "You might be interested to know that Frank's not dead."

"What?"

"I made a couple of calls after I talked to you. The guy you found — his name is Frank Baron — is at county hospital. He's got AIDS, Ben. You know what that means? If he was screwing the kid, the kid might have it, too."

"You're lying."

"Get him ready, okay?" Gomez said. "Let's make it easy on everyone."

II

"Mr. Weiss? Good morning. I'm Elizabeth Lloyd."

Ben looked at the silken-haired woman who'd entered the small windowless room where he'd been waiting for fifteen minutes. She wasn't at all what he'd expected from their brief conversations over the phone. To him, child psychologist conjured up the grandmotherly woman to whom he'd been sent at nine for his bed-wetting. This woman wore a tailored wool suit of deep lavender and was as carefully coiffed and made-up as a model. It was easier for him to imagine her querying a wine steward than counseling troubled children.

"I'm sorry to keep you waiting," she said, clearly conveying to him that her time was valuable. She regarded him skeptically. "Bobby calls you the 'pretty man'. He's right."

Ben didn't take it as a compliment.

"I'd like to see him." For the past two weeks Bobby had been at McMahon Hall, a holding facility for kids declared wards of the court.

"Why don't we talk for a few minutes."

"That's all I've been doing since the cops took him," Ben complained. "I talked to the D.A. for four hours yesterday."

"You're the D.A.'s star witness."

"But I heard on TV that there's no evidence."

Frank Baron had been charged with child molestation even though he was dying of AIDS. The charges made headlines. "Boy Allegedly Molested by AIDS Victim," the tamest one had read. Baron's lawyer, a man named Henry Rios, told the press that there was no medical evidence either that Bobby had been molested or that he was positive for the AIDS virus. Rios was one of the people who wanted to talk to Ben. The D.A. had told him not to.

"The medical evidence is inconclusive," Elizabeth Lloyd was saying. "It frequently is in these cases. Physically, children heal quickly. On the other hand, he does display some of the classic symptoms of sexual abuse."

"Like what?"

She smiled without meaning it. "There's a pattern of behavior in children who've been abused which we call the accommodation syndrome. Initially, there's secrecy and denial. The child understands that what's happened to him should not be disclosed. This is followed by feelings of helplessness because of the violation in the child's relationship with the adult. Quite commonly the adult molester is someone the child trusted, often a parent."

She looked at Ben as if she knew that he was thinking about Reverend Paul. After the first few times, Ben had learned to submit to sex as the price he paid for the man's attention. It was only when Ben began to enjoy the sex that he threatened the chaplain with exposure, and the sex stopped. Shortly after, Ben transferred to another school.

She was saying, "Eventually the child accommodates himself to the situation. If it's bad enough, though, he will at some point tell someone."

Ben had never told anyone. "Does he always?"

"No, particularly if it's a male child. The shame is too great. He finds other ways to deal with it."

"How?" Ben asked, wondering if she suspected what was behind his interest.

"Well, the way Robert has dealt with it is to create an alter ego."

Ben said, "I don't know what that means."

Her smile said, no, of course not. Aloud, she asked, "Did he ever mention someone named Georgie to you?"

"Georgie? Yeah, he said that Georgie was his brother, but I figure he was either a pimp or just another kid he met on the street."

"He was neither. Georgie is what Robert calls the part of himself that he admits was abused."

"Did he tell you that?"

"Working with abused children, one learns to read between the lines. He thinks Georgie really does exist and told me, as he did you, that Georgie is his brother. When I asked him what happened to Georgie, he said that Georgie had been beaten by his uncle and run away. Isn't that what happened? He was abused and he ran away."

"It was because Frank was sick."

"No, Ben, that was only Robert's opportunity to get away from him. You found him on the streets. Do you know for sure how long he'd been out there?"

"No," Ben said, uncertainly. What she said made sense, but some part of him remained unpersuaded. "But you said he talked about being beaten, not molested."

"Men," she said, "even little ones have a need to protect their masculinity. It's easier for them to admit they've been physically abused than sexually abused."

He decided that even if she was right, she was still a bitch. "What if there was a Georgie?"

"He's been at McMahon for two weeks," she said, "and no one has stepped forward to claim him, even with all the publicity surrounding the case. There is no Georgie. He's Georgie. I know instances of children who actually split into multiple personalities as a way of coping with their sexual abuse. This is just a milder form."

"Can I see him?"

She got up. "Tomorrow. I'll arrange for it. Around ten. By the way," she added, "he may be angry at you for abandoning him."

"I didn't abandon him."

"That won't make any difference."

❏

On his way home, Ben stopped at Iris Wong's office. She'd told him she wanted to talk to him about Bobby, a request that surprised him since she had only been briefly involved. Her office was in Century City, in a glass tower, with a commanding view of the west side of the city. It had been drizzling all day and there was nothing to be seen from the windows of her waiting room but gray and white. The weather deepened the gloom Ben felt after talking to Elizabeth Lloyd. He tried to persuade himself it was on account of his concern for Bobby, but it wasn't Bobby he was thinking about as he studied his reflection in the window.

Brief but vivid recollections of Reverend Paul flashed through his head; the weight of the man's body, his smells, the things he said as he prodded Ben's anus with a greasy finger, ". . . does this feel good, do you like it. . ."

"Ben?" Iris stood at the door to the waiting room, her white smock covering a black wool dress.

"Hi," he said, unclenching his fists.

"Come into my office."

He followed her into a small office. He sat down in a leather chair with a view of her desk and, on the wall behind, a faded Chinese scroll depicting two tiny human figures ascending a mountainous landscape.

"Are you just getting back from seeing Bobby?"

"I didn't get to see him, just the psychologist."

"Elizabeth Lloyd?" she asked, with distaste.

"Yeah," he said, surprised. "Did you talk to her?"

"That's why I wanted to see you," Iris said. "She called me since I was the first doctor to examine Bobby. She insisted on telling me what I saw."

"What do you mean?"

"She wanted me to tell her about physical signs of sexual abuse. I told her," she said coldly, as if still talking to Lloyd, "I didn't find any. All I saw was a hungry, sick, frightened kid." She shrugged. "I don't think the prosecutor is going to ask me to testify."

"But did you look at Bobby for abuse?" he asked awkwardly.

She nodded. "After what you told me, I examined him thoroughly. There just weren't any signs of the trauma that I'd expect to see where there's been sexual abuse."

"Like what?"

"Scarring or enlargement of the anus, or tenderness around his abdomen, or signs of veneral disease. Nothing."

"She told me that kids heal fast."

Iris raised a dismissive eyebrow. "You don't heal without scars."

"She said the scars were inside."

"You would know that better than anyone," Iris replied.

"What do you mean?" he asked sharply.

She blinked. "I just meant that you spent time with him. What did you think I meant?"

Ben shook his head. "Nothing. I'm a little on edge. Sorry."

Her gaze was skeptical but also concerned. "You really care for him, don't you?"

"I just want to do the right thing."

"I'm sure you will, Ben," she said.

❏

He and Bobby were walking across the grounds of McMahon Hall toward the high wire fence that surrounded the place. Behind them, obscured by mist, was a lumpy brown-brick edifice with turrets and guard towers. He heard dogs barking and he and the boy began to run. Heart beating frantically, he saw a fence ahead of them and put out his hand, grasping it. An electric shock knocked him to his knees. He pulled himself free and shouted to Bobby, "Don't touch it."

The dogs were closing in. Glancing over his shoulder, Ben

could make out their dark forms cutting through the mist.

"Fly!" he yelled at the terrified boy, and flapped his own arms to show him how. "Fly!"

The boy flapped his thin arms wildly, like a cartoon character. They began to rise from the ground, slowly at first, but with increasing speed.

"Fly!" Ben shouted, ecstatic now as they easily surmounted the fence, rising above the mist into the clear blue sky. He looked over at Bobby who laughed wildly as he darted through the air, his arms beating as fast as a hummingbird's wings.

"Fly," Ben said. "Fly, fly. . ." He woke to the darkness, a hand over his crotch and the rattle of someone else's breathing. He turned his head in the direction of the breathing. A woman. Her bare breasts looked pale and misshapen in the shadowy light. Her hand gripped Ben's balls. He jerked it away, awakening her.

"What's wrong?" she muttered, a blast of whisky on her breath.

"You just about castrated me, that's all," Ben said, sitting up. She'd once been an actress, he remembered, as she emerged from her stupor. Twenty years earlier he'd watched the TV series in which she played the sweet young daughter in a family sitcom. Now she sold real estate in Brentwood and claimed to be thirty-five. He was sure she had been, once.

"We wouldn't wanna do that, would we?" she said, patting his leg. "Here, let me make it all better."

❏

"Hi, Bobby," Ben said. "I brought you a present."

"Hi," the boy said, accepting the brightly colored package, sullenly.

"Aren't you going to open it?"

Without replying, the boy unwrapped the present, opened the box, and examined the Masters of the Universe sweatshirt that Ben had brought him. "I don't like it," he said.

"Sure you do," Ben replied. "Here, put it on."

Bobby jerked away from him. Unlike the place in his dream, McMahon Hall didn't have turrets and guard towers. It looked like an elementary school, boxy rectangular buildings connected by covered hallways. They were sitting in the cafeteria, a high-ceilinged building that smelled of stewed tomatoes and disinfectant. From its banks of windows was a view of the grounds. And a fence. It was not as ominous as it had been in Ben's dream, but it was there.

"Look, I'm sorry they made you come here. I tried to stop them."

The boy looked stubbornly away.

"I came to see you as soon as I could."

"I hate it here," Bobby said. "The kids call me names."

"I know," Ben said. "Let's go for a walk."

He got up and stood at rigid attention. "I hate you."

"Here," Ben said, extending the sweatshirt in his hand. "It's cold outside."

Bobby stared at it, and then at Ben. He grabbed the sweatshirt and pulled it on.

"I hate you," he repeated, but with less conviction.

Ben said, "I heard you, Bobby, and I'm sorry. Let's go outside, okay?"

They went out, walking across the grounds toward the fence, not speaking. When they got to the fence, Ben put out his hand and brushed his fingertips against it, half-expecting a shock, but felt only damp metal.

"I know you want to get out of here," he said.

Bobby grabbed the fence and pulled himself back and forth against it. "How come I can't stay with you?"

"I want you to," Ben said, "but these people think your family might come to take you home. Would you like that?"

"Just Georgie," he said.

Ben sat down on the cold grass. Bobby stood next to him, looking at him gravely. Ben reached up his hand and pulled Bobby down, hugging the boy to him. "I miss you."

Bobby echoed, "I miss you."

"I have a secret to tell you, Bobby," Ben said. "When I was a little boy there was a man who did something nasty to me. I never told anyone and it still makes me sad when I think about it." He paused. "Do you understand what I'm saying?"

Bobby shook his head. "What did he do?"

"Do you know what a penis is?" Ben asked awkwardly. "The thing you pee with?"

"My pee-pee?"

"It's called a penis."

Bobby looked at him skeptically. "A penis?"

Ben nodded. "This man, he put his penis into my butt."

Bobby giggled. "Why?"

"Because it felt good to him, but not to me. It hurt and it made me feel bad. Do you know why I'm telling you this?"

Bobby shook his head.

"It's okay to tell them about what Frank did to you."

"He didn't do nothing."

"Bobby, he can't hurt you now. Just tell him."

"Then can I come and stay with you?"

Ben kissed him. "I hope so."

❏

When he got home, Ben found Wade pacing the hall, having graduated from a walker to a cane. Today he wore a maroon running suit of plush velour and a pink bandanna tied ascot-style around his neck.

"Just in time for tea," Wade said, reaching out with talon-like fingers to grip Ben's hand.

"Sure, come on in," Ben said, opening his door. He helped the old man to a chair and went into the kitchen to put the kettle on.

"How was your visit?" Wade asked when he returned to the living room.

Ben lit a cigarette and sat down. "I didn't do Bobby any favors by turning him over to the court."

"You didn't have any choice."

"That place is like a jail and the poor kid is scared shitless."

The tea-kettle whistled. He went into the kitchen and prepared a pot of Twining's Earl Grey, bringing it and two cups out on a tray.

"Iris doesn't think that Baron did anything to him."

"What do you think?"

"That's what she asked me. I don't know." He poured tea into the cups. "All I wanted was to take care of him, and instead I keep fucking up. He's going to end up really hating me."

"He would have died if you hadn't found him," Wade said, blowing over the surface of his tea. "I don't think he's going to hate you."

He studied his friend's face. It was a map of someone who had seen everything. "There's something I want to tell you, Wade," he said, getting the words out quickly. "When I was twelve, there was this guy. He raped me."

Wade sipped his tea. "You told me that the first time I met you, honey. Don't you remember?"

Ben shook his head.

"Well, you were pretty drunk." Wade set his cup down. "You probably don't remember what I told you, either."

"No."

"I told you it wasn't your fault. Now that you know what happened to Bobby, maybe you'll believe me. Maybe you can stop trying to kill yourself."

"I don't know what you mean."

"The drugs, baby. The booze. The sex. That's what that's about."

The cup in Ben's hand rattled, spilling tea onto his leg, but he felt nothing.

❑

The following afternoon he made his daily call to Elizabeth Lloyd to check on Bobby.

"Ben, I'm so glad you called me," she said, her cool tone belying her enthusiasm. "I've got some great news about Robert."

"What's that?"

"Well, first, he's finally able to talk about the abuse."

"Yeah, when did that happen?"

"At our session this morning," she replied. He detected real feeling in her voice, and he disliked her a little less. "He just opened up, Ben. I hardly had to say anything. In fact, it's the most he's said the whole time he's been here."

"What exactly did he say?"

"Well, it was rather general," she said, reverting to her tone of cool assessment, "but he did say — I'm using his words — that Frank put his penis in Bobby's butt. Now we'll have to pin him to dates and times for his testimony at the trial."

"Is that exactly what he said?" Ben asked.

There was a pause. "Yes, Ben, did he say something different to you?"

He tried but could not bring himself to tell her that Bobby's words may have referred not to something that had happened to him, but to Ben. Not only was she the last person he would confide in, but it seemed possible that Bobby was merely borrowing Ben's words to describe what Frank had done with him. Wanting to believe this, he tried to ignore his doubts.

Carefully, he said, "When I saw him yesterday I told him that if he'd talk to you about Frank, maybe he could come back and stay with me. You don't think because I said something—"

"Did you say that really?" she asked, then added decisively. "No, I don't think there's a connection."

"But maybe," he insisted.

She held her ground. "The time was right, Ben. Trust me, I've dealt with hundreds of these cases. Anyway, there's other news, too. His mother has come forward."

It took a moment for Ben to understand. "His what?"

"Robert's mother. She identified his picture in the newspaper. . ."

"His picture's been in the paper for weeks," Ben said.

"Not in San Luis Obispo county," she said. "That's where Robert's from, a small town called Guadalupe. Apparently, some neighbor of Mrs. Velez saw Robert's picture in the Santa Barbara paper and brought it to her. She's coming down today."

"To take him home?"

"Presumably," Lloyd said.

"Are you sure she's his mother?"

"Well I can't be sure until I talk to her," she replied, a bit tartly. "You know, Ben, your attitude toward all this is really quite curious. I thought you'd be happy."

"I am."

"You don't sound it," she said. "I have to go now—"

"Wait, will I be able to see him?"

"Once he's back with his family, that's out of my hands," she said. "I'll tell his mother you asked. It'll be up to her."

❑

"Tonight we have a happy ending to a sad story."

Ben turned up the volume on the TV and leaned back into the pillow, glass of bourbon in hand, watching the white-haired idiot anchor arrange his face into happy crinkles.

"Tonight, little Bobby Velez was reunited with family. Bobby, you will remember, is the child who was allegedly sexually abused by a man suffering from AIDS. We go to Tom Jasper for the story."

The scene switched to McMahon Hall. A coiffed male mannequin — whom Ben had seen at a leather bar in Silver Lake — looked sincerely into the camera.

"Four weeks ago, eight-year-old Bobby was brought to McMahon Hall after police discovered that he'd been living with a man, Frank Baron, dying of AIDS."

"Bullshit," Ben slurred at the screen. "I found him."

"Subsequent investigation revealed that Bobby had been sexually abused by the man who is now in critical condition from the disease at the jail ward of county hospital. Even though Baron is dying, the D.A. decided to press child molestation charges against him."

There was a quick shot of the press conference at which the D.A. had announced charges. "Heinous," he was saying. "Unbelievable."

"Since then, Bobby has been here, at McMahon Hall, while investigators hoped that publicity surrounding the case would turn up Bobby's parents. Today their hopes were realized when Bobby's mother, Mary Velez, stepped forward to claim her son."

There was a shot of a heavy woman in a dark dress, tears running down her face, embracing Bobby, who looked dazed.

"Tonight, Bobby, now Bobby Velez, is en route home. This is Tom Jasper at McMahon Hall."

"Tom," the anchor said, "will this affect the case against Frank Baron at all?"

Jasper said, "No, the D.A. will go forward with the charges. However, I understand that Baron is very sick and not expected to survive much longer."

"Thank you, Tom, " the anchor said.

"Thank you, Tom," Ben mimicked, drunkenly.

III

After a week of not hearing anything, Ben called Elizabeth Lloyd. It took him several tries to get through to her. When he did, she was even brisker than usual.

"I wanted to know if I can see Bobby," Ben explained. "You were going to talk to his mother."

"I did," Lloyd said. "Obviously if she hasn't contacted you it's because she doesn't want you to see him."

"Why?" he asked. "What did you tell her?"

"I beg your pardon?"

"Sorry," he said, "I didn't mean anything. Could you at

least give me her phone number, so I can talk to her?"

There was a pause. "I'm sorry, Ben, I really can't do that."

"What the hell's going on here? I'm the star witness, remember?"

"Mrs. Velez and I had a long talk with Detective Gomez about you," she said. "Evidently, she's decided it wouldn't be in Robert's best interests for him to have any further contact with you."

"Yeah? Well I'll remember that when you people need me to testify at the trial."

"I don't think you'll have to worry about that," she replied.

"What is that supposed to mean?"

"You'll have to excuse me," she said curtly.

"Fuck you," he replied to the dial tone.

❏

That night he had Wade over for dinner. Angrily tearing pieces of lettuce for salad, he shouted from the kitchen to the living room where Wade was watching television, "I don't understand that bitch. She just cut me loose."

"Ben, come out here for a minute. Hurry."

Wiping his hands on his jeans, he went to the doorway. "What?"

"The news," Wade said, pointing at the screen.

". . . with Baron's death, charges will be dismissed and the case officially closed," the reporter was saying. "That's according to his lawyer, Henry Rios."

The scene changed to a thin, dark, dishevelled-looking man standing in a hospital corridor. He said, "I expect the prosecutor will drop the charges. I'm sorry to see it end this way because I was prepared to prove that there was no truth to these allegations."

Back in the studio the anchor said, "To repeat, Frank Baron, the AIDS victim accused of sexually molesting an eight-year-old boy, died today in the jail ward of county hospital."

Ben stared at the screen. "That's what she wouldn't tell me. She knew he was about to die. I've got to talk to that lawyer."

❏

Henry Rios's office was in a three-story building on Sunset, just west of Vine. The building was square and pinkish. Banks of dirty windows looked out upon the street. In the little foyer a tiled wall mosaic depicted a school of fish swimming in the direction of the elevator. Ben pushed the elevator button and waited. After a couple of minutes he went up the stairs to the third floor.

In Rios's office, a black woman in cornrows sat at a desk working at a computer. She glanced up at him, stopped what she was doing and asked, "Are you here to see Mr. Rios?"

"Yeah, I'm Ben Weiss. I called this morning."

She picked up the phone and pressed three digits. "Mr. Weiss is here." To Ben she said, "The end of the hall."

"Thanks," he said, and stepped around her desk. At the entrance to Rios's office, the shiny green linoleum that covered the hall gave way to tweedy gray carpeting. Rios sat behind a glass-topped table cluttered with books and papers, shirtsleeves rolled to his elbows, tie askew. The credenza behind him was also piled high and on it, beside a vase filled with wilting carnations, was a framed picture of a young man.

"Sit down, Mr. Weiss," he said. "It's nice to finally meet you."

Ben sat and said, defensively, "The D.A. told me not to talk to you before."

"Yes, I know. That's how they try to protect their witnesses. Of course, they don't have any right to do it, and sometimes it backfires. As in this case, for instance. All I wanted was to give you some information."

"What information?" Ben asked.

Rios said, "I have another appointment in a few minutes, so I'll get right to the point. Did Bobby ever talk to you about his brother, Georgie?"

Startled, Ben said, "Yeah, but Mrs. Lloyd said there wasn't any Georgie. She said Bobby made him up."

Rios managed a smile that was both polite and dismissive. "Mrs. Lloyd is what you might call a professional witness in child abuse cases. She can be very persuasive. That's why the D.A.s love her. The downside is that she's wrong as often as she is right." He leaned back into his chair. The noise of traffic drifted up from the street. "She's certainly wrong about Georgie. At this moment, Georgie Velez is serving a sentence in county jail for burglary."

"Bobby's brother?"

Rios nodded. "Just as Bobby said: his brother Georgie brought him to L.A. to escape their uncle."

Ben said, "Why? I don't understand."

"I'm afraid that that's been the problem all along, Mr. Weiss. Let me explain. Georgie and Bobby lived with their mother and uncle in Guadalupe. The uncle is apparently a violent alcoholic who liked to use Georgie as a punching bag. Two years ago, when Georgie was sixteen, the uncle put him in the hospital for a month. When Georgie got out he decided that he'd had enough and he ran away. He took Bobby with him because he was afraid that his uncle might start in on Bobby if he left him there. Also, Georgie knew their father was in L.A. They came here to find him."

"Why did he leave?"

"For more or less the same reason that Georgie did," Rios said. "To escape being murdered by his brother-in-law. You see, he was gay. When his brother-in-law found out, well, Mexican men aren't known for their tolerance of homosexuality. Anyway the father took off but he occasionally wrote his wife, sending money or asking for it. Georgie found one of the letters and that's how he got his father's address in L.A."

"What was his father's name?" Ben asked.

Rios smiled, "Let me tell you this in order, Ben. It doesn't make much sense otherwise. Georgie and Bobby came to L.A. to the address on the letter. Unfortunately, the address was for county jail." He looked at Ben. "Their father had become a junkie. Sad life," he said, reflectively. "Really a waste, and all because he couldn't accept being gay. But that's another story." Rios re-arranged some papers on his desk. "Anyway, his name was Emilio Velez, but when Georgie tried to find him, he was told there wasn't anyone by that name at county. Georgie was understandably afraid to go home so the boys stayed in L.A. Eventually, they drifted to Hollywood, like a lot of runaways. Georgie supported them the way street kids do, petty crime, hustling. They did this for about a year. Then, one of Georgie's friends got picked up and sent to county. Georgie asked him to look for his father. He found him."

Ben interrupted. "What about Bobby? Did he do that stuff? Hustling?"

"Georgie says no, and I believe him," Rios replied. "I think he tried to shield him from the worst part of living on the street but I imagine Bobby saw a lot of things anyway. He's not a tough kid, from what I saw."

Ben nodded.

"When Emilio got out of county, he tried to persuade Georgie to go back to Guadalupe. Georgie said no and they ended up hiding from Emilio, too. Then Georgie was arrested for burglary, trying to break into a Taco Bell or some such thing. When they sent him up to jail, he got word to Emilio and made him promise to take care of Bobby until he got out." Rios paused and looked at Ben. "Emilio was a man of many names. The one he was going by after he got out of jail was Frank Baron."

"Frank? The same one?"

"That's right," Rios said. "Unfortunately, Frank was dying of AIDS though he didn't know it at the time he took Bobby. That's where you came in, and misunderstood the situation. Frank was Bobby's father. In his own way he was doing the best he could to take care of the boy."

Ben said, "What about Bobby's mother?"

"Ben," Rios said quietly, "she stood by while her brother beat Georgie half to death. You think she'll do any better by Bobby?"

"What the hell's wrong with her?" he demanded.

"She's afraid," Rios said. "I gather the uncle's a real nightmare."

"Why did you want tell me all this, Mr. Rios?"

"Because I hoped that, once I talked the D.A. into dismissing the case, you'd agree to take Bobby while I tried to get the mother declared unfit, and to get custody of Bobby with

Frank." He leaned back in his chair, fatigue informing the lines around his eyes. "But then Frank died."

"Can't you still try to get Bobby out of there?"

"I don't have a client any more, and Georgie's in jail."

"What about me? You wanted me to have him in the first place."

"Only as long as Frank was alive," Rios said. "I had hoped that he would last until Georgie got out of jail and there was another family member to step in. You don't have a legal claim on Bobby by yourself."

"I'm not talking about legal."

Rios looked at him thoughtfully. "I can't participate in anything like that, Ben."

"You'll just let his uncle keep him."

"Guadalupe is a town of two thousand," Rios said, after a moment, "just south of San Luis Obispo. The uncle's name is Esteban Torres. A phone book would give you his address."

"Thank you."

Rios shrugged. "For what? I'm not advising you to do anything illegal. I just thought you might want to visit Bobby."

Ben nodded and got up to leave.

"Ben," Rios said, stopping him at the doorway. "Georgie will want to know how his brother is. You can reach him through me."

❏

Two days later, Ben turned up at Iris Wong's office. He waited for almost an hour before she was able to see him, greeting him with, "Hello Ben, is something wrong with Wade?"

He shook his head. "No, it's about Bobby." They went back to her office.

"What about him? Isn't he's back with his family?"

"Iris, listen to me," he said urgently.

"Sure, Ben. Talk."

Ben told her the story that Henry Rios had told him two days earlier. "The day after I talked to him, I went up there, to the town."

"To Guadalupe?" she asked.

"Yeah. I found the house. The mother was there and I told her who I was and all, and asked to see him. She acted real nervous and told me that he was at school. Well, it was Saturday, so I knew he wasn't at school. Then the uncle came home and told me to clear out."

"Bobby wasn't there?"

He shook his head. "Rios was right. The uncle is a nightmare," he said. "I could tell that just from the five minutes I was around him and from how weird the mother was acting, like anything would set him off. No, I didn't see Bobby. I drove around the corner and parked and walked back. I went around to the neighbors and asked if they'd seen him. Finally, one of them told me an ambulance had been there a couple of nights earlier and she thought she'd seen them take him away. There aren't any hospitals in town. Can you help me find him?"

"I don't know what you mean," she said.

"Could you call a doctor in Guadalupe and ask him what hospital he would send someone to."

"Just like that? It would be a strange question."

"It would be stranger if I did it," he said. "At least you're a doctor."

She drew her brows together. "What will you do when you find him?"

"Take him away from there."

"That's kidnapping, Ben," she said.

"Didn't you hear anything I told you?" he snapped. "He's in the hospital because his uncle put him there."

"You don't know that for sure."

He got up angrily. "I won't know anything for sure unless you help me. We might be saving his life. Isn't that what doctors do?" He slapped his hands down at the edge of her desk and leaned toward her. "Isn't it?"

"I think you better go, Ben, " she said quietly.

❏

He and Wade were watching "Gilda" on the VCR when Iris called.

"He's at a hospital in San Luis Obispo," she said, "called St. Martin's. They took him in with a broken arm and a concussion. His mother said he fell. He's due to be released in a couple of days."

"Thank you," Ben said.

She hung up.

Wade looked over at him from the bundle of blankets and afghans with which he'd covered himself. "Who was that?"

"Wrong number."

Wade raised a disbelieving eyebrow.

"I'm going away tomorrow, Wade," Ben said. "I don't think I'll be coming back."

"Bobby?"

"The police will ask you questions. The less you know the better." He smiled at his friend. "I've decided to stop killing myself. I've decided to live."

"Welcome back, baby," Wade replied.

❏

Ben lay awake that night devising elaborate plans of how to

get Bobby out of the hospital, but in the end, simplicity won out. He went up to San Luis and spent the day at the hospital, observing the shift changes and mealtimes, watching for the moment of maximum confusion. It happened just after lunch. The halls were crowded with orderlies pushing carts of dirty dishes, doctors making their rounds, and visitors coming in for afternoon visiting hours. Everyone moved with a specific purpose, blind to the traffic around them.

The day after, Ben went to a uniform store and bought a pair of orderly's whites. Putting them on at the hotel, he arrived at the hospital at 12:30 with a sack of Bobby's clothes. He found Bobby's room and told him they were leaving. Bobby nodded, as if he'd known Ben would come all along. The boy got dressed and they walked out, scarcely noticed in the din and bustle, a little boy with a broken arm and an orderly, taking him somewhere, to do something. No one saw them get into the car or saw the car drive off. It wasn't until much later that afternoon, when Mrs. Velez came to visit, that the disappearance was discovered. To the hospital administration's embarrassment, no one could say what had happened. It was days before Mrs. Velez remembered the man who had come asking about her son. It was even later than that when the L.A. police got involved and by then, Ben's apartment had been rented, and his possessions scattered. The old man who lived next door to him claimed to know nothing. Without any leads to link Ben Weiss to the boy's disappearance, the police dropped their investigation and Bobby entered the statistics of missing children.

❏

The letter arrived in Rios's office with his name neatly typed and no return address, postmarked from San Francisco. He opened in and removed a single sheet of paper. Unfolding it, he read:

Tell Georgie he can stop worrying. We're fine. I got a job. Bobby's in school. No one asks any questions. To our neighbors we're just father and son. There's an old man named Wade London who lived next door to me. Would you go and visit him sometimes? Thank you.

There was no signature. Rios wrote down the name Wade London, then torn the letter into indecipherable pieces and scattered them in the trash. He buzzed his secretary.

"Arjay, see if you can find me a phone number for a Wade London in West Hollywood."

A moment later she buzzed him back with the information. Rios picked up the phone and dialed.

VINCENT LARDO
All About Steve

K erry Kerrington stood by the French doors, peering surreptitiously through a chink in the curtain. He watched the Bentley make its regal way down the curved driveway that divided the perfectly manicured grounds like the proverbial garden path. The elegant black car could have been carrying the queen of England on her appointed rounds. When it disappeared around a final curve Kerry dropped the curtain and sighed, "Finally, they're gone, and won't be back for hours. Or however long it takes to play eighteen holes of golf."

Michael Harris was half sitting, half leaning on an antique desk of great value. A portrait of the escritoire's owner hung above it. Noel Becton, depicted in oil on canvas, looked down upon his study, and on the two young men who presently occupied it, with a mixture of pride, disdain, amusement and lechery. The artist, as they say, had captured the inner man. Michael pushed himself from the desk and advanced to the center of the room where Kerry waited with open arms. The two embraced with enthusiasm if not passion. "Do you think he knows?" Michael mused.

"What?" Kerry responded. "That we're lovers? Or that we're going to murder him?"

"Don't say that." Michael moved out of Kerry's reach.

"Say what?" Kerry teased. "That we're lovers, or that we're going to murder him?"

"You sound like Lady Macbeth," Michael chided as he snooped about the room, uncovering little decorative boxes and opening drawers whenever one presented itself.

"Really? I was aiming for Tony Perkins in *Psycho*. I'd better brush up for my Hollywood debut."

"*If* you get to Hollywood," Michael answered, giving up his search. "Where does he keep his cigarettes?"

"I will get to Hollywood," Kerry insisted, "if you keep your promise and help remove your lover from this vale of tears." He opened his arms in a gesture denoting that the vale included the study of Noel Becton's Connecticut mansion. "And he doesn't smoke."

"He does when no one is looking. In company he tells everyone how he gave up the weed years ago without a moment's misgiving or discomfort." Michael explored the inside of an empty jar. "And I didn't give you my word — and I thought you were my lover."

Kerry shrugged. "Whose lover you are is academic, but your word is sacred. I mean your lover is whoever you happen to be in bed with when the question arises."

"If that's the criteria," Michael grinned, "you're it. Noel is at the age where going to bed is synonymous with going to sleep."

"Really?" Kerry raised an eyebrow. "When I was the chosen one he must have been in his fucking prime. No pun intended."

"Do you think Vera knows?" Michael speculated.

"What? That we're lovers or. . ."

"Oh, shut up, Kerry. It wasn't funny the first time."

Kerry now placed his posterior against the priceless desk, folding his arms across his chest in the manner of a lecturing professor. "Do I detect a case of nerves? Yes, I do. Young hopeful on the eve of stardom expresses doubts." Here he turned into a barking army sergeant, wagging a commanding finger at Michael as he continued. "Well you had better get it together and fast, unless you want to be a stage manager for the rest of your life. Of course Vera doesn't know. What we have planned for Noel isn't fodder for a press release."

Michael waved his hand in annoyance. "I meant does she know about Noel's. . ."

"Predilection?" Kerry broke in. "She's his wife and wives are always the first to know. Sometimes even before gossip columnists."

"Why does she put up with it?"

"Because she loves being Mrs. Noel Becton, wife and partner of the legendary Broadway team of Becton and Becton. He writes 'em and she produces 'em. They're the flip side of the curtain to Taylor and Burton, and Noel isn't the only Becton to play the casting-couch game. Vera has had her share of aspiring Marlon Brandos."

"Do you speak from experience?" Michael asked, laughing.

"I did what I had to do to further my career."

"Noel told me he found you in a bar. You were hustling," Michael stated rather than accused.

"He didn't pluck you out of Actor's Studio, love."

"I was hungry," Michael explained.

It was the cue Kerry had been waiting for. "And you still are," he thundered dramatically. "But for more than just a fancy meal at a posh pub. The roar of the grease paint and the smell of the crowd is what you crave, Michael — the truth?"

"Not enough to kill for," Michael replied with equal vigor.

"Bullshit!" Kerry hissed. "I bet you can feel the heat of that spotlight and hear the applause of an adoring audience." Kerry moved around Michael as if examining a sculpture or a floor model reduced for immediate sale. "Have you practiced taking your curtain calls? Don't be embarrassed, of course you have. And wondered what you'll say to the housewives who just happen to be passing the stage door when the matinees break? Not to mention the pretty boys who'll stare and the waitresses who'll flaunt and the sales girls who'll ask you to autograph their receipt pads." Kerry pointed at the portrait mounted in a gilded baroque frame. "You've been dreaming all those dreams since the day Noel Becton picked you off a bar stool and promised you the world in return for a little heavy breathing and playing acolyte to his bishop."

"He said. . ." Michael tried to interrupt, but not quickly enough.

"Stage manage first, Michael me boy, to get the feel of it and then you'll be ready for the next go-round." Kerry mimicked Noel Becton's faux British accent, which was more reminiscent of Katharine Hepburn than Cary Grant. "Oh, I can just hear him, the bastard."

"He made you a star," Michael reflected. "You can't hate him for that."

"Not a star, Michael. His star. Something to parade across the boards to enhance Becton and Becton and then put back into his pocket between creative intervals. When I first met him I'd been in New York two years and the closest I'd gotten to a stage was the rear of the orchestra, when I could afford it. I was tired of waiting tables to pay the rent and selling my tail for the extras. I would have signed a pact with the devil for a break and sometimes think I did. An exclusive contract, he said, but I was too delighted to read the fine print. I didn't know I couldn't perform anyplace without his approval, and the bastard won't even let me appear on the Carson show or do a fucking commercial. I'm a star that comes out when Becton and Becton present, but when they don't present I might as well be dead. Did you know I was offered the role of Steven on 'Dynasty'?"

"Christ," Michael moaned in sympathy.

"And a few other plum roles amply filled by Gere and Travolta. Then he discovered you, fresh meat on the hook and took yours truly off it. He promised you this new show, didn't he?"

"You know he did. But it was conceived for you and a rewrite would take months. He explained. . ."

"He explained nothing," Kerry cried impatiently, "except that I'm back on the hook and you're still waiting in the wings. Conceived for me? We're as alike as peas in a pod which says a lot about Noel's predilection and little else."

Kerry's accusation was more than justified. Both young men were in their mid-twenties, tall and lean with light brown hair, clean-cut features, and the kind of smiles that sell toothpaste by the ton.

"Noel thought Hollywood and everyone else had forgotten all about me," Kerry continued, "so he plays the magnanimous benefactor and gives us what we both want. You get a starring role in the new play and I get put out to pasture where the only place my name will arise is in a zippy game of Trivial Pursuit. He's in control of his discoveries and no one but Becton and Becton profits from his labors.

"Then I get an offer for a big role in a mini-series that promises to be next season's sensation and Noel's retirement plans for me backfire. Once again I'm viable, therefore the contract stands. I'm back in the new play and you're back in the wings waiting for the next go-round. Only by then, he'll have found someone a little younger and a little prettier and I can be safely given the boot — you can say no to Hollywood just so many times — and you will have missed the boat, having been caught between lovers, so to speak."

"If he pulled something like that I'd. . ."

"You'd what, Michael?"

"I'd kill him."

A sigh of relief, barely audible, escaped Kerry's smiling lips. "And so you will. Just as we planned." Kerry raised his head skyward and recited from memory, "'Upon the demise of either party, this contract is rendered null and void.' It's the only clause I don't need a lawyer to interpret."

"I can't do it, Kerry." Michael turned his back on the other man, hanging his head as if in shame.

"Nonsense. You just said you would."

"Talk is cheap," Michael mumbled. "And he hasn't screwed me yet."

"But he will. You can be damn sure the scenario will play exactly as I just outlined it. Look what he's done to me. Do you really think he'll have any more regard for you? If we're going to commit a crime, and we are in this together, it's better done for profit than revenge."

"You make it sound so justifiable and plausible. But when

I'm alone I think that I'll have to live with it for the rest of my life."

Kerry went to him, placing both hands on Michael's shoulders and pressing himself against Michael's back. "Would you rather live with failure," he whispered, his lips just touching Michael's ear, "and without me?" Slowly, he turned Michael around so that they stood face to face. "Look at me," Kerry insisted. When Michael obeyed, Kerry kissed him lightly on the lips but when Michael sought to turn affection into passion, Kerry gently resisted the advance. "It's going to be wonderful, Michael. Everything we've ever wanted is ours for the taking. New York. Hollywood. The world. The world, Michael, the whole fucking world."

"Are you sure I'll get the part?" Michael asked, unromantically.

"Christ," Kerry moaned, "Vera adores you and Andrew Evans, our estimable director, listens to Vera because if he didn't he'd be directing traffic at school crossings. Vera knows as well as you and I that the bloody play was written for you, not me. By the way, did you know that Andrew was my predecessor, or hadn't you noticed that he only directs when Becton and Becton present?"

"Like royalty, I'm at the end of a long line."

"Just make sure the line ends with you."

"Suppose the play is a flop?" Michael whined.

"Really," Kerry said impatiently. "You're guaranteed a leading role in a Broadway show by the most successful writer-producer team to come down the pike in this century and now you want a clause that states it's got to be a hit. A certain risk, Michael, and in this case a very small one, is inevitable. You're going to be a star."

"And all I have to do is commit murder," Michael said glumly.

"Think of it as one small murder for man and one giant kindness for mankind."

"Suppose Vera finds out. . ."

"No one is going to find out anything. And if Vera did suspect what we were about she would want to get in on the act. There's no love lost between Becton and Becton. She stands to inherit the kingdom, including a spanking new Noel Becton play, and disinherit her competition on the casting couch which has always been a bit crowded to suit Vera. Now, shall we talk it through once more?"

"We've talked it to death," Michael groaned.

"That, I believe, is the general idea." Kerry rubbed his hands together and all but waltzed across the room. "By God, we can even block it all out while we're here."

"You're enjoying this," Michael accused.

"Time — Saturday, one week from today," Kerry announced. "Place — right here. We've already been invited for the weekend for a long-awaited look at the new script. I'll come up early Saturday morning, say the ten a.m. train. Vera, as usual, will have her hair done at Kenneth's and make the five p.m. back, arriving in Harbor View at six. You. . ."

"I," Michael picked up the thread, "will invent something I have to do in town and arrange to come up with Vera on the five o'clock. At three I'll call Kenneth's and tell Vera that I'll be longer than expected and will have to take the six o'clock train. She won't offer to wait for me and I won't ask her to. Then I'll get my ass on the four o'clock and get into Harbor View at five. I'll walk to the house — that's one hell of a hill out there," Michael digressed.

"The climb will do you good."

Michael went to the French doors and opened one. "I'll hide behind those bushes," he said, pointing.

"At about fifteen to six I'll drive to the station to pick up Vera and you," Kerry continued. "Noel will stay right here because Noel never goes to the station unless he's going into the city. Vera will get off the train and tell me that you didn't make the five o'clock but you will be on the six o'clock. I'll say it's foolish to drive back to the house only to turn around and come back to the station to get you."

"You'll invite Vera to have a drink at the town pub while waiting for me to arrive at seven, and Vera never refuses a drink," Michael added to the plot, "especially at the town pub where the locals will ogle the lady producer and the handsome Broadway star."

"And soon to be handsome Hollywood star," Kerry said joyously. "When we get to the pub I'll ask Vera to call Noel to tell him what's happening while I order our drinks." Kerry now appeared very excited, pacing as he spoke, as if charged by his own cleverness. "And that's the beauty part of it, Michael. Vera will talk to Noel and swear that he was alive and well while I was with her, which corroborates my story that he was alive when I left the house to drive to the station."

Michael now began to catch Kerry's enthusiasm. "I'll be behind those bushes, listening for the phone. As soon as Noel finishes talking to Vera I'll come in through these doors. . ." Michael pretended to enter the room through the French doors. "Make sure these damn doors are unlocked before you leave."

"They're never locked when the house is occupied." Kerry

snapped, indignant at the interruption. "You'll carry the gun in an overnight bag along with burglar tools."

"Noel is usually sitting at his desk. I'll walk quietly toward him," Michael rehearsed his movements as he spoke, "raise the gun, take aim, and — BANG, BANG, you're dead."

"Don't forget to mess the room up to make it look like an attempted robbery."

"I'll exit the way I entered and begin my jog back to the station," Michael concluded.

"Don't forget to toss the bag and gun into the gorge as you go down the hill. That's what a frightened burglar would do. I figure the police will think the burglar didn't expect to find anyone at home. Remember, I'll be out with the car. When he encounters Noel he loses his head and fires. Then he beats it down the hill."

"I'll be back at the station before seven. . ."

"Where it will appear that you just got off the six o'clock from New York." He smiled, smugly. "I'm with Vera at the time of the murder and you're on a train. The widow Becton will back our alibis. It's foolproof, Michael — foolproof."

"Everything contains an element of risk, remember?"

"But in this instance I've minimized the risk to near zero. Which reminds me, have you got your disguise for the train?"

"Wig and mustache. Cute, but rather melodramatic."

"I don't want anyone to say they saw you on the four o'clock train."

"But there'll be no one to say they saw me on the six o'clock train either, because I won't be on it. And didn't you say that no one remembers strange faces on trains — even conductors?"

"Especially conductors," Kerry assured him. "Regardless

of what you've seen in the movies, they see so many faces, some familiar, some not, on so many runs they would never match a face to a specific train and then swear to it. The same goes for passengers. But someone might say they thought they saw you on the four o'clock. I don't want even that shadow of a doubt to cloud our story. Hence the disguise. Agreed?"

"It's your plot, Kerry. I'm just an actor following directions."

"And if you follow them as written, 'Upon the demise of either party, this contract is rendered null and void.' Hello, William Morris — I accept, I accept, I accept."

"It might be prudent to wait till next Monday before calling William Morris," Michael remarked caustically.

"I suppose you're right. But then it's Hollywood time for Kerry Kerrington."

"I'm going to miss you," Michael said, looking longingly at the future movie star.

"Oh, we'll keep the long distance wires humming, as they say. But you'll be too busy with the new show to think about me."

"I wish I had your confidence," Michael lamented.

"You have to believe in yourself, Mike. If you don't you'll never make it as an actor."

"I believe in you, Kerry."

"Thanks. And you know what? I love you, Michael."

"And I love you, Kerry."

II

The portrait of Noel Becton looked down upon its once animated counterpart with a mixture of pride, disdain, amusement, and lechery. If it could weep it would have shed tears more for Noel Becton's ungainly appearance than for his untimely demise. The writer was sprawled across his precious desk in the manner of a student who had fallen asleep over some incomprehensible tome. The blood flowing from the wound in his chest had begun to form a red reservoir in the cul-de-sac of his armpit. Would the stain lower or enhance the antique's value?

The room was, not surprisingly, deathly still, making the sound of the Bentley coming up the gravel drive inordinately definable. So, too, the car's doors opening and slamming shut and finally the incongruous strains of laughter and convivial chatter floating on the flower-scented summer air, rudely assaulting the silence in the death chamber.

"And no bar tab," Kerry was saying. "I think our bartender was trying to put the make on you, Vera."

"Then why," came the seductive tone of a sophisticated female voice, "did he ask you for your autograph and why did you scribble your phone number under your signature?"

"I thought the hand was quicker than the eye," Kerry answered.

"Not when it's had two martinis," Michael joined in. "Vera, would you get that door open so I can catch up?"

"Where are my keys?" Vera complained. "You know, I think I left them in my other purse."

"Well, ring the bell," Michael advised.

"If Noel hasn't heard us by this time he never will," Vera stated. "We've made enough noise to wake the dead."

"Bite your tongue, Vera," Michael laughed.

"Shut up, Michael," Kerry admonished, clearly not amused.

The door chimes echoed again and again throughout the

house but Noel Becton was as incapable of responding to them as the portrait which stood vigil over his corpse.

"The terrace," Vera exclaimed. "Let's try the terrace doors."

"Good idea," Kerry said, "they're usually open."

Vera led an orderly line, like a school fire drill, around to the side of the house where the light coming through the double doors cast a jaundice glow on the flagstone terrace. The doors opened at a touch and Vera entered the room calling, "Noel? Noel? We're here." She stopped when she saw her husband asleep at his desk. "Noel?" Vera advanced cautiously toward the unusual spectacle. "Noel? Are you all right?"

Kerry had entered behind Vera and raised his arm to keep Michael from advancing past the doorway. Kerry's eyes darted about the room. To his unpleasant surprise, it was as neat and orderly as when he had left it a few hours earlier. Before he could catch Michael's eye, Vera's scream shattered the silence and all else was forgotten.

"He's dead," Vera cried. "My God, he's dead. And there's blood — blood all over."

Kerry looked more confused than startled, like someone who's won a whopping lottery and is not quite sure if the moment is real or imagined. He stumbled forward only to collide with Vera who staggered backward, retreating from the bloody sight of her dead husband. Kerry, the consummate actor, immediately drew supportive arms about Vera as if this was why he had rushed to her.

"Blood — blood all over," Vera chanted.

"What is it? What's going on?" Michael had entered the room and was advancing toward the desk, paying scant attention to Vera and Kerry. "Noel?"

"I think he's dead," Kerry exclaimed.

"Think?" Vera shouted. "Look — look — blood — blood all over."

"Try to control yourself," Kerry said, still holding Vera in his arms while at the same time trying to prevent Michael from reaching the desk.

"Christ," Michael cried, "he *is* dead. Someone's. . ."

"Get away from there, Michael. Don't touch anything and help me with Vera."

"I'm all right. I'm all right," Vera rallied, squirming her way out of Kerry's embrace. "He's been murdered. My God, Noel's been murdered."

"A robbery," Kerry offered but no one was listening.

"We've got to call the police." The decisive words announced that Vera was once again in control of herself and therefore of the situation.

The three looked at the telephone which stood inches from Noel Becton's bent elbow as if the instrument was a bomb. "Not here," Michael ordered. "Let's go to the drawing room."

Again the two young men and the woman marched in a line, exiting the room without a backward glance. The so-called drawing room was Edwardian in decor and formidable in ambience, but it did boast a telephone and lack a corpse. Vera made the call while Michael filled three brandy glasses with scotch, carefully avoiding eye contact with Kerry.

"We all need this," Michael offered along with the drinks.

"What did the police say?" Kerry asked.

"They'll be right here. It's awful," Vera sobbed. "Just awful."

"Drink," Michael ordered, "and let's not go to pieces again."

Harbor View is a very small town and already a siren,

eerily reminiscent of an air raid warning, could be heard a great distance off, but growing louder with each mournful wail. The sound changed the trio's camaraderie of a few minutes earlier to the uneasy companionship of strangers huddled inside a shelter. Sudden death was a woeful reminder of the fragility of our mortality, and the original party pooper.

"A robbery," Kerry tried again.

"I don't think anything was missing," Vera replied, "but I can't be sure. All I looked at. . ."

"The police will tell us what happened," Michael said, giving Kerry a nasty look. Kerry returned the sentiment.

"I can't believe it." Vera seemed to be speaking to herself as she picked up a book and opened it to reveal a pack of cigarettes nestled within the hollow of the phony pages. Michael refrained from exclaiming in surprise but managed to help himself before the pack once again disappeared into *Great Expectations*. He lit Vera's cigarette and then his own, enveloping both of them in a cloud of smoke as the siren rose to fever pitch before it stopped abruptly at Noel Becton's front door.

Both men looked at Vera as if awaiting instructions but she bounded from the room, pausing only to toss her newly lit cigarette into a scrupulously clean fireplace hearth. A moment later she could be heard greeting the new arrivals. In her absence Kerry grabbed hold of Michael's arm. Michael immediately shook off the grasping fingers as if offended by the touch, and raised a cautionary hand to discourage any communication between them. When Vera returned, followed by a man in civilian dress and two uniformed policemen, Michael and Kerry were as far apart as the palatial room allowed.

"This is Detective Hart," Vera announced, "and — and..." she waved at the men in blue, "and his staff. In there," she then added, gesturing toward the study. The three men trooped between Kerry and Michael and into the adjoining room.

Vera began to follow, then paused. "I don't think it's necessary," Michael said.

"No, I suppose not," Vera answered. She picked up her glass and finished what remained of the scotch. "Should we offer..."

"I don't think so," Kerry spoke up. "They're on duty."

"Christ, this isn't a play," Michael exploded. "When they get a look at that..."

"Please, Michael," Vera cried, clutching her heart.

"I'm sorry," Michael apologized, stubbing out his cigarette in a crystal ashtray and immediately reaching for *Great Expectations*. "But we're all acting as if we had something to hide."

"We're acting," Kerry answered, "like people who are not accustomed to dealing with violence. And I thought you gave up cigarettes."

"Extraordinary times call for extraordinary..."

"Shut up, both of you," Vera injected. "You sound like a pair of cackling hens. Michael, I will have more scotch even if we can't offer it to inspector what's-his-name."

"Hart, ma'am, and it's detective, not inspector." He was suddenly there, among them, flanked by his two blue shadows and looking like the answer to a casting director's prayer. Fortyish, graying at the temples, tall, thin, and in need of a shave, detective Hart lacked only a raincoat to step into the role of Mike Hammer, Philip Marlowe, or Sam Spade. "Who was the last person to see Mr. Becton alive?"

"I think I was," Kerry answered.

Hart looked at him questioningly and Vera stepped forward. "This is Kerry Kerrington," she said to the detective.

"The actor," Hart acknowledged.

"Thank you. I do, on occasion, act."

"Go ahead, Mr. Kerrington. Tell us the circumstances of your last meeting with Mr. Becton up to the time you discovered him dead."

Kerry, holding tight to his brandy glass of scotch whiskey, squared his shoulders and drew himself up to his full height, his head raised as if playing a scene to lord and lady balcony. "I arrived here this morning," Kerry began, knowing that every eye in the room was upon him and making the most of the situation. Michael especially paid close attention to Kerry's performance as if preparing to understudy the improvised speech. "We're all — that is Michael and I — guests of the Becton's this weekend. I left here about twenty to six and drove to the station to pick up Mrs. Becton and Michael who we expected to arrive at six. Noel — Mr. Becton — was fine when I left. He was seated — well, he was seated where he is now, looking at a script. Mr. Becton is a playwright. Vera — Mrs. Becton — was on the five o'clock for New York but Michael wasn't with her. She explained that Michael had been delayed in town but would be on the next train, arriving in Harbor View at seven.

"It would have been foolish to come back here and then drive back to the station for Michael, so Mrs. Becton and I went for a drink at the local. Vera called Mr. Becton to tell him what was happening and about seven we went back to the station to pick up Michael, drove directly here, and — well, the rest you know."

"Does that sum it up?" Hart asked, turning to Vera.

"I'm afraid not."

"What?" Kerry cried.

"Please, Mr. Kerrington. You had your say." The detective looked once again at Vera. "Mrs. Becton?"

"The shock of all this seems to have affected Mr. Kerrington's memory — or else he's completely lost his mind."

"I think that it's Mrs. Becton who's in a state of shock," Kerry stated, his delivery less theatrical than his opening salvo. "She was hysterical when we discovered the body."

"Once again, Mr. Kerrington," Hart interrupted, "I'm asking you politely to be quiet. If you continue, I'll have the officer here take you outside until we're finished. Mrs. Becton?"

"Thank you," Vera answered with a regal nod. Vera Becton was one of those women whose age could be anywhere between thirty and fifty, possessed of a presence that was demonstratively physical. Long blond hair, green eyes, and a figure that did justice to straight-lined skirts and high heels, she was keenly aware of her attraction to men like detective Hart and not above pandering to their baser instincts.

"Michael and I arrived together on the five o'clock from New York and Mr. Kerrington did pick us up at the station at six. He — Mr. Kerrington — insisted that we stop at the town pub. I think he wanted to see the bartender. At least he gave the bartender his phone number but I'm sure you can check on that for yourself."

Here, Kerry waved his arms in frustration and took a step toward Vera but was physically restrained by one of the officers.

"I wanted to call Noel," Vera was saying, moving closer to the detective as if for protection, "but Mr. Kerrington insisted that we'd only be a few minutes and said it wasn't necessary. As it was we stayed for several drinks. Michael — Mr. Harris — didn't come in the bar with us. He didn't want a drink so waited in the car. We left the bar about seven and drove directly here."

"Bullshit," Kerry shouted at Vera.

"Mr. Kerrington, I told you not to interrupt."

"Bullshit," Kerry repeated. "I'm not going to keep quiet while she tells a story that's pure crap. What the hell is wrong with you, Vera? Mike, tell him what happened."

Now all eyes were on Michael. "You're Michael Harris?" Hart asked.

"Yes," Michael answered. "I work for — worked for Mr. Becton. Stage managed, that is."

"For three people who spent the last hour in each other's company two of you can't seem to agree on how or when you got from there to here. Perhaps you can tip the scale, Mr. Harris," Hart said to his last witness.

"Two of us agree," Michael said.

"Thank you, Michael," Kerry sighed.

"I arrived on the train with Mrs. Becton. The rest is exactly as she told it."

Kerry lunged for Michael and this time it took both policemen to hold him back.

"Tell them," Kerry shouted, straining to free himself like a mad dog on a short leash. "Tell them that Vera called Noel from the bar and then we picked you up at the station at seven. Dammit — we did."

"Mr. Kerrington," Hart said calmly, "today is Saturday. The last hourly train from Grand Central is at five p.m. After that they run every two hours. You could have met a train at six but the next one," the detective looked at his watch, "is just pulling into Harbor View, if it's on time, which I seriously doubt. If you picked up Mr. Harris at seven he must have walked from New York and made better time than the train usually does, which is possible but highly improbable."

"But you checked the schedule," Kerry said to Michael who had retreated to a position somewhere between and behind Vera and the detective. "Oh, I get it," he grimaced. "The old stab in the back. And what a charming pair they make. Now you'll get the truth, Inspector."

"I'm not an inspector, Mr. Kerrington."

"You will be when you bring in this little bugger for murder. He wasn't on the train with Vera and, as you so cunningly deduced, he wasn't on the six o'clock from New York because there is no six o'clock from New York. But he was here long before Vera, hiding in those bushes just beyond the terrace."

"How do you know that?" Hart asked.

"Because I saw him when I left the house to pick up Vera. We waved, dammit. Don't you understand? We planned this?"

"Planned what, Mr. Kerrington?"

"To kill Noel," Kerry screamed, losing what little poise he had left.

"I think I had better warn you, Mr. Kerrington. Anything you say may be used against you and you have the right to legal counsel."

"This isn't a confession, asshole," Kerry ranted at Hart and then pointed an accusing finger at Michael. "He killed Noel, not me. We planned it, but he killed him. When I left for the station he waited till after Vera called to keep me from getting suspicious."

"Why should you be suspicious if you planned it?"

Exasperated by his efforts to make the detective understand, and still physically restrained, Kerry was now noticeably disoriented. "It was supposed to look like a break-in. Now those two are trying to frame me."

"But you said you planned it," Hart insisted.

"No. I mean, yes. But I didn't kill Noel. Michael did and she's in it with him."

"But Mrs. Becton told us that Michael Harris was on the train with her."

"He came up on the four o'clock train. Ask the conductor. Ask the passengers. He was wearing a wig and a phony mustache."

"If he was wearing a disguise, Mr. Kerrington, how can he be identified?" Hart asked quietly.

"He came straight here and waited in those bushes till Vera called. The way it worked was I could be with Vera when she spoke to Noel and everyone would believe Mike was on a train. That was the beauty part of it, Inspector."

"How could he be on a train that doesn't exist?"

"We didn't know there wasn't a six o'clock from New York," Kerry screamed. "At least I didn't. Michael was supposed to check the schedules. How the fuck did I know he was going to double-cross me? Him and that bitch. They're both murderers. Arrest them and leave me alone."

Vera and Michael regarded Kerry like parents forced to view the antics of their mentally ill offspring. All during the exchange between the detective and Kerry they had stood, side by side, like spectators to a drama, their expressions rotating between pity and outrage at precisely the right moments in the duel.

"Mr. Kerrington, I don't think you should say anything more until you talk to a lawyer," Hart said, after the last outburst.

"I don't need a lawyer. He does. They do," Kerry pointed. "Noel was alive when I left here. Vera called him. Look for the gun — the wig. He must have tossed them down the gorge. He waited in the bushes for Vera to call then he came in through the terrace doors and shot Noel."

"With a knife?" Hart asked, imperturbably.

"What?" Kerry exclaimed.

"Mr. Becton was stabbed in the chest, not shot."

Kerry, now hysterical, kicked and squirmed to free himself from the cops and get at Vera and Michael. "The gun," he ranted. "Where's the gun? He was supposed to toss it down the gorge on his way back to the station. Don't you see, he had to be at the station by seven so it would look like he just got off the train."

"Mr. Kerrington, you're going to have to come with us."

At these words from their superior, the two policemen dragged a raving Kerry Kerrington from Noel Becton's poshly appointed drawing room as the widow Becton and Michael Harris tried to conceal their relief.

"I'm sorry," Hart spoke to Vera Becton.

"Is he under arrest?" she asked.

"Let's say he's under a great deal of suspicion. I take it you're both sticking to your versions of the events prior to the discovery of Mr. Becton?"

Hart looked at Vera with a mixture of longing and cynicism. Kerrington's ravings, though unbelievable, had got Hart thinking about the lady and the handsome young man at her side. Lust was a powerful motive.

"Of course," Vera answered indignantly. "Why would we alter the truth?"

Hart shrugged. "A detail from the station will be here to clean up." He nodded toward the study. "Until then, please don't touch anything in there."

"Have no fear," Vera assured him.

"No need to show me out," Hart said, unnecessarily as neither Vera nor Michael had made any move to do so. When he left, they stood very still, fearing even to breathe too loudly, until the sound of a car, minus siren, could be heard skidding over gravel. When the shrill noise faded and a symphony of crickets rushed in to fill the void, the two finally turned cautiously toward each other.

Vera, smiling, curled her arms languidly about Michael's neck. "We did it," she whispered with a great deal of restraint.

"Don't count your chickens," Michael answered, his arms circling her waist as he pulled her closer. "They haven't arrested him yet."

Vera laughed. "He'll talk himself into the electric chair before the night's over. Kerry made the mistake of telling anyone who would listen that he was indentured to Noel by a contract that only death could break. It will be the first thing I tell the police when I'm asked to make my statement."

"You're a bitch," Michael laughed.

"A bitch in heat," she replied, grinding her pelvis into the crotch of Michael's gray flannels. "Let's go upstairs, darling, and celebrate."

Michael disentangled himself from Vera's arms and went in search of *Great Expectations*. "The police will be back, as our friend told us, along with an ambulance and the press, I'm sure. If the new widow is found prostrate it should be due to grief."

Vera laughed, accepting Michael's offer of a cigarette. "Of course, you're right. And we have all the time in the world, don't we, Michael?"

"Right now I'd say we have about ten minutes before the proverbial shit hits the fan. I think you should take off your make-up before the photographers get here. 'Mrs. Becton appeared pale and shaken' should be the wire services' lead."

Vera vetoed the idea, refilling their glasses. "Too obvious. I think tear-streaked mascara would be more effective, and natural."

"But not the whiskey breath," Michael advised.

"I'll gargle with cologne like Scarlet O'Hara. Remember that scene?" Vera began to babble.

"Easy, Vera. I think you're losing it."

She took a good swallow of scotch. "Perhaps a little heady from success. But never fear, I'll play my part when it's necessary. Wasn't I convincing at the discovery of murder most foul?"

Michael pretended to ponder the question. "To start — yes. But you recovered too quickly, giving orders when you should have been in shock. Only Kerry looked genuinely surprised, which I guess is a compliment to his acting acumen."

"What surprised him was that his favorite daydream had actually come to pass," Vera speculated, then quickly added, "and giving orders is what I do best. That's why I'm a pro-ducer, the person with the final say. If you remember that, Michael, we shall get along famously."

Fearing that he had gone too far in his new role of partner

and confidant, Michael immediately reassured Vera of his loyalty. "Didn't I come straight to you with Kerry's ingenious plan?"

"You came to me, Michael, because you knew damn well I would have seen right through Kerry's ingenious plan." Vera spoke the word 'ingenious' so as to leave no doubt that Kerry Kerrington's scheme was anything but clever. "I would have seen to it that the both of you were blacklisted by the profession if I couldn't get a judge to put you behind bars for the remainder of the best years of your lives. The only thing ingenious about Kerry's plot was the fact that we could so easily adapt it to suit our purposes. Killing two faggots with one blow, so to speak."

She tossed off the rest of her drink. "You came to me because with Noel dead and without my backing your ass would be in a sling or back on a bar stool. Like most actors, Kerry couldn't see beyond the fall of the final curtain. That's why I like you, my pet — street smarts coupled with a great deal of ambition and a paucity of scruples."

"You left out my licentiousness," Michael boasted.

"Don't tell me. Show me."

Now it was Michael who played the passionate lover. Taking Vera into his arms he declared, "A relationship founded on ambition and a paucity of scruples. Where does that leave romance?"

"In the movies, where it belongs," Vera answered. "Truth without illusion is the only sensible approach to any partnership. It was the guiding principle of Becton and Becton."

"And look where it got him," Michael said, glancing toward the study.

She kissed him coolly. "Noel was getting too cocky and too

possessive. I didn't mind his passion for pretty boys but when our dinner table began to take on the appearance of a prep-school cafeteria I decided to draw the line. Enough is enough."

"The man was going to dump you," Michael said cruelly.

"Don't be vulgar," she warned.

"Truth without illusion, remember?" he replied, smiling cynically. "Noel had the talent, therefore the upper hand. Like Kerry, he had his eye on Hollywood and needed someone familiar with tinsel town. Someone, preferably, with a less competitive spirit. In short, he no longer needed you, Vera."

"And look where it got him?" She echoed Michael's words.

Annoyed by her clumsy threat, Michael tried to extricate himself from her embrace but she only clung tighter. "How did it feel," she taunted, "to murder?"

As if in response, a siren once again began to shatter the tranquility of the suburban town.

"I don't want to talk about it," Michael replied.

"But I do," she insisted, insinuating her hand between their tightly pressed bodies. "You're a criminal, Michael. A rogue. A social outcast."

She spoke, not accusingly, but as if recalling girlhood fantasies of sexual abduction by irresistibly handsome villains. The siren grew louder as her hand grew more insistent, the fondled object hardening in spite of Michael's reluctance to participate in the macabre post-mortem.

"I did what I had to do," he allowed.

"But you did it so well."

"I'm an actor. Imagination is my only reality and right

now I'm imagining, like the police, I hope, that Kerry Kerrington is the culprit. My conscience is clear."

"You are the cool one," Vera replied with admiration. "We're going to be a great success, my pet."

The siren sounded as if it were inside the very room as she tugged on the tab of his zipper.

"The house will be overflowing with police," he pleaded, trying to shake her off.

"That's what makes it so exciting," she panted. "Like Russian roulette."

Her hand was inside his parted fly as cars swarmed up the gravel drive, headlights turning night into day. Screeching brakes, muffled shouts, and heavy footfalls surrounded the house like an invading army. In a panic Michael roughly forced Vera to relinquish her grip. "You're crazy," he gasped, turning to adjust his trousers.

She laughed, tossing her head back and opening her arms in greeting to the horde. "If they could see us now."

"Fuck you," he cried.

"You're getting the idea."

"Open the front door."

"We're home free, Michael."

"If you don't get us arrested."

"And all those faggots out of my life."

"Don't count your chickens, Vera. Don't count your chickens."

III

The New York office of Becton and Becton was located on the top floor of a tenement in what Noel Becton euphemistically called the theatrical district. Native New Yorkers know the neighborhood as Hell's Kitchen, a battleground of ethnicity for the past hundred years. The windows of the fifth floor walk-up were dirty and unadorned, the furnishings as uninspired as the failed Broadway shows they had originally been designed for and the air, cold in winter, hot in summer, was always spiced with the unpleasant aromas of the building's dank hallway.

In sharp contrast, a bedroom and bath, located at the rear of the railroad floor-through, was as smartly furnished and commodious as a suite at the Plaza. It was here that Noel and Vera, never together, but never alone, stayed when 'detained' in town.

The surviving Becton had called a meeting to initiate the myriad steps necessary to open a new play on Broadway four months hence. Assembled in the depressing front room office were the producer, Vera Becton, her leading man, Michael Harris, her director, Andrew Evans, and What's-his-name. The latter was a young man brought into the inner family of Becton and Becton several months earlier by Andrew Evans and given the title Assistant to the Director. This position, as even an usher knows, is as remote from the job of Assistant Director as a bit player is from a star. How this young man assisted the director was unclear. Since, however, his stipend came out of Andrew's wallet, and not the coffers of Becton and Becton, a job description had not been requested by Mrs. Becton or offered by Andrew Evans. In show business such arrangements are not unusual and often vastly more entertaining than anything happening in front of the skeins.

The Assistant to the Director had a proper name which those bearing loftier titles pretended to forget, giving the impression that they couldn't care less. These lapses in memory fooled no one, least of all the object of this perverse attention. What's-his-name wasn't exceptionally handsome or exceptionally well put together or, in fact, exceptionally anything. His face neither startled nor repelled but rather titillated in some indefinable way, vaguely evoking memories of high school crushes and touchdowns in the last minutes of the fourth quarter. Probably twenty or perhaps twenty-one, he could have played eighteen without help from lighting and make-up, and appeared as eager to please as a recent graduate on his first job. His smile tugged at the heartstrings and his eyes, to paraphrase Browning, 'liked what e'er they looked upon and his looks went everywhere.'

At that instant, those eyes were looking at Vera Becton like a puppy in a store window looking at a prospective owner. Vera, in a smart Chanel suit, resembled a haute couture mannequin who had wandered onto the set of *Les Miserables* and decided to make the best of it.

"We are fully subscribed," Vera was saying, "which isn't surprising. Noel wrote five plays, all of them financial if not critical successes." She held up a neatly bound script and wielded it like a fan. "And I think Noel's swan song is going to prove his masterpiece."

"I think so, too," Andrew Evans offered, "but how it comes across, as opposed to how it reads, depends on the male lead. The work is a very delicate balance between comedy and tragedy and the actor has to toe the line like a tightrope walker."

The puppy-dog eyes moved to Michael Harris, whose own eyes shot daggers at his incipient director.

"It's the sort of thing Kerry could have done so well," Andrew concluded.

Vera, seated behind a table that substituted for a desk and

looked as if it couldn't support a typewriter, started at the mention of the unmentionable.

"He's otherwise engaged," she replied curtly.

One wasn't supposed to even think the name of the murderer in the presence of the bereaved, let alone compliment him. (Taking no chances, the offender's assistant closed his eyes and bowed his head as Vera spoke.)

Andrew, like a blind man traversing unfamiliar turf, continued cautiously. "His lawyers want him to plead temporary insanity and I can understand why. Imagine concocting that inane story in front of you two and expecting you to back him up. I would have thought Kerry had more sense than that."

"As you said — temporary insanity. It's the result of harping too long on a single and morbid theme," Vera answered.

Andrew refused to take the hint. He was enjoying the gossip and the fact that it was clearly upsetting Vera didn't deter his pleasure.

"The contract, of course," the director nodded, turning his unwavering stare from Vera to Michael.

"Were you saying that you don't think I can handle the part?" Michael asked, coming to Vera's rescue.

Andrew shrugged. "I was saying that the male lead is an exceptionally demanding role."

"I am the male lead," Michael stated, as if introducing himself, "and I wish you wouldn't talk about me in the third person. In case you haven't noticed, I'm present."

Andrew smiled indulgently. Entering middle age, his hair was graying at the temples, which he thought distinguished, and thinning on top, which he tried to hide with a tricky hair-do and enough hair spray to remove whatever was left of the planet's ozone layer. Exercise and a careful diet kept him in good form and vestiges of the handsome young man that he had been were still clearly visible.

"I am talking about our character," Andrew explained with mock patience. "And I hope, Michael, that once rehearsals begin you assume a more professional attitude. My job is to interpret and criticize. Yours is to listen and learn."

"This is a business meeting, Andy, not a classroom or a rehearsal hall."

Vera did not interfere in the debate. Knowing that healthy competition was the best way to get the most out of her drones, she allowed the two to nit-pick while she tried to appear disinterested and bored. The best way to do this, naturally, was to look at What's-his-name as if she were looking through him. When artistic temperament rose to fever pitch and droll innuendo turned to shrill accusations, Vera went so far as to acknowledge the boy's existence with a smile of noblesse oblige that could have given HRH Elizabeth II a run for her money. The boy responded with a blink and a blush, leaving Vera to wonder if the bedroom suite was in readiness. Did he know about it? Surely, when he was here alone with Andrew he had explored — or had Andrew led the expedition? In show business, where a totally heterosexual male was an endangered species, virgins (of either gender) were virtually extinct. Vera sighed without flexing a muscle.

"What do you think, Vera?" she heard Andrew ask.

"About what?"

The argument, it appeared, had abated and the business meeting reinstated. Both men smiled smugly, as if saving his trump card for higher stakes. This, after all, was still the honeymoon. The sparring was simply a test to determine long suits and weaknesses. The clash of titan egos was still a long way off. Men wrapped up in themselves, Vera thought, make small packages, indeed.

"Stage manager," Andrew repeated. "We can't expect our star to ply his old trade. I was thinking my assistant could fill the vacancy."

"If he's competent," Vera answered, stuffing the script and loose papers into her leather briefcase.

"He's very versatile," Andrew told her.

"I'll bet," Michael sneered, rising along with Vera.

"Whatever you think, Andrew. The decision is yours." She smiled contentedly as she packed her gear. War had been declared and the lines of scrimmage clearly drawn. The director was in one corner and the show's star in the other. She would play double agent, thereby assuring herself of being kept informed of every maneuver by either faction. This, plus the new stage manager, were harbingers of exciting times ahead for the lady producer.

"We're late for our meeting with my legal people and I did want to see at least one set designer to get some preliminary sketches in the works. I think we'll have to skip lunch." Vera played the busy executive on the move with great elan.

"I'm starved," Michael pouted.

"Sacrifice is the actor's lot in life," Andrew preached.

"And gluttony, the director's."

"Come along," Vera called, trying not to touch anything as she made her way to the door. Michael followed her out, closing the door on Andrew and his assistant without a nod, wave or fare-thee-well.

"So," Andrew Evans exhaled when the sound of Vera's heels on the bare wood steps faded to a faint click-click. "I wonder how long that's been going on?"

"What?" the boy questioned.

"Vera and Michael. Do you think the affair began before or after Noel's departure?"

"I thought Michael was Noel's lover."

"He was," Andrew said, walking to one of the room's bare windows. "But he was double-crossing Noel with Kerry and, I think, double-crossing Kerry with Vera."

"That's what *I* call versatile."

Andrew tried to rub a peephole into the window's soot in a futile attempt to see the street. "Really? I would call it the perfect breeding ground for premeditated murder."

The boy arched his eyebrows in surprise. "You think Kerry's innocent? That he's telling the truth?"

Andrew could just about make out the blond head and its brunette companion scurry out of the building and move rapidly toward Broadway. "With Vera Becton all things are possible. Teamed up with the likes of Michael Harris I think the worst and doubt if I would be disappointed. I know Kerry, sane or insane, is too smart to have done what he's being accused of. He was either coerced or framed. I was just playing a hunch but did you see how upset they were at the mere mention of Kerry Kerrington?"

"Maybe they don't like to be reminded."

"I'll bet they don't," Andrew grinned. Noel Becton's empty seat was certainly big enough for two and the time to strike was when the iron was hot.

"Thanks for the promotion." Andrew felt a comforting arm drape his shoulder and a finger drawing circles at the nape of his neck.

"You deserve it," Andrew complimented.

"My first step up the ladder." The boy leaned into

Andrew's hip and the director shuddered at the turgid urgency being pressed upon him. More than just the iron was hot.

"I love you," the director confessed.

"And I love you, Andrew."

IV

The late Noel Becton, oil on canvas, continued to survey his study, much to the chagrin of the room's new master. "He stares at me," Michael complained.

The mistress of the house refused on grounds of propriety to have the portrait removed. "It's been there forever," Vera argued, "and people would talk."

Michael was hard pressed to come up with something about Noel Becton that had not already been said. "It gives me the creeps."

She who had the final word, spoke it. "Imagine it's not there."

Michael sat in the study because, despite its ghost, it was the most comfortable room in the house. The bookshelves lined with morocco-bound treasures, the worn leather furniture, and the French doors opening to the formal garden made it ideal for reading, browsing, nodding, and dreaming. But for Michael the magic was gone. The room that had once inspired dreams of fame and fortune now evoked unpleasant memories and thoughts of escape from the woman who kept watch over her domain like a paranoid despot. Michael felt neither guilt nor remorse over the events of the past month — only indignation. He knew everything had its price but, thanks to Vera, he felt certain he was being fleeced.

It was a wonder Noel hadn't done her in long before she

administered the final solution to him. Noel Becton had been the heart and soul and breadwinner of Becton and Becton. Without him Vera would be, at best, a lady theatrical agent to second-rate talent. Vera knew this and must have toed the line with her husband, allowing him all the space he needed or wanted. Michael, alas, could not afford the luxury of standing up to Vera. Right now he needed her and that meant tolerating, with a laugh and a smile and a song, her bullying, her dominance, and her insatiable sexual appetite.

All the things he was so sure he could live without now took on the aura of sentimental nostalgia, like youth viewed from the distance of old age. His little walk-up in the Village, the bars, the boys, the banter and, by God, even Kerry Kerrington. But no need to dwell on that. Like Kerry, Michael, too, had done what he had to do to further his career, and he knew damn well that, were their roles reversed, Kerry would not have spared Michael. Hadn't Kerry designated Michael the murderer, keeping his own hands clean? Now Michael used this as justification for sending Kerry to jail for the crime. After all, Noel's death was a direct result of Kerry's manipulations. Who struck the fatal blow was a moot question. One didn't accuse a gun of murder, but rather the person who pulled the trigger.

In spite of this somewhat convoluted rationale, Michael dreaded coming face to face with the accused. To date he had been lucky. Thanks to Kerry's courtroom threats to kill both Vera and Michael, his lawyers had been unable to get a judge to set him free on bail pending the trial. Not only that, but because of his insistence on swearing to his bizarre scenario of the murder night, he'd been declared non compos mentis, unfit to stand trial. So, once again, Vera had been right. Kerry

Kerrington was talking himself into the electric chair, or a padded cell, without the prosecution so much as pointing an accusing finger.

Michael sat in the Becton study, avoiding Noel's portrait and clutching the script that would make him a star. The sun had not shown itself on this chilly spring morning and now the rumble of thunder could be heard coming from the direction of Long Island Sound. Billowing black clouds trimmed in white gathered overhead like a coven of nuns caught in a high breeze. Michael neglected to close the French doors. He enjoyed watching nature turn the landscape into a foreboding set, like a scene from a Hollywood film. The type of film that could make handsome and ambitious young men rich and famous and legends in their own time.

He held the script tightly against his chest, secure and confident in his perfectly appointed womb. He felt the lights, warm as the invisible sun, on his cheeks; he heard the persistent whir of the camera inches from his face and behind it the intent stares of the director, the sound men, and the script girl. A salvo of thunder, like the roar of spontaneous applause, came in right on cue as a spiral of lightning. . .

"Are you mad?" Vera closed the doors against the impending rain, obliterating the set and banishing the camera and crew in one sure, swift motion. "It's about to pour — the rug will be ruined — and aren't you supposed to be taking a golf lesson?"

"In this monsoon?"

"Just a summer shower, I'm sure. The pro tells me you're not taking your golf seriously. You must try, Michael. Many a deal is consummated on the golf course."

More than deals are consummated on a golf course,

Michael thought in response to mention of the club's pro. "He's a pompous ass," Michael replied, venting his annoyance at Vera on the pro.

"But quite a looker," Vera smiled. She was wearing a simple shirt-waist dress and, with her hair pulled back and tied into a ponytail, looked closer to thirty than fifty. Romance, especially young love, was Vera Becton's salvation. Vera firmly believed that fornication, rather than cosmetic mutilation, wiped away the years, and her presence was proof of the tactic. She now stood with her back to the patio doors, a jumble of typewritten pages in her hand. The lady executive took her role, like her sport, very seriously, and a jumble of papers had become more or less a prop she was seldom without since becoming Chief (and sole) Executive Officer of Becton and Becton.

"Since the moment you told me about Kerry's fantastic plot I've been trying to remember where I heard it before." Having chastised him, she plunged into the purpose of her intrusion upon Michael's Hollywood reverie. "Like an old movie you see on television you know you've seen before but can't quite place."

"You think Kerry borrowed from Agatha Christie?"

"No. From Noel." Vera waved the papers in her hand at Michael. "It's the plot of a play Noel was writing when he met Kerry. I discovered it this morning while going through Noel's papers."

Michael, who, as usual, hadn't been paying very close attention, now sat up and took notice. "You mean Noel was the engineer of his own demise?"

"Can you imagine the audacity," Vera exclaimed, helping herself to one of Michael's cigarettes.

An added boon from Noel's demise was that now anyone who wished to could smoke openly in the manor. *Great Expectations* was no longer furtively perused every half hour.

"Taking such a chance," Vera exhaled, along with a stream of smoke. "If the police had done a thorough search and come up with this," again she waved the sheets at Michael, "his entire idiotic cover would have been blown."

"Not his cover," Michael reminded her, "mine. And the bastard knew it." Now Michael was surer than ever that justice had been served with Kerry's formal indictment. "How does it end?"

"It doesn't," Vera answered. "Noel never finished it. Now I remember him saying it wasn't right for Kerry. Noel thought an audience wouldn't accept Kerry as a murderer."

"So a role he didn't get to play on stage he now assumes in real life," Michael said thoughtfully.

Rain began to pelt the windows and patio doors, the sound at once chilling and menacing. Michael forced himself not to look at the portrait hanging over the desk. Instead, he concentrated on the aborted script in Vera's tightly clenched fist. He knew he had to get hold of it and destroy it. Unfortunately for Michael, Vera knew it, too.

"What's-his-name should be here any minute," Vera announced, artfully diverting the subject from Noel's script as if it were nothing more than an amusing discovery, a moment's diversion on a rainy day.

"Who?"

"Andrew's so-called assistant," Vera answered. "He's coming with drafts from several set designers. We'll have to make a decision, and very soon." She moved to the French doors. "He's supposed to call from the station and one of us will have to go fetch him. With any luck this rain will let up. . ." The phone, loud and shrill, rang as if mocking Vera's plea for luck. "So much for that," she said, making her way to the antique desk and telephone. She paused near Michael and laid the script on a table next to where he was seated, hesitated a moment, and then picked it up again and proceeded to the phone.

Bitch! Michael almost muttered aloud.

". . . yes, of course," Vera was saying, butter firm in her mouth. "About fifteen minutes and do stay inside — I'll sound the horn — a black Bentley — no, no, I don't mind driving in the rain, in fact I rather like it."

Michael rose as Vera rang off. "I'll go."

"No," Vera stated. "I have a few errands I can take care of on the way to the station."

"Then I'll come with you," Michael offered.

"No," she insisted sharply and then changed her tone. "I don't think we should be seen constantly together so soon after the — the incident. It's a small town and little rumors into steamy novels grow."

It was all Michael could do not to wince at her aphorism. He was not fooled by her explanation as to why she wanted to go alone. Vera had other reasons and Michael knew all of them.

"As you wish."

"I've been very happy these past weeks," Vera cooed, caressing Michael's cheek with the now-rolled-up outline for the perfect murder. The touch of the paper to his face made Michael's hair stand on end. It would be so easy to reach for her throat and. . .

"So have I," he lied unconvincingly.

She smiled, her lips forming a red heart. "I love you, Michael." She managed to sound offended at having to remind him.

"And I love you, Vera."

❏

Michael sat, depressed and dejected, blowing cigarette smoke in the direction of Noel Becton's frozen gaze and listening to the rain. When he heard the Bentley drive past the flagstone terrace, he didn't run in search of the script because he knew she had locked it away in the safe in Noel's bedroom, which, of course, she now occupied. Tantalizingly near but untouchable, that would appeal to the lady. She wanted him to stew but he wouldn't give her the satisfaction. Nonetheless, she knew that he knew and he knew that she knew. It wasn't a standoff, but more like a sadomasochistic two-step with Michael the unwilling bottom man.

The French doors rattled in a sudden gust, the rain pelting the glass with the force of hail. Michael got to his feet to secure them when they began to open, slowly and deliberately, driven not by the wind but by a human hand. He froze and quickly calculated the distance between himself and the inside door. If he screamed no one would hear. If he fled he would expose his back to whoever or whatever was out there. The car was gone. The intruder thought no one was home. When he saw Michael he might lose his head and attack.

Michael began his retreat, propelled by a gale that threatened to blow the room into disarray, when a figure in a raincoat and fisherman's hat entered the drawing room, shaking himself like a dog escaping its bath. The hat came off and a shiny, wet face appraised the room. "What a dump!"

"You!" Michael cried.

"Who were you expecting, love, Clint Eastwood? Or did you think I was at the station, waiting for poor Vera? It would have been a futile wait, let me tell you."

He held up his hand and cocked an ear toward the open doors. A sound like a scream in the night competed with the summer storm. The more discerning would recognize it as the grinding screech of failing brakes. Then there was the sound of metal being crushed, and finally an explosion that could not be mistaken for thunder.

"Even a Bentley has brake fluid and when it leaks out the brakes don't work. And if you have some loose bolts on the front wheel, driver's side, and a hill that's a bitch even when everything's in working order, what you get is an unfortunate accident."

Michael, dazed, walked slowly to his visitor and threw his arms around him, jumping in joy as he bellowed, *"You're a genius, Steve! A fucking genius!"*

They kissed. A long, wet, passionate kiss. "A genius," Michael repeated. "A genius."

"You're getting soaked," Steve laughed.

"Who cares? Who gives a hoot in hell? All I know is I love you and you're a genius. She's out of my hair, out of my life, and out of my career. Do you know I almost killed her myself ten minutes ago."

"We mustn't rush. I told you that. We had to wait till the play was fully subscribed. The angels, remember, were on Vera's side." Steve took off his coat and dropped it where he stood. "My feet are all soggy."

"Take off your shoes and socks," Michael pampered, "and I'll light a fire. How long have you been out there?"

"An hour at least. I walked from the station and worked on the car. Don't worry, there won't be a trace of anything anywhere. They'll think the fluid's been leaking for days and never notice the bolts. It's a hell of a drop down that gorge."

"Should I call the police?" Michael suddenly asked.

"No. No. Pretend we heard nothing. I think that would be best."

"But suppose she had managed to get the car down the hill?"

Steve shrugged. "No harm, really, except that we would have had to try again." He removed his shirt, soaked in spite of the raincoat, and loosened his belt. "I called from the public booth up the road as soon as I finished playing mechanic."

Michael was shoving newspapers under a stack of kindling. "She found one of Noel's old scripts and would you believe it was the blueprint for Kerry's scheme."

"Kerry was foolish but not stupid. If he got the idea from one of Noel's plots I'm sure he didn't know a draft still existed. Christ, if it had gone according to his plan and then the script was discovered it would have put his head in a noose." Steve unzipped his fly and allowed his jeans to fall down his legs. He stepped out of them and stood in his jockeys, displaying a body as ordinary and enticing as the placid face above it.

Michael put a match to the paper. "Not him, Steve. Me. I did the dirty work. She's got the script locked in the safe upstairs and I don't know the combination."

Steve blew on his fingertips and then rubbed them across his bare chest. "I think I can extract it."

"You're a jack-of-all-trades."

"I prefer 'a man for all seasons.'" Steve went to the fire and extended his hands over the blaze. "When you told me about Kerry's plan and I told you to tell Vera, you thought I was crazy."

Michael rose, running his hand over the length of Steve, from ankle to neck. "I stand corrected." He kissed the flushed cheek.

"I knew she would arrange step one," Steve said, "and once we were sure the play was a go, all I had to do was move in for operation mop-up." Michael's hands tugged on the jockey shorts.

"Do you think Andrew knows?" Steve sighed.

"What? That we're lovers or that we catapulted him into the enviable position of producer/director?"

"He suspects you and Vera of framing Kerry."

"I thought as much. But now that he's in for a good fifty percent of the show, not to mention the prestige, I think your lover will suffer a memory lapse."

Steve backed out of Michael's reach. "I thought you were my lover."

"Who's lover you are is academic," Michael said, with a flourish of his hands. "I mean your lover is whoever you happen to be in bed with when the question arises."

"Is that what you told Vera?"

"I didn't tell Vera anything. She told me, and she always had the last word. She was a letch, just like her husband, and would never have let me go until she chewed me up and spit me out. Well, she's had her last word. A-fucking-men. She stuck to me like fly paper but that wasn't enough, not for Vera. She had her eye on you, mister. The only reason she wouldn't let me come to the station. . ." Michael stopped abruptly, his eyes wide with terror, the color draining from his face. "Good God, I almost went with her."

Steve left the comforting hearth and went to the table that held the script of the new play. He ran his hand over the cover page.

"Did you hear me?" Michael shouted. "I almost went with her. Why the hell didn't you warn me it was going to be today? Why didn't you tell me what you had planned? Suppose I had gotten into the car. . ."

"I would have stopped you," Steve said, sounding more bored than concerned.

"How? How would you have stopped me? You would never have known. Where the fuck were you when she drove out of here?"

"Up the road a bit. I would have seen. I would have thought of something."

"You think fast, but not that fast. And leave my script alone."

"I love reading it. It's so damn good." Steve flipped through the pages, his back to Michael, his buttocks round and taut beneath the stretched cotton fabric. "I have it all memorized."

"Memorized?" Michael took a step forward. "Why the hell do you have it memorized?"

"Andrew is coaching me — Oh, didn't you know? I'm to be your understudy."

Michael felt dizzy. He reached out for something to lean on and encountered only the hot air above the grate. Did he hear a police siren or was it the wind?

"But — but — I love you, Steve."

Steve turned and smiled at Michael with his puppy-dog eyes. "And I love you, Michael."

CONTRIBUTORS

Phil Andros is the author of several collections of stories in the picaresque tradition describing his adventures as a hustler in the gay world of the fifties and sixties. These stories were among the earliest gay fiction and were told through his amanuensis Sam Steward, himself the author of two mysteries featuring Gertrude Stein and Alice B. Toklas, whom Mr. Steward numbered among his friends. The most recent of these mysteries, just published, is *The Caravaggio Shawl*. Mr. Steward lives in Berkeley. Phil Andros is on the road.

Ivy Burrowes writes: "I was born in Wyoming, a state of depression most notorious for Cris Williamson (who is from there, too), conservative folk, and lots of wind. I fled the Great Plains first to Florida, then southern Spain, and now live in a cabin in the Rocky Mountains of Colorado. I graduated from Metropolitan State College in Denver with a B.A. in English and History, and have published, and won minor awards for, both short stories and verse. Currently, I am at work on a novel."

Katherine V. Forrest is the distinguished author of several novels including *Curious Wine* and *An Emergence of Green*. She has also written two mysteries featuring Kate Delafield, *Amateur City* and *Murder at the Nightwood Bar*. Currently, she is at work on a third Delafield mystery. She lives in Los Angeles.

Richard Hall was born in New York City and grew up in New Rochelle, New York. His books include *The Butterscotch*

Prince, the first gay mystery, as well as two collections of short fiction, *Couplings* and *Letters From a Great-Uncle & Other Stories*, and *Three Plays for a Gay Theater*. He was a contributing book editor for the *Advocate* from 1976 to 1982 and has written for many major periodicals. His essay "Gay Fiction Comes Home" appeared in the *New York Times Book Review* in June, 1988. He recently completed a coming of age novel, *Family Fictions*.

Alan Irwin was born in 1952 in Woodland, California and grew up in the Sacramento Valley. Currently, he lives in the Russian River area and works as a court reporter. He is working on his first novel.

Vincent Lardo is the author of three previous novels, *China House*, *The Prince and the Pretender*, and *The Mask of Narcissus*. Currently, he is at work on another novel. He lives in New York City.

Gerald Lebonati is the author of *Tropic Lights*. His writings have appeared in newspapers and periodicals including the *Advocate*, the New York *Native*, the *Artist's Magazine*, and the Miami *Herald*. He wrote the Metropolis column for *David* magazine, and is now working on his second novel. He lives in Coral Gables, Florida.

Michael Nava is the author of two previous mysteries featuring gay attorney Henry Rios, *The Little Death* and *Goldenboy*. He is currently at work on a third Rios novel. He lives in Los Angeles.

*Alyson Publications publishes a wide
variety of books with gay and lesbian
themes. For a free catalog, or to be placed
on our mailing list, please write to:
Alyson Publications
40 Plympton St.
Boston, Mass. 02118
Indicate whether you are interested in
books for gay men, for lesbians, or both.*